Steph Vizard is an Australian writer and lawyer. After studying literature at Oxford University, she worked in publishing in London. Her debut romantic comedy, *The Love Contract*, won the 2022 HarperCollins Banjo Prize. She is a connoisseur of salt and vinegar chips and lives with her family in Melbourne.

The Love Contract

STEPH VIZARD

HarperCollins*Publishers*

HarperCollins*Publishers*
Australia • Brazil • Canada • France • Germany • Holland • India
Italy • Japan • Mexico • New Zealand • Poland • Spain • Sweden
Switzerland • United Kingdom • United States of America

HarperCollins acknowledges the Traditional Custodians of the land upon which we live and work, and pays respect to Elders past and present.

First published in Australia in 2023
by HarperCollins*Publishers* Australia Pty Limited
Gadigal Country
Level 19, 201 Elizabeth Street, Sydney NSW 2000
ABN 36 009 913 517
harpercollins.com.au

A catalogue record for this book is available from the National Library of Australia

ISBN 978 1 4607 6398 8 (paperback)
ISBN 978 1 4607 1618 2 (ebook)

Cover design by Louisa Maggio, HarperCollins Design Studio
Cover images: Pram and doors by shutterstock.com
Author photograph by Miranda Stokkel
Typeset in Bembo Std by Kirby Jones
Printed and bound in Australia by McPherson's Printing Group

To Hugh and Poppy

PROLOGUE

Everyone was wrong – the world was full of lovely men and I wasn't going to be alone forever. Dating in your mid-thirties wasn't the horror show or battlefield that so many people had warned me about over the past three months. It was entirely possible to find a guy – the proof was sitting opposite me in Don's, an intimate bar that had recently opened a few streets from my house.

'Tomato sauce – fridge or cupboard?' I asked.

'Fridge. As directed by the bottle,' Matt replied.

'Ah, so he's a rule follower. Interesting.' I did my best attempt at coquettish.

'Okay, I've got one. I owe you a dollar in change. Do you want five twenty-cent pieces, or a fifty, two twenties and a ten?'

'Five twenties, obviously.'

'Correct answer!' he said and we both grinned.

See – we were perfect together.

Matt was better looking than his Hinge profile, in real life. Even in the bright midday light streaming through the windows, he was gorgeous – his chambray shirt set off both his early summer tan and grey-blue eyes, which crinkled when he laughed. With his flop of blond curls, he resembled a lion – albeit the friendly ones featured in the board books I read my niece and nephew on demand.

'Okay, your question,' he said.

I took a sip, well a slurp, really, of my yuzu gin and tonic. There wasn't going to be a better segue than this. It was my moment. And it was going to be fine – since we'd met we'd been messaging nonstop, this was date number four and there was a definite zing between us.

'Kids – sooner or later?' I asked, as nonchalantly as possible.

'On the fence,' he replied. There were suddenly no crinkles around his eyes.

'About ... sooner or later?'

'More about kids in general. You know, whether they're for me or not. I haven't decided yet. I'm possibly open to the idea, maybe at some point,' he said, fidgeting with his cardboard coaster.

'Okay,' I said slowly. Matt was a 38-year-old surgeon with a mortgage, at least two of his profile photos featured a kid on his shoulders and he'd ticked the 'I want kids' box on the dating app we'd met on. I didn't expect him to pull me into his arms and say, 'I can't wait another moment to start thinking about attachment styles and school waiting lists.' But I'd thought he was probably just searching for the right person (i.e. me), not that he was completely ambivalent.

'What about you?'

'I'm more in the "sooner" category, I guess,' I said.

Matt necked the rest of his schooner, then he reached across the table and put both of his hands on mine.

'Zoe, I think a relationship needs to unfold at its own pace ... not at the speed of a ticking biological clock.'

The words sat comfortably in his range – he'd definitely performed this speech before. 'I think you're amazing: beautiful, smart, fun. But I don't think it's fair for me to ask you to choose between us or a baby.'

'Um … thanks,' I said, because it was clearly the response he was seeking.

He gave a modest shrug, as if it was a shame that most men weren't as enlightened as he was. 'But we can still have fun together, if you want,' he said and winked. 'Another round?'

Two hours later, I was sweltering in the thick December heat, dressed as an elf. It was my street's annual Christmas party. Months ago, I'd been asked to help with the photo booth. It had felt like a nice way to contribute to the community. And saying no to people wasn't my greatest strength.

Today the inner-city street in Prahran – a long one filled with former workers' cottages in various states of rejuvenation occupied by octogenarian Greek couples, ageing millennials and most recently terrifyingly cool twenty-somethings – could have competed with the Myer Christmas window. Tinsel had been draped on fences ar[illegible] poinsettias dotted around en masse. A hint of a bre[illegible] wafted around the smell of mulled wine and g[illegible] biscuits, while 'Let It Snow' taunted me as my [illegible] became flushed and my hair stuck to my neck.

'Where's Santa?' The innocent face of the fi[illegible] who lived a few doors down peered up quizz[illegible]

'Santa broke up with me three months [illegible] tc[illegible] years of dating,' I wanted to reply. Or a[illegible] ex-boyfriend, who was meant to be melting next to me in an equally humiliating costume, had.

'He's busy at the North Pole making toys. But you can take a photo with me?' I replied.

'No, that's okay,' he said. His dad shot me an apologetic look. I shrugged and attempted a wobbly smile.

I knew I should reply to the messages my sister, Camille, and best friend, Sofia, had sent me. The three of us had been excited about my date with the supposedly miraculous Matt for days. But I knew what they'd say.

Camille would tell me off in a long message full of lawyerly bullet points. Why did you ask him about babies?! No man (a) wants to think about fertility, (b) ever thinks they're ready for kids ...

Whereas Sofia would rage at the system. If Matthew was Matilda it would be now or never ... not 'I haven't decided yet'! But don't stress – my tarot reader said that you're going to have luck with a guy who has a connection to the Northern Territory. You'll find someone.

Except, I didn't have her optimism anymore. All I'd done in the last few months was date. And Matt was the fifth guy I'd met, since my breakup with Adam, who'd gone cold after I'd raised the question of kids. I'd been ghosted, dumped by message and now in person, by a man who'd made it clear that his idea of commitment was dinner before we rolled back to his place. And these guys weren't (all) sociopaths. They were (mostly) good guys. Just good guys who didn't want to have a baby. Yet.

But I couldn't wait for 'yet', not when I was racing towards thirty-six with sticky ovaries.

'Whoever chose that outfit doesn't like you.'

I turned around and sighed. It was Will Flemming, my exceedingly pleased-with-himself, judgemental, irritating next-door neighbour. The guy who never acknowledged Jess, the barista at our local cafe, because he was too self-important to tear his eyes away from his omnipresent phone. The guy whose tradies had taken up all the parking spots outside our houses for months – all for a renovation that no doubt was turning his house into a shrine to white and beige.

The guy who was currently staring at me as if I was a freak-show exhibit.

I suddenly wished I was wearing anything other than too-tight gold spandex leggings, a green felt tunic and a red floppy hat, that all smelled like the ghosts of Christmas past.

'What are you doing here? I thought you were allergic to parties,' I said.

'I brought my EpiPen,' he replied.

'Oh, can I stab you?' I asked. 'I'm in the mood to stab a guy.' I felt the riptide of frustration and humiliation that had been swirling through me all day churn into anger.

'What a heartwarming sentiment from our neighbourly Christmas elf.'

'There's a Santa costume if you feel like contributing to something other than your individual success on thi planet,' I said.

A smirk appeared on his face, which despite the wasn't shiny or flushed. The extreme humidity even affected his perfect hair. 'As tempting as that I'm working,' he said. Of course he was, that's did. Even on the Sunday before Christmas. do flammable fabrics. Or children.'

We were interrupted by the most recent arrivals to our street – a couple, around my age, with a pram.

'Could we have a photo?'

'Sure. But it's just me – no Santa, sorry,' I said.

'That's okay. Why don't you sit down and we can stand around you,' the friendly mum suggested.

I sat down on Santa's throne, as directed, feeling a tug of guilt as my golden bottom hit the gilded wood. As a mere elf, I hadn't felt entitled to sit on such a lavish chair all afternoon. God, when had I internalised this stuff?

They handed me their baby – a newborn dressed in a mint-green romper covered with koalas in Santa hats. She was tiny – all fuzzy hair, peachy skin and rosebud lips. As I stared at her, all the embarrassment and anger that had been washing around me dissipated. I felt calm again.

'Would you mind taking the photo?' The dad turned to Will, who was still lurking by the Christmas tree.

'I guess. Quickly,' he replied.

God, he was rude.

The baby girl wriggled in my arms and I glanced down to check she was okay. At the same time, the baby's mother kneeled next to me – and she gazed at her baby with such tenderness and care and … love.

I felt my heart begin to pound. I'd always thought that other people were the answer. But where had that left me – a sweaty, rejected elf.

I looked back up, straight into the camera lens, and smiled.

Because I knew exactly what I wanted. And I also knew, for the first time in my life, that I could do it without anyone else.

CHAPTER 1

Eighteen months later

We were late, Hazel was on the verge of losing it and an enormous skip was covering our driveway. I'd struggle to get our pram past it, let alone the car.

This couldn't be happening. Not today.

I took a deep breath, hiked Hazel further up my hip and marched us both the few metres down our street to the house next door.

Ignoring the electronic doorbell, I banged on the freshly painted slate-grey front door. I knew he'd still be home – he left for work at the same time (8.15 am) every day. Footsteps began to move down his hallway, then the door swung open to reveal Will.

The expression on his face was the one I imagined he used when food-delivery drivers dared to knock on the door rather than leave his dinner on the doorstep.

'It's my first day back at work and Hazel's first day at childcare. We need to leave. And we can't, because your skip is blocking my driveway.'

He peered suspiciously past me and Hazel, as if I'd invented the story to interrupt his carefully calibrated morning routine. 'The idiots at the hire company have stuffed up,' he said, clearly not willing to take any responsibility. 'They'll have to come back and move it.'

'I don't have time to wait. I needed to leave five minutes ago,' I said, my voice now an octave higher than normal.

'I'll order you an Uber,' he said.

'I know you've never encountered a baby in the wild, but they need car seats,' I said. 'We'll take your car.'

I said it without really thinking. But actually, it made sense. There was no way I could survive today without a car. Will had caused this problem, so he could fix it. He'd probably specifically told his landscapers (who'd appeared on the scene the minute his torturously slow house renovation had finished) to position it across my driveway, just to annoy me. Well, today he'd pay for it.

'You just said you need a car seat,' he said, with a smug 'gotcha' expression.

'I can put ours in your car,' I said, with more confidence than I felt. The man in Baby Bunting had given me a master class on car-seat installation when I'd bought it, but I wasn't sure how much I'd retained.

'I need my car this morning. I've got a big meeting in the city.'

Of course he did. This man's whole sartorial vibe, from his law-firm-branded puffer vest to the R.M. Williams boots that had never been near a farm, screamed, 'I always have somewhere more important to be.'

'Take an Uber? Or there might be a free e-scooter on Chapel Street. You could scoot to your meeting?' I suggested, in a faux helpful voice. 'Or there's this thing called a train.'

He shot me a withering look.

'I need to join a call in a few minutes. A confidential one.'

Of course he worked on his commute – this was the guy who'd called the police and had my thirtieth birthday party shut down because we were interrupting his work calls. On a Friday night.

'The childcare centre's on St Kilda Road. I can drop you off right on the edge of the city. You can make all the calls you want, and as scintillating as I'm sure they'll be, we promise not to listen. I'll return your car tonight.' It wasn't a question.

He didn't say anything – which was probably one of his lawyerly negotiating techniques. Hazel and I both glared at him. I'd never been prouder of my progeny.

'Fine,' he said finally.

By the time I'd dragged my handbag, laptop case, bag of emergency snacks, breast-pump bag and Hazel's jammed backpack from next door, almost losing circulation to my left arm en route, his garage door was up and the boot of his gleaming black Audi open.

Will stood in his driveway head down, furiously typing. He didn't offer to help. It was clear he saw himself as the inconvenienced party. I coughed pointedly and he begrudgingly looked up from his screen.

'Can you hold her for a second? I need two hands to get the car seat,' I said. He stared at me like I'd asked him to hold an undetonated bomb. Which to be fair, was often what caring for Hazel felt like.

He gingerly put his phone in his vest pocket, then held out his arms like he was a forklift. He stiffened as I carefully handed her to him.

'Just … don't drop her, okay? I'll be back in a minute.'

I extracted the car seat with worrying ease, lugged it up the street, then I hauled it onto Will's pristine leather seat.

'So, you just strap the strap into the hooky thing,' I coached myself. Hazel, who'd clearly had enough of being held like Simba being shown to the Pride Lands, began to wail.

'I'll do it,' Will said impatiently. I hesitated for a second then grabbed Hazel and began to gently jiggle her.

In one swift movement, he looped the straps into place and gave them a gentle tug.

'It's really not that complicated,' he said, with an infuriating shrug.

I sighed. As if Will, whose life was so regimented he had a subscription underwear service (which once had been delivered to our house by mistake), knew what *complicated* meant.

I popped Hazel in her seat, hoping that every strap of what seemed like a 28-point car-seat harness would slide smoothly into place. Alas, it was not to be. I was convinced this car seat had only earned its super-high safety rating because it put people off actually driving anywhere.

As I struggled to clip and tighten, Hazel, wedged into a prison of foam, became increasingly fractious. I pulled the safety strap again before realising the thing blocking it was her chubby leg. She cried out, her face scrunched up like an angry kewpie doll.

'Sorry, baby girl,' I said in my most soothing voice and gently moved her leg. I tightened the final strap with a yank, as Hazel stopped crying.

'Okay, get in. We have to hustle,' Will said, jerking his head towards the passenger door.

'No way. I'm driving. That's my daughter in the back,' I said.

'You look like you've had about three hours of sleep – which is basically the equivalent of having the blood-alcohol level of a uni student in O Week. I'm driving.'

'Did you just call me haggard and negligent in one sentence?' I felt a Dyson-hairdryer-strength blast of anger surge through me. What kind of monster told a new mum she looked exhausted and was putting her child at risk? And I'd had five hours of sleep – three of them unbroken.

'Okay, my alternative submission is you're late, I'm late and Hazel's upset. If I'm driving and she starts crying again, you can calm her down,' he said, pointedly checking the chunky silver watch poking out of his crisp white shirtsleeve.

I'd promised my sister, Camille, I'd meet her at 8.30 am on the dot. If we left now it was possible we wouldn't be disastrously late. And Hazel had calmed down. But who knew how long that would last.

'Fine, you can drive,' I said. 'But only because I don't have time to argue.'

He smirked as if he'd won. Everything was a competition for him. He ran by my window every morning, with the focus and determination of a Melbourne Marathon entrant.

I slid into the passenger seat as Will brought up the navigation page on the shiny screen of his dashboard. I typed in the address of Camille's childcare centre.

'I have to join that call now,' he said, as we drove down our street. I rolled my eyes, though I was secretly relieved that we wouldn't have to make small talk or drive in awkward silence.

'Before I jump on the DDC call, I need you to email me the latest version of the report. Then while I'm offline, finalise the ASIC Relief application. And I want that taxi pack I emailed you about last night on my desk by the time I return from my meeting – see if there's a grad free to help. Okay?' Will rattled off commands in his deep, measured voice.

'And thanks so much for your help – really appreciate it,' I said, in a stage whisper.

He tapped the 'mute' button on his phone. 'Let me guess – you end all your emails with "Thanks! Please let me know if you need anything else! Smiley face."'

'I bet your sign-off is "Thnks" – no "a" because you think you're too important for vowels,' I shot back.

He turned to face me for a second, and I could tell that I was right. I hoped he couldn't read me as easily. Not that there was anything wrong with a friendly sign-off.

He unmuted his call without acknowledging me, and resumed peppering his minion with more work.

It was amazing how three minutes trapped in a car could affirm everything you'd long suspected about someone. Will was self-entitled, self-assured, self-everything. And it wasn't a mystery why. The world was literally built for guys like him. When he arrived at his gleaming office, the air-conditioning would be set at the exact temperature to optimise his comfort in his tailored merino-wool suit. Standard office hours would always suit him – he would never have to worry about drop-offs, pick-ups, maternal nurse appointments, vaccinations or school holidays. He'd never have to stay in a mediocre job, treading water, because he wasn't sure he could get a part-time role anywhere else. He'd be promoted and promoted and promoted, and one day he'd run the show. One day, he'd get to make decisions that affected the lives of real people. But he'd never use that power to make any real change because he'd never truly understand the struggles of ordinary people, people who weren't like him.

Okay, so maybe I'd made a few assumptions based on a couple of minutes of eavesdropping. But I'd known enough guys like Will to bet I was right.

I snuck a sideward glance at him. Adam had called him Dweeby Will, because he never stopped working. From my kitchen, most nights and weekends, I could see a glowing computer screen lighting up his pale, bespectacled face.

But actually, as I watched him authoritatively negotiate, I decided that *dweeb* wasn't the right word. Beneath his acetate glasses, his chestnut eyes flashed as his colleague tried to push back on his deadline. He made my own Miranda Priestly-esque boss seem like Leslie Knope.

He caught me staring. I quickly turned my head, then closed my eyes and took a deep breath to compose myself. For the first time this morning, I felt a sense of calm. I needed to cling to this feeling because I hated first days. I'd hated first days for most of my life.

'Zoe!'

I woke up with a start. Where were we? Ah, we were already here. I must have drifted off for a few moments. I checked the clock on the gleaming dashboard. Well, about fifteen minutes. I swung my head around. Hazel was calmly staring at her hands. Was it my driving that usually made her so unsettled in the car?

Will was scanning the tiny car park for a space.

'There's one,' I said, pointing at an empty spot at the end of the row.

'I can get closer,' he said.

'I'm not letting you park in the disabled spot.'

He ignored me. 'I don't believe in settling,' he said as a Porsche pulled out of the park closest to the entrance. Will swung his car in, failing to suppress a victorious smile as he turned off the engine.

As I unbuckled Hazel, parents converged upon the childcare centre, exiting their SUVs in crisply ironed shirts and tasteful, dry-clean-only dresses, and ferrying their children in UPPAbaby Vistas and iCandys, each worth more than my car. It was like an army of Camilles. In fact, one of them was Camille.

She spotted me then marched towards us. I smoothed down my hot-pink coat, feeling like a flamingo in a bazaar of sleek falcons.

'You're on time. Miracles do happen.'

She softened as she leaned in to kiss Hazel, who beamed up at her beloved aunt, revealing both of her recently acquired bottom teeth (and the cause of our sleep deprivation). I gave my three-year-old niece and nephew, Artemis and Remy, who trailed behind her, a squished hug with my half-a-free arm.

The driver's door opened and Will climbed out.

Camille looked expectantly at me for an introduction. What was I meant to say? 'Camille, this is my awful next-door neighbour who is reliably rude and often hostile, whose car I've commandeered.'

'Will Flemming! And Camille Harper!' A voice boomed behind us and broke the awkward silence.

An older man with a balding pate ringed by stringy grey hair and mottled skin wearing a well-cut suit waved at us. He held the hand of a toddler, who I guessed was a grandson.

'What are the odds! My former and current acolytes in one place,' he said.

'Robert! This is my younger sister, Zoe. Mother of Hazel,' Camille said. 'Zoe, Robert was my first boss. I learned everything at his feet.'

Will's phone rang before the introductions could continue.

'Sorry. Good to see you, Robert,' he mouthed at us, as he walked off.

'It's Zoe's first day back at work,' Camille said to Robert, as she checked her watch. 'And she's going to be late.' She redirected her attention towards me. 'I'll get her settled in. Trust me, it'll be easier for everyone that way.'

'It's okay. I've got time,' I protested. I didn't, but I couldn't leave her yet. In fact, I was pretty sure I couldn't leave her at all. She was a part of me.

'Go!' Camille ordered, reaching out for Hazel, who was giggling as her cousins pulled silly faces. 'I promise I won't leave until she's happy.'

'Right. Okay.' I gave Hazel a kiss, then another dozen. 'Bye, my Hazel-girl. Have a good day. I'm only going because I absolutely have to. I love you.'

'She'll be fine,' Camille said firmly. 'Oh, and I spoke to the manager. They can't do me any more favours. You have one week to sort out proper childcare.'

I managed to reach the driver's seat of Will's car before I burst into tears. I could count on one hand the number of hours I'd been away from Hazel since she was born, and I already felt a physical absence. Normally, she was within reaching distance at all times.

But it wasn't just sadness that was pouring out of me. It was something else. Relief. I felt like a weight, one that I hadn't even noticed had become quite so heavy, had been lifted off my shoulders. For the first time in six months, I wasn't wholly responsible for another, extremely dependent human. I was free. Today, I just had to look after myself. I could do whatever I wanted. Well, I couldn't. I had to go to work. But it was just me again, back in the real world.

Before I could stop it, my tears turned into a laugh, quite a loud, slightly hysterical one. I guiltily looked out the window to make sure no one could see me. Despair I could admit to. Relief I could not.

Will, still on his call, stared straight at me. He'd left his keys in the car. But I could hardly abandon him in the childcare centre car park. I wound down the window.

'Can I drive you a bit closer to the city?' I asked.

He shook his head, clearly annoyed that I'd interrupted his train of thought. 'I'm on a sensitive call. I'll get myself to my meeting from here,' he said, then turned and walked away.

The car suddenly felt very empty. I pulled the driver's seat forward and took stock. Here I was – a sole parent going back to work, her daughter barely six months old. With no childcare sorted. And one week to fix it. This hadn't been the plan.

But nothing had really gone to plan for the past few years.

CHAPTER 2

'My dance-class orientation's about to kick off,' Sofia said. I could hear muffled music and a hum of exuberant chatter in the background.

'You're sure you can dirty-dance at ...' I did some quick calculations, '... six months?'

'My doctor said I shouldn't let growing human life slow me down. But this isn't about me – I wanted to check you survived day one?'

'Barely,' I replied.

'Any childcare breakthroughs?'

Over the last few weeks, Sofia had been my partner in outrage and panic. During my second trimester, I'd put Hazel on a stack of waiting lists for local childcare centres. A grand total of none of them had been able to offer us a place in time for my return-to-work date.

'Nope. At pick-up, I basically begged Camille's centre to take Hazel. But they said they can't magic up a spot. Not that I expected a different answer. Camille's entire maternity-leave project was getting the twins in there. I'm pretty sure she offered to do all their legal work pro bono to secure not one but two coveted places! Either that or sexual favours.'

'God, it's a bloody jungle out there.'

'The only places that have space right now are awful,' I said.

We'd got as far as attending orientation at one of them last week. I shuddered at the memory – soporific toddlers slumped on sticky beanbags glued to screens, food that would be sent back on a budget airline, announcements from the nearby supermarket that penetrated the thin walls. We'd fled.

Before I could stop her, Camille, who'd insisted on coming with us to orientation, had jammed in her AirPods and convinced (well, bullied really, possibly blackmailed) her twins' centre into taking Hazel for a week.

But after this week, I had nothing sorted – zero care for any of the three days I worked. I'd spent the last week ringing and emailing every half-decent childcare centre within driving distance, but had had no luck.

'What a total joke!'

'I know. The end of my maternity leave has coincided with a nation-wide shortage of childcare workers.'

'Imagine people not flocking to an underpaid, under-appreciated profession.'

'Imagine,' I said, with a dark laugh.

'I need to write a story about this,' Sofia said.

'Just don't ask me to be the human-interest angle,' I said, before she could. My nightmare was being a poster girl for the struggling single mum, trying and failing to do it all. Particularly when Adam read Sofia's paper, religiously.

'And even if I could afford more maternity leave, which I can't, Monica made it very clear that if I didn't return to work this week she could find another copywriter more easily than I could find another part-time job,' I said.

'Which is totally illegal.'

'Only technically.'

'Thank God I won't have to deal with this.'

I felt a familiar uninvited sting of jealousy. Sofia's baby hadn't even been born and her mum could barely wait for her to go back to work so she could care for her grandchild all day.

'Is there any chance your mum could—' Sofia began.

'Absolutely none,' I cut her off. 'I better go. I need to try a few more places before they close. Enjoy getting your *Footloose* on.'

'So … Would you like to pay the seventy dollar non-refundable deposit to put Hazel on the waiting list?'

The voice on the other end of the phone was professional but tinged with impatience. It was 6.01 pm. I sensed that as soon as this phone call ended, she'd be able to clock off.

'What's the current wait-list time?' I asked, trying to sound like a friendly prospective mother rather than desperate.

'We never know exactly how long,' she said, trotting out what sounded like a much-used line.

'Ball park?'

'We make most of our offers at the start of each year. We suggest you check in then.'

I bit my lip to stop myself from letting out a squeal of frustration.

'Look. I'm a single mum. I have to work or we'll starve. My boss is as inflexible as a metal pole. And I can't afford a nanny. So, I really need to sort out childcare by the end of this week. Please just give it to me straight,' I pleaded.

There was a long pause at the end of the line.

'You have more chance of winning the lottery than getting a spot in our baby room.' Her professional phone voice had been replaced by a conspiratorial whisper.

My heart sank. And this place wasn't even that great. There was an official government website that graded childcare centres. This one only 'Met Expectations'. I'd tried a heap that 'Exceeded Expectations' (apparently, the government used the same grading system as Hogwarts) and had had no luck.

All I wanted was to get Hazel a spot at a half-decent childcare centre. But evidently, I'd run out of options. Was it my expectations that were out of touch? Or was this system completely broken?

As soon as the call ended, I poured myself a glass of wine. Hoping it would take the edge off my frustration, I took an enormous swig then checked my watch. When did I need to stop drinking, so that Hazel wouldn't get drunk?

There was no agreed-upon rule dictating how much you could drink while breastfeeding. I knew because the brains trust had told me.

First Camille, who did everything by the book and who'd passionately researched every possible pregnancy and post-partum conundrum, had imparted her wisdom. 'I mean, not a lot of research has actually been done. But the official position is that it's safest not to drink at all. No coffee, either,' she'd said firmly. Almost too firmly.

I'd asked Sofia, whose superpower was the ability to digest and analyse enormous amounts of information, for a second opinion. If you can drive, you can breastfeed, she had texted back.

In a later text, she'd added, At appointment with my midwife and asked. She told me that if you can speak you can breastfeed, which sounded a bit apocryphal.

I'd done my own research, too, of course. I'd discovered (amongst other things) that Beyoncé had drunk wine when she breastfed her twins. Obviously, I didn't give this the same weight as Camille's and Sofia's research, but I'd be lying if I said this didn't tip the balance. I decided that I was allowed to drink a single glass of wine a couple of hours before a feed. However, this often required some serious speed drinking.

My phone lit up. I checked the screen – 'Mum'.

I inhaled the rest of my glass of very budget chardonnay and considered not answering. This morning, I'd sent her a bunch of photos of Hazel, in her nicest pair of overalls, her few wispy strands of blonde hair tied up in a bow – surely I'd done my bit.

'Hi, Mum.'

'So, Camille had to bail you out on day one.'

I felt my stomach tighten at the thought of Camille, sitting in her corner office, calling Mum in her less salubrious cubicle. I could imagine Mum's lips, coated with a colour that matched the logo of the bank branch where she worked but not her complexion, thinning with disapproval as Camille said, 'Zoe had a bit of a hiccup with Hazel's childcare.'

'No. I just assumed—'

'You can't afford to assume anything, Zoe!' she cut in. 'You have to be ahead of the game. I always had to be twice as prepared. And she said some total stranger gave you a lift?' Her voice was thick with disapproval and condemnation.

I felt my hackles rise. 'He wasn't a stranger! I wouldn't let a stranger near Hazel. He's our neighbour. I've known him for years,' I responded, gazing longingly at the now forbidden bottle of wine on the bench. I didn't have the strength for this conversation. Not today. 'Mum, I have to go. Hazel's woken up. But I promise you – I'm totally on top of things, ahead of the game. I've got it all under control. Bye, Mum.'

I hung up before she could answer and checked the monitor. Hazel was still fast asleep.

Why had Camille mentioned Will to Mum? 'You can't rely on anyone' was practically her life motto – she'd said it often enough when we were growing up.

A ripple of unease ran through me as I remembered the state I'd been in this morning – exhausted, anxious and emotional. And Will had seen it all up close. Why did it have to be him of all people?

We basically lived on top of each other, and this necessitated boundaries. And ours had been clearly defined. We staunchly pretended we knew nothing about each other's lives, despite knowing nearly everything. This had been our system for years, and it had worked.

He was Dick Next Door. Sofia had bestowed this moniker when he'd had my birthday party shut down.

I'd taken the baby seat out of his car when we'd got home (though I'd left the shower of biscuit crumbs from Hazel's snack as a souvenir of our road trip), but I still had the key. When Hazel woke up I'd return it – before he appeared on our doorstep demanding it back. Then we could resume our system of mutual enmity.

After Hazel's dinner and bath, we tiptoed across Will's freshly tiled verandah, bordered by a newly planted line of anaemic-looking birch trees, to the front door of his painstakingly renovated cottage.

I bent down and posted the key through his letterbox. But before I could retreat, Hazel wailed and I heard steps coming down the hallway. The front door swung open.

'Hi. I, um, was returning the key.'

'How'd the rest of the day go?' he asked.

'She smelled different.'

I'd meant to say 'fine' – the answer I'd have given to anyone else. But while I could attempt to maintain a veneer of perfection – well maybe not perfection, but at least one of sanity to the rest of the world – there was no hiding the truth from him.

He could hear Hazel crying through the night. He could see me walking the pram up and down the street in the early hours. He saw me stumbling out of the house in the morning, deep bags under my eyes, stains on the front of my hoodie, dirty hair in a bun.

'What do you mean?'

'When I picked up Hazel, she smelled like another woman's perfume. It was on her hair and in her clothes. Which is good! It means someone must have cuddled her today. But it made me realise – she'll never be totally mine again.'

'She's all you.'

I paused. As much as I wanted to believe Hazel was all me, I knew she wasn't. Being reminded, even indirectly, made me feel unsettled.

'Her eyes, for one – they're identical to yours. The exact same shade of blue,' he said.

I took a moment to work out how to reply to a comment that wasn't laced with frustration or sarcasm.

'And she's inherited your lack of volume control,' he added.

'We have to be loud to drown out the Classical FM constantly blaring out of your house.'

'How else is she going to be exposed to culture?'

'Hey – The Wiggles won Triple J's Hottest 100 – they're true artists.'

'You say potato, I say hot potato,' he said dryly.

A burst of laughter shot out of me before I could stop it. 'You should log off. You look like you need to be plugged back into your mainframe soon, or you'll revert to factory settings.'

'Now who's calling someone haggard?' he replied lightly.

But there was a heaviness in his voice. And I recognised his expression from my own mirror – sheer exhaustion. I knew how hard he worked – I saw the light on in his study until the early hours of the morning most nights. Honestly, I'd found it quite comforting to know that we were both up during those lonely hours. That in an emergency, I could knock on his door and he'd be conscious. But in the glare of his harsh security light, I saw the effect of this work ethic. His face was drawn and his eyes bloodshot.

'Before I finish for the day, I have to deal with this,' he said. He pulled his phone out of his pocket, tapped it a few times and handed it to me with a glint in his eyes. An open email was on the screen.

Will. I've put time in your calendar tomorrow. A belated congratulations on baby Hazel.

I've attached the firm's new gender-neutral parental-leave policy. I've checked with HR, who confirmed you haven't taken any time off yet.

I know you probably feel that taking time off now would impact your chance of making partner – I want to assure you that this is incorrect. The firm wants its fathers to be seen to be taking leave. We want our future male partners to be Champions of Change. The partners are incredibly excited that one of our male lawyers is actually going to use our new policy.

Tomorrow, we'll discuss how we structure your paternity leave.

Robert

I burst out laughing. 'That guy in the car park this morning, the Mr Burns doppelganger, is your boss?'

Will nodded, as he tried to suppress a smile.

'And he thought you were Hazel's dad?'

'She's clearly a very intelligent baby. Very alert. So, he naturally assumed she was my daughter,' he said. The smile transformed into a cheeky grin. It was disarming, when I was so used to seeing him frown.

'I guess you both have the same comb-over. Maybe that was it?' I replied, dragging my fingers through Hazel's wispy strands.

'It's not the craziest assumption,' he said. 'We did drop her off for her first day of childcare together.'

'Technically, we gave you a lift,' I said, still bristling from Mum's comments.

'Fine, but you can see how it seemed to him.'

I could. Why else would he have been there?

'He must think you're insane, not telling anyone at work you'd had a baby!'

'I'd be joining a long line of men at the firm who didn't miss a day of work after they had a kid. And I wouldn't be the first to not say anything.'

I boggled, once again, at how different the world could be for men. I spent the day after I'd given birth being regularly hand-milked by various midwives to extract colostrum because Hazel hadn't yet learned how to latch. While their wives were navigating this, their husbands had turned up to work and blithely announced, 'I had a baby,' or not, and continued on with the day-to-day.

'So, why would your boss be encouraging you to take paternity leave?' I asked. From what Camille had told me, law firms made astronomical profits because they worked their staff to the bone. Encouraging lawyers to take time off, paid time off, surely didn't help their bottom line.

'The top law firms all compete with each other for talent. And the current playing field is parental-leave policies. To win, all the firms want to be able to say we have the best policy and all of our women and men took loads of leave. It's the new frontier.'

'How long do you get?' Camille's husband, Ed, had gone back to work two weeks after her C-section. Against

Camille's protests, Ed's mum had moved in because my sister couldn't lift her babies.

'Twelve weeks.'

'What!' I knew when I chose to go it alone I would, by definition, be unsupported. But there were mothers here in this city who had a partner taking care of their babies for three whole months.

'I know. And I could do with a break.'

I guessed this was the first time he'd said this out loud, even though it was obvious from the deep bags under his eyes that he needed one. I wasn't sure which of us looked worse. He seemed so exhausted that I didn't even mention that wrangling a baby was the opposite of a holiday.

Hazel grizzled in my arms.

'Right, it's her bedtime, I better get her home.'

'Night.' He began to close the door, then paused. 'It's bin night tonight. If you forget again you cannot put any more dirty nappies in my bin.'

Without thinking, I raised the middle finger on the hand that wasn't holding Hazel. Whoops.

I caught a death stare before the door shut. Our peace accord was broken. Nature had healed. I breathed a sigh of relief, then smiled. The whole love-thy-neighbour situation, even for one conversation, had been exhausting.

Once I'd put Hazel down, I collapsed into bed with my laptop. I was desperate for sleep but very aware I only had a one-week grace period at Camille's childcare paradise, before we were on our own again.

I furiously googled childcare centres and wrote desperate email after email outlining my case, begging to be considered if a spot was available. I must have fallen asleep emailing, because when I woke up with a start my laptop, now dead, was on my pillow.

It was the first time since Hazel had been born that I hadn't woken up to her cries. I checked her cot, next to my bed. She was still sleeping soundly – curled up like a croissant, her chest gently moving up and down.

The sun hadn't risen yet, but I didn't feel heavy with exhaustion. Instead, I felt something that I hadn't felt in a long time – hope. Because I'd had a vision.

Now I just had to convince Will that my vision was inspired.

CHAPTER 3

A few hours later, at 8.20 am on the dot, Hazel and I were installed at the table next to the door at our local cafe, conveniently located in a former milk bar at the end of our street. I knew Will came here every morning – he had one of their distinctive yellow-and-black cups permanently attached to the hand his phone wasn't in – at the exact same time.

And of course, this was his local. Everything was gleaming and slightly curved, as if iPhones had attained sentience and a builder's licence to design a cafe for themselves. We could have been in Scandinavia, if you ignored the enormous vase filled with artfully arranged sprigs of deep-yellow wattle sitting at the end of the oversized blond-wood bench.

I rarely bought coffee and never came here. The regulars were suits like Will and mums decked out in figure-enhancing PE Nation, Outdoor Voices and Lululemon Lycra. Adam had loved this place. Not that I wanted to be thinking about Adam now, or ever.

The door swung open and I turned my head. Nope – not Will. Just another guy with a groomed beard and a Boston Red Sox cap. I checked the time – he'd be here any second.

I ran through it all again.

If Will's work thought he was Hazel's dad, why shouldn't he take three months of paternity leave? I'd have more time to sort out proper childcare, to scale the dizzying heights of their waiting lists. His firm could boast that a guy actually had used their new, flashy policy. And Will would make his boss happy and get the break he so obviously needed. It was genius – a simple transaction that benefitted all parties.

Will was insufferable. But he was also reliable (he had his car washed every Saturday morning, without exception), a perfectionist (his shirts were so crisply ironed that they could be used as a weapon) and exceedingly particular (I'd overheard him force his landscaper to replant a box hedge that wasn't equidistant to the others). Surely someone who exhibited these qualities in spades wouldn't let anything happen to Hazel.

You had to be ahead of the game – that's what Mum had said yesterday. If I convinced Will to agree to the plan then I could tell her and Camille that I had everything under control. The only issue, the sticking point, was I'd be lying. And Will would be lying. We'd both have to lie to make it work.

The menu board behind the barista set out the options in copper lettering – BLACK ($4.50) or WHITE ($5). But life wasn't that simple. Sometimes life demanded grey.

'Hi, Will.'

I greeted him as he stood at the entrance of the cafe. He gave me a curt nod by way of reply. He was dressed in his uniform – a navy suit and polished black leather shoes.

The ends of his dark hair were still wet from his post-run shower and he smelled of a cologne that was fresh and woody.

'Come join us. I've got an extra coffee!' I trilled, and waved him over.

He looked suspiciously at me. 'I can't drive you. Again. I have a big day.'

'I know,' I said. 'Can you please sit down for a second? There's something I want to talk about.'

I pushed a coffee towards him. He raised an eyebrow and sat down, but on the edge of the sleek tripod wooden stool, as though he might spring up and flee at any moment.

I took a deep breath. I was a copywriter at a giant real-estate agency, where I wrote the marketing spiel for people selling their houses (which nobody ever read, scrolling down to the photos, instead). It was my job to persuade people to buy whatever we were selling. But the idea I was about to pitch to Will wasn't exactly a double-fronted weatherboard Edwardian ('superbly renovated with every modern amenity!').

'I know you're a busy man, so I'll make this quick. I've had an idea. And I think it's pretty brilliant and mutually beneficial,' I began. I'd practised this line.

'Okay …' he said warily. He sipped his coffee and his eyes narrowed. I could tell he wanted to ask how I'd got his coffee order (a magic) right. But I wasn't going to tell him that I'd asked Jess, the barista, for one of what 'the anally retentive workaholic with the nice suit and floppy hair orders' (Jess had replied without missing a beat, 'Which one?').

'I think you should take parental leave and help me look after Hazel.' I paused for a moment to let the suggestion sink in. He stared at me like I was certifiably crazy.

'The key part of parental leave is ... being a parent,' he said in a slow voice, as if talking to a particularly dim-witted toddler.

'Yes, I understand that. But ... anyone could be Hazel's dad, you see,' I said. It was clear from his blank stare that he didn't, so I went back a step.

'The spot on the birth certificate for her father's name is blank. As far as anyone knows, it could be you.'

'Right.'

'I used a donor,' I said, feeling my cheeks heat up and my stomach begin to churn. 'Long story short. I dated Adam – the vertically challenged guy who always wore cycling Lycra – for five years. I saw an engagement ring in his sock drawer and then waited around for another two for him to give it to me. When he didn't, I told him straight out that I wanted to get married and have a baby. Then ... he basically ghosted me.'

I didn't give him time to make the inevitable expression of sympathy and/or horror the recap of my relationship with Adam usually solicited.

'And so, after a few months of dates with men whose role model in life was Peter Pan, I decided to have a baby on my own using a sperm donor.'

I paused. I didn't like to dwell on Hazel's conception. In fact, I'd pretty much blocked it out.

'I had a plan about how it would all work. I saved up enough money for six months of maternity leave. And I'm going to work part-time for a while. But the kink in my plan is that there's a decent-childcare drought in this city. And so, here I am … proposing a temporary alternative plan to you. And this isn't really even my plan, it's almost your boss's plan. I mean, he thinks that you're a parent, and parents are entitled to parental leave.'

'Right,' he repeated. 'Okay—'

I could tell he was about to explain why my plan was flawed, so I cut him off. 'No one would ever know. Ever,' I said, almost in a whisper, as if to prove my point. 'The only thing I ever tell anyone is that I don't know who Hazel's dad is. The only person who knows about the donor is my best friend, Sofia. Not because I think using a donor to have a baby is anything to be embarrassed about. It's just – it's no one's business.'

He paused for a moment, and I could almost see the cogs in his mind ticking over, methodically working through the information I'd told him. He hadn't outright rejected the idea.

'Zo—' he began.

I interrupted him again, deciding to go in for the kill. I'd also rehearsed this part.

'You're up for partner, right? Well, a million studies show that fathers are far more likely to get promoted.'

'Really?' He raised an eyebrow, interest piqued. I could see the hunger in his eyes. He really wanted to make partner. Then he looked irritated with himself for engaging with me, and the eyebrow lowered. But I'd hit upon something.

'There's a study that shows fathers are more desirable job candidates than non-fathers. People think they're better at their jobs. More committed.'

This was true – I'd read up on it this morning. Also totally unfair because while fathers often got promoted, the opposite happened to mothers. The same study had shown that being a mother worked against a woman. They called it the Motherhood Penalty. Not that that was the point right now.

'You need an edge to make partner. This is it. Your boss is desperate for a guy to use their new policy. The firm is encouraging it. They already think you're Hazel's dad. So, make everyone happy!'

He opened his mouth to interject.

'Here's my thinking,' I continued. 'You meet with your boss and tell him you'll do as he suggests – that you'll happily take all your leave starting straightaway. Next week.

'I'm working Monday to Wednesday at the moment. You watch Hazel while I'm at work. Which will be a total breeze – she's an angel baby,' I lied through my teeth. But it didn't feel like the time to mention pooh-namis, or the specific combination of terror and brain-shrinking boredom of staying at home with a baby all day, or how my last month had been formally dedicated to trying to teach Hazel to reinsert her dummy to save my sleep and sanity.

'Then the rest of the time, the other four days of the week are yours. You can sleep, read laws, work out how you'll decorate your corner office – whatever you do to relax.'

He still appeared cynical, like he couldn't believe he was listening to what I was saying, but his concentration had drifted off slightly.

'You buy me more time to find Hazel a spot at a childcare centre that isn't a total cesspit,' I ploughed on. 'And you impress your boss. Maybe even catch up on some sleep. A classic win-win situation.'

I exhaled and stepped off my metaphorical soapbox. Hazel was still, miraculously, gnawing on the piece of toast I'd given her. Will turned towards her – his potential fake daughter. She reached out her pudgy hand and offered him her piece of slobbery, gummed toast. I intercepted it.

Maybe Hazel would clinch the deal? She was especially cherubic today in her best outfit – a hand-me-down romper from the twins covered in daisies.

'No way,' he said. 'Not a terrible pitch. But you're mad!'

I felt my face fall with disappointment. The adrenaline that had pumped through me since I'd had the idea seemed to instantly evaporate.

Suddenly, the day ahead of me – dropping off a crying Hazel, worrying about her while racing through another to-do list at work, expressing in an empty office without a lock, slinking out of the office in time for pick-up, frantically heating up and then trying to cool down vegetable mush, bath time, many attempts at bedtime and a night broken by feeds – stretched before me like an exhausting, unrelenting marathon.

'If anyone found out I knowingly lied about having a kid, and took an entitlement, my career would be over.'

'They wouldn't find out.'

'Even if they didn't, I have a duty to the court – a duty to be ethical.'

'Would this really be so wrong! I mean, it's a transaction where everyone gets something – including your firm. Sure, they lose a bit of money. But you said they're desperate for some of their men to take parental leave. So, they win too.'

His face remained cynical. I felt a surge of anger bubble to the surface. I tried to push it down, but when I was around Will I seemed to lose control.

'Well, there's nothing bloody ethical, or moral, or even just right about our leave system. If we're lucky, we get paid minimum wage for a few months. And most of us have to return to work and use a childcare system whose sole purpose seems to be to cause nervous breakdowns and bankruptcy.'

I took a deep breath, realising that I'd gone a bit off-piste and needed to swiftly change tack.

'Hazel only has me, which means that she won't get as much time as lots of other babies to be at home. Which just doesn't seem fair,' I said. 'And obviously, that's my problem. It's for me to deal with. But it's my job to make sure I give her everything I can. And I just thought … your firm is trying to do the right thing. And that even though we'd be telling a small lie, well, when you looked at the bigger picture it'd be the right thing to do.'

'I'm sorry,' he said, more gently this time, draining his cup and standing up. 'But I just … It wouldn't … No. I can't.'

I nodded and bit my lip.

'I'm sure the whole … childcare thing will sort itself out,' he said. He spoke with the confidence of a man who'd never met a roadblock he hadn't been able to leap over, of a man who always got the best parking spot.

'I'll work something out,' I said, willing myself to believe it.

Why had I thought I'd be able to convince Will to do anything – let alone this? Hadn't Adam taught me pretty comprehensively that convincing men to do, well … anything, wasn't my forte?

Strapping Hazel to my chest, I gathered up the detritus from her breakfast, spread over the table. I stepped through the door Will impatiently held open for us, just in time for the council rubbish truck to drive past, leaving its distinctive pong in its wake. We both knew I'd forgotten to put out my full bin.

CHAPTER 4

'See, that's how desperate I am! I have until Monday to sort out something, otherwise I'm totally screwed. I need a new plan.'

The next day, I called Sofia as I inhaled lunch in the office kitchen and told her what I'd done.

'It wasn't totally crazy. Taking some leave could help Dick Next Door's career – one of my colleagues is writing an article about it. And it's not just law firms who are suddenly on board with men taking parental leave – it's across the corporate world.' She sighed dramatically. 'I knew I should have fallen for a nice hedge-fund manager or equivalent. Morgs thinks he'll only be able to take a few days away from the shop after the baby's born.'

Sofia's boyfriend, Morgan, owned a small florist. Trained as a sculptor, he lived to create giant floral masterpieces. It was a source of much anguish that outside of fashion week or gallery openings, most people wanted fewer visionary pieces and more often than not asked for a simple bouquet ('She likes roses!') and white weddings.

'Are you okay with that?' I asked.

'Yeah, I'll be fine. The baby will mainly be sleeping at the start. And Mum'll be around.'

'The first few weeks can be … a lot. Are you sure he can't get someone to cover the shop for a bit longer?'

'Ohhh, I reckon he's got hotter! Look at your phone,' Sofia said, ignoring my question.

I opened the photo she'd sent me. It was Will's new LinkedIn profile picture.

'They probably photoshopped it,' I said.

'God – he's impressive! Did we know this?' Sofia asked, skimming his profile. 'Undergrad degree in maths. JD, BCL from Oxford. Associateship on the High Court. He must be some kind of genius.'

'Maths and law – a laugh a minute.'

'How would having Dick Next Door in your house half the week sit with your vow to never let a man into your life, ever, ever again?' Sofia asked.

I'd expected this question. She hadn't won a Walkley by not being direct.

'First, it was a vow to steer clear of relationships, at least until Hazel is all grown up, which is hardly an issue with Dick Next Door. Second, this would be a straight-up business arrangement. Third, it's irrelevant because he's said no. And fourth, it's not as if I'm a catch at the moment.'

'Don't be ridiculous. You're a babe and Dick Next Door would be so lucky. Also, you have the world's cutest baby!'

Monica, my boss and head of marketing, stalked into the open-plan, ergonomically designed kitchen, decorated with motivational posters in company colours ('We're so much more than co-workers – we're family!').

'I've got to run. Sorry. Love you,' I told Sofia and ended the call.

'I've just heard from the agent for forty-six Garden Street. You need to be there at five.' Monica didn't look up from her phone as she spoke, or acknowledge that I was eating.

Kajal, our receptionist and sunshine in human form, called Monica 'Eeyore' behind her back, because she was permanently miserable. Her emotional range spanned from put upon (when the managing director wanted her to do something), to let down (when one of us did anything for her).

'Is there any chance we could get access earlier?' I asked, trying to disguise my panic.

'Is there an issue?' she asked, finally looking up.

She knew there was. Yesterday, I'd had the conversation I'd been dreading – the one where I had to spell out that I was on my own and was pretty much unavailable outside of working hours. I'd hoped to last longer than two days, but when she'd scheduled a breakfast meeting and then asked me to meet a client at a twilight photoshoot, my hand had been forced.

'I need to pick up Hazel by five-thirty.'

'Could someone else do it?' she asked, in the simpering voice she used when she was being unreasonable.

'No. There's no one else. Just me,' I said, my throat tightening. I could ask Camille – she'd be picking up the twins. But she didn't have a baby car seat anymore. And I could just imagine another phone call from Mum asking why I'd dropped another ball, yet again. 'Could I do it tomorrow?'

'Fine. See if they can give you access,' she said, already halfway out the door, voice loaded with her standard mix of exasperation and benevolence.

'Isn't Thursday a non-working day?' asked Kajal, who'd arrived mid-conversation, as she filled up her rainbow metallic drink bottle.

'Yep.' I sighed into my sushi roll. I'd have to take Hazel along. It would no doubt be in the middle of one of her nap times. Or meal times. Or feeding times. At least I'd been doing this job for so long that I could knock it out easily enough.

'Will you get paid overtime?' she asked. I raised an eyebrow and we both giggled. We knew Monica would prefer to set fire to a pile of cash than authorise overtime payments.

'I have access to her calendar.' Kajal lowered her voice. 'This afternoon she's got a site visit in Toorak, then she's going straight from there to get a facial. Don't stress about leaving today – Eeyore will be too busy having her face Botoxed into submission to be riding your arse.'

'Thanks,' I said, both intensely grateful for the intel and a one-day reprieve from sneaking out of the office at five on the dot, pretending to ignore Monica's death stares.

But I was also a bit surprised. I knew that working mums ranked in popularity somewhere between the guy in accounts who questioned every expense claim and the person who ate a tuna-based lunch at their desk every day. We were the cohort who always called in sick at the last minute, who didn't volunteer to join the committee to organise the EOFY party, and who snagged all the annual leave over the school holidays. The last person I'd expected to be an ally was our glamorous Gen Z receptionist.

She must have seen that I was a bit confused because she said, 'I don't like bullies.' Then she winked one of her

Euphoria-esque eyelids at me as she sashayed out of the kitchen.

After lunch, I was furiously finishing the copy for a 'period gem' when my mobile rang.

Monica, from across the open-plan office, stared at my flashing screen like a hawk. She'd caught me scrolling through photos of Hazel earlier in the day, and hadn't been able to disguise her disapproval. She spent a good chunk of her day online shopping, but it was clear that if I wanted breaks to pump and to leave work on time my phone was off limits.

Annoyance turned to panic as I saw an unknown number. Was it childcare? Had something happened to Hazel? Anxiety began to twist around me as tightly as an ergonomic baby wrap.

'Hello, Zoe speaking,' I answered.

'It's Will Flemming,' he said, in his deep, steady voice.

I hadn't seen him since the ambush. Honestly, my current plan was to avoid him forever.

'I've been reflecting on your … proposal.'

'Yes?' I replied, feeling my heart begin to pound. Was this conversation really happening?

I stood up and walked away from Monica's pricked-up ears.

'After our conversation, I read our firm's new parental-leave policy. As I said yesterday, I'm not willing to say I'm Hazel's biological father …'

'Right,' I said. Where was he going with this?

'… But one of the key principles of our policy is that to be a parent isn't just a function of biology. And … some of the definitions in the policy have been drafted broadly. For example, if we'd begun a relationship after you got pregnant and I'd effectively become a co-parent or a guardian to Hazel with plans to adopt her, then, on my reading of the policy, I'd still be eligible for parental leave.'

'Right. So … we'd have to pretend that we're together? And that you've been helping me with Hazel since she was born?'

'Exactly.'

'But isn't that just a different lie?'

'Well, yes,' he said. I could hear impatience in his voice, as if I were a difficult client. 'But this version of events makes more sense because it's closer to the truth. It accounts for the donor if anyone found out about that. We're not misrepresenting Hazel's biological parentage, just … the precise nature of our relationship. It's lower risk. And more logical.'

So, instead of being enemies, we'd be pretending to be in a relationship. I could now feel my heart pounding in my ears, and I took a deep breath.

Of course, Will had made a counteroffer – one that hinged on an interpretation of a policy. But I didn't necessarily hate his plan. I'd felt uneasy that Hazel was the focus of our lie, whereas now the lie was about … well, us. And, at the end of the day, the only people who were ever going to hear Will's version of events were his boss, Robert, and whoever processed the paperwork in their HR department. No one else ever had to know about our arrangement.

'Okay,' I said.

There was a pause. I could practically hear him pacing around his office, which I bet was high up above the city, all glass windows and neat piles of paper, as he ordered his thoughts. From his lofty height, he probably looked down on my office building in Cremorne, a wedge of the city between the MCG and the river that housed the city's marketing and advertising agencies in former factory buildings.

'Okay. I'll speak with Robert this afternoon and lock everything in. Just to check the terms of the agreement, you're prepared for me to tell my firm that I'm your partner and Hazel's co-parent. And you'll corroborate this story if required. I'll take three months' leave and care for Hazel, Monday to Wednesday inclusive. And the other days are unencumbered. Are you comfortable with these terms?'

He was using his serious negotiating voice. In his mind, this was clearly a straight-up-and-down transaction. Which, as I'd told Sofia, it was.

I paused for a moment. Now my head was pounding too.

What if I said no? Today was our last day at Camille's childcare. Then, nothing. My inbox had been flooded with centre managers politely telling me they might have a spot available towards the end of the year, which was still months away.

I'd known from the minute Hazel was born and passed to me – wrinkled, still covered in gunk but alert – that I'd do anything to protect her. I'd promised her that I'd build a safe world for just the two of us. But practically, to do this I needed childcare and a job, which meant I was going to have to let someone into our world.

Maybe it was perfect that this someone was Will. He was my nemesis. We both knew that this was a transaction. And once it was finished, it would be easy to pull up the drawbridge. We could go back to ignoring each other. Or I could move – rent somewhere else that didn't desperately need new stumps.

If I said yes, I'd have some breathing room to find a childcare centre that wasn't a dive. And I could, hand on heart, tell Mum and Camille I'd sorted everything out.

'Yes, I am comfortable with these terms.'

'Okay. We've agreed in principle. We can iron out the details over the next few days,' he said. 'Speak soon.'

'Wait,' I said before he could hang up. 'Why are you doing this? Why did you change your mind?' I asked. It felt important to know.

There was a long pause at the other end of the line.

'Today, Robert popped by my office for a chat. He wanted to know how Hazel's first few days of childcare had gone.'

'That's nice of him,' I said, not following how some office small talk had changed his mind.

'That's never happened before. Not in the eight years I've worked for him. It was the first time he'd … well, seen me as a proper human and not some super-law nerd who could answer all his twisty technical questions, urgently.' He paused. 'I want this promotion. And the lawyers who actually know the law, and work their arses off, aren't necessarily the ones who make it across the line. At the end of the day, they have to like you. I read the research – you're right, people like dads.'

I nodded, even though he couldn't see me. I knew he was telling me the truth, though I suspected there was more to the story. But it was good enough, for now.

A new email popped up as I fed Hazel dinner – 'Draft Contract' from Will Flemming. I spooned some pumpkin puree into her mouth, which like the rest of her face was fluorescent orange, then clicked on it. The email was from his personal account.

Z. I've drafted up a basic agreement between us. Pls review contract and make proposed amendments, if any. Thnks. W

His abrupt style, which brutalised vowels, was nothing if not consistent. A Word document was attached.

For a moment, I felt a bit taken aback. Hadn't we reached an agreement on the phone? A contract was so formal. So black and white – literally.

I clicked on the attachment and scanned the first page.

Contract between
William Flemming
and
Zoe Harper
dated [Insert]

Recitals: The purpose of this agreement is to set out the terms of the arrangement ('The Arrangement') between William Flemming ('The Carer') and Zoe Harper ('The Mother') for care of Hazel Harper ('The Baby').

I skimmed over the 'Definitions' and 'Interpretations' sections, until I reached the interesting part.

Section 3 – The Carer

The Carer agrees for the term of The Arrangement to:

(1) care for The Baby on Mondays, Tuesdays and Wednesdays from 8.30 am to 5.30 pm and at such other reasonable times as mutually agreed between the parties;
(2) follow reasonable directions of The Mother as to the care of The Baby; and
(3) The Carer will, as required, publicly do all things consistent with being in a personal and co-parenting relationship with The Mother.

Section 4 – The Mother

The Mother agrees for the term of The Arrangement to:

(1) provide support as reasonably required for The Carer to seek paid parental leave from The Firm; and
(2) The Mother will, as required, publicly do all things consistent with being in a personal and co-parenting relationship with The Carer.

I had to admire Will for managing to make 'pretend to be your fake girlfriend' sound both so pretentious and dull. And despite my initial hesitation that this was overkill, I liked the idea of having everything about our set-up set out with the boundaries clearly established.

I scanned the rest of the two-page contract. Will had asked for my thoughts, if any. I very much had some.

Once Hazel was in bed, I printed a copy on the only piece of printing paper I could find – on the back of a Woolworths delivery receipt. Then I scribbled my thoughts on it, as requested, and popped it under Will's door.

CHAPTER 5

Subject: Response to Draft 2 of The Contract
From: William.Flemming@flemming.com
To: Zoe.Harper@gmail.com

Z,

<u>* Do not accept addition of inserted clause:</u>

3A The Carer's vibe

The Carer promises, ipso facto, to:

(1) smile more than frown at The Baby;

(2) not to be judgey about The Mother's house, outfits, life et al.; and

(3) not use his phone at The Mother's house except for the following reasons:

  (a) checking time, weather, setting timers ('Boring Phone Things');

  (b) sneakily checking Instagram, Facebook, BeReal, TikTok ('Social Media') when The Baby's awake windows drag on; and

  (c) playing the following music: The Wiggles, Baby Lullaby Playlist, Cocomelon (if desperate).

For the avoidance of doubt, habeas corpus, this means that The Carer will not do any of his normal legal job during The Arrangement.

* Do not accept below amendment to Clause 3 – The Carer:

(2) follow reasonable and unreasonable directions of The Mother as to the care of The Baby.

* Do accept below clause:

Section 8 – Life after The Arrangement

When The Arrangement ends, The Mother and The Carer will go back to living their own separate lives. They will not be required to acknowledge it ever happened, or each other.

Consider and revert. Refrain from using Latin in further revisions – it makes no sense and we do not live in 1552.

W

Subject: Response to Draft 3 of The Contract
From: Zoe.Harper@gmail.com
To: William.Flemming@flemming.com

Hi Will,

Fine, delete the vibe clause, but FYI – I'll be informally enforcing it. ☺

Hypothetical question – is there a way to make a friendly greeting each morning legally enforceable?

Thanks!

Best, Zoe

Subject: Response to Draft 6 of The Contract
From: William.Flemming@flemming.com
To: Zoe.Harper@gmail.com

Z,

Would appreciate serious comments only. It's Friday night and The Arrangement is scheduled to begin on Monday morning. We need final execution version to sign over weekend.

W

Subject: Response to Draft 6 of The Contract

From: Zoe.Harper@gmail.com

To: William.Flemming@flemming.com

Hi Will,

Execution version sounds a bit intense, doesn't it? Like you're about to put on a hood and sharpen your axe. Think term needs a rebrand – maybe the 'You finally agree with me' version? You can use that if you want.

Happy to sign this one. Thanks! ☺

Best, Zoe

Subject: Final version of The Contract – for your records

From: William.Flemming@flemming.com

To: Zoe.Harper@gmail.com

Please find attached final executed version of The Contract.

Subject: Final version of The Contract – for your records

From: Zoe.Harper@gmail.com

To: William.Flemming@flemming.com

Thanks!

I've just told Hazel – she responded by eating her sock – I'm taking that as a big thumbs (toes?) up.

So, I guess this means … we're doing this.

Best, Zoe

On Saturday morning, I called an emergency summit with Sofia. Negotiating the contract hadn't felt real – more like one of our normal neighbourly sparring sessions. But since Will had sent through the final version replete with our signatures (his predictably spiky), the weight of the plan I'd conjured up, of what we'd agreed to, had hit me. I needed her to tell me that everything was going to be fine.

I'd invited Camille, too. I'd toyed with telling her the plan, but in the end settled on a version of the truth, one that glossed over Will and our faux relationship. Tactically, I was banking on the fact that she was less likely to stage an inquisition in front of Sofia.

It was a crisp, blue-skied morning, and we'd decided to walk The Tan, the track around the Royal Botanical Gardens that skirted the edge of the city and the river. As I pushed Hazel's pram towards South Yarra, past darkened nail salons and hairdressers, primary-coloured hot-air balloons sponsored by shopping centres and radio stations floated overhead, puncturing the quiet morning with hisses of gas. They were probably filled with couples about to stage social media–friendly engagements. But this morning, I was too exhausted and distracted to feel cynical.

Sofia and I met early so we could talk candidly. She'd nabbed a table at Gilson, a cafe heaving with both the suburb's retirees and yummy mummies, united by their love of blonde hair dye, filler and Lycra. It wasn't really our scene, but they made nuclear coffee and accommodated prams.

Sofia stood out from the sea of black-and-beige active wear in a tangerine leotard peeping out from under a lavender sweatshirt, her dark perm held up by a lime-green scrunchy. She was only five feet tall and had a snub nose that meant she'd forever be able to pass as twenty – but with her bob of curls and cheeky smile, you couldn't miss her.

'Love your outfit,' I said, as I awkwardly manoeuvred the pram, where Hazel was finally napping (after a night of partying), next to our tiny table.

'I've got dance class after this.'

'Oh, how's it going?'

'I'm obsessed. Everyone is beyond extra and you spend the semester learning a dance routine for a massive concert. You'll come, right?'

''Course,' I said, already dreading it.

'No, I promise it'll be objectively amazing. Here's a video from the last one.'

She passed me her phone, and we both watched a clip of a group of lithe adults in Eurovision-style costumes and makeup gyrating under professional lighting across the stage of an enormous theatre. It was very extra, and very Sofia.

'The teacher's choreographing the whole dance around me and the unborn. My belly's going to be planet Earth – they're going to paint it and everything.' She cradled her bump, affectionately. 'But enough about my grown-up Rock Eisteddfod journey. We're here to talk about you.'

'Well, the main agenda item is how I convinced my nemesis to become my small, helpless baby's manny, and am now having all the doubts,' I said. 'God, I'm an idiot. I blame sleep deprivation.'

'I blame the structures of the patriarchy,' Sofia said. 'But blame aside, I think you're a genius. This is the manny-cure to your problems. Instead of paying $180 a day for Hazel to get hand, foot and mouth disease, which by the way is an illness that needs a rebrand, she'll be cared for by someone with a graduate degree in her own familiar environment. For free!'

I exhaled. This was exactly what I needed to hear.

'I'm not worried about Hazel. I'm more worried about how you're going to cope having a hot nerd in your house all day, when you're not getting any?'

'You can cross that worry off your list. Last night, we signed a contract setting out very clear boundaries for the next three months.'

'How very *Fifty Shades*, except in reverse,' she said. 'So, there's a "no sex" clause in this contract?'

'That's one contingency we did not need to prepare for,' I said. 'Between everything Will does, says and is, and my lack of sleep, every interaction we have is a "no sex" clause.'

'Hello, I'm here!' Camille appeared beside our table, early.

Sofia and Camille hugged.

'Should I go up and order coffees? Takeaways so we can get moving?' Camille bounced up and down on the spot. She was pulled together – every strand of her dark, straight hair was in place and she was wearing a running shirt that I suspected had been ironed, but her energy was even more manic than usual.

'What can I get you, Sof? Something decaf?'

'Nope – just a regular caffeinated long black for me,' she replied.

'Oh, right.' Camille failed to hide her disapproval. When she'd been pregnant with the twins she'd followed every rule, and then made up a few more. 'I guess we all have our own risk appetite.'

I felt a flicker of annoyance. I was used to her being critical of my life decisions, but she didn't have to impose her super-high standards on my friends, too.

'I'm nothing but appetite at the moment,' Sofia said lightly. 'And my doula said a coffee a day is totally fine.'

'Maybe grab some muffins?' I suggested, before Camille shared her thoughts on doulas. I knew when it came to pregnancy, she didn't trust anyone who hadn't spent most of their twenties, and ideally their thirties, in a medical training program.

Coffees secured, we began to walk.

'Are the kids with Ed?' I asked. It was rare to get Camille alone on the weekend – after a week in the office, she spent most of her time with the twins.

'Yep, he volunteered to do swimming lessons this morning. He was at a conference all week and he's playing golf this afternoon, so he wanted to have time with them,' she said.

I wondered, not for the first time, how Ed got away with such an 'opt-in' parenting style.

'Now – have you sorted childcare for next week?'

I was impressed she'd lasted this long – we'd covered a whole hundred metres.

'I have.'

Her arched eyebrows shot up. 'Which centre?'

'Not a centre. There's an older lady on our street who loves Hazel. We got talking and she's keen for some part-time work. She's going to come to our house on my working days.'

I was very aware this was slightly more than glossing over the truth – that I was in fact actively conjuring up a tale of a *nonna* with too much time on her hands.

'Okay …' Camille said slowly. I could see her methodical mind working through this new development. 'Does she have a lot of experience with babies Hazel's age? References? And a Working With Children Check?'

'I haven't asked. Maybe, probably,' I said.

I saw Sofia try to smother a smirk. Camille gave me a look. She knew me too well.

'I've known my neighbour for years. Surely, that's the best test,' I said.

Camille pursed her lips but didn't say anything further. I knew she thought the best thing for Hazel was somewhere with qualified, uniformed staff, checklists to be ticked and endless policies. Well, I'd tried.

We reached the end of our lap – Camille and Sofia barely pink-cheeked, me huffing and puffing.

'I better hustle. I've got dance class north side,' Sofia filled in Camille.

'Oh fun. Good to get hobbies out of your system now before they become a distant memory,' Camille said.

'Is Ed playing nine or eighteen holes today?' I asked.

'I better go too. He'll be wanting to head off soon.' Camille ignored me. 'Now, are you sure you can trust this person you met on the street with your Hazel?'

'They're a neighbour, not someone I met on the street,' I said, aware that I sounded like a petulant child, as I felt the sting of her disapproval.

'Sometimes you just have to trust people,' Sofia came to my defence.

I nodded gratefully. Although, trusting people wasn't exactly my strong suit anymore.

'Exactly,' I said, with more confidence than I felt, ignoring Camille's concerned stare.

CHAPTER 6

By Monday morning, the enormity of what I'd done had fully hit me. I'd solved our childcare crisis, sure. But I'd agreed to hand over my precious baby to a man who was an expert in equity capital markets (which I assumed were less fun than farmers' markets), but who I suspected had never willingly held a baby.

While Sofia's vote of confidence had been reassuring, it was inevitably Camille's concerns that had wormed their way into my psyche. And she didn't even know about Will.

Since our walk, I'd worked myself into an anxious frenzy. Even if Will showed up this morning (and part of me doubted he would), would I be able to bring myself to leave Hazel with him?

There was a knock on our front door. He was right on time.

I finished wiping yoghurt off Hazel's face and took a peek at myself in the window behind her highchair. I'd left my hair out today. I hadn't had time to wash it, but I'd sprayed in some dry shampoo, which had pulled it back from the edge. I wondered if anyone would notice that I was sort of … bald at the front? No one had told me that the payment for luscious, flowing hair throughout pregnancy would be chunks of it falling out when the baby arrived.

There was another, slightly louder, knock. I scrunched my hair into the bun it'd been in since Hazel had learned to grab and pull, and opened the door.

Will had dressed for the part – the suit was off and he was wearing a pair of jeans and sneakers – the outfit screamed 'casual Friday in the office'. His white T-shirt gleamed, box fresh. I felt another sting of anxiety – he really hadn't spent any time around a baby. Hazel would turn it into a Pollock painting by the end of the day.

'Hello! Ready for paternity leave?' I asked, a bit too brightly, repressing a strong urge to shut the door in his face.

'The *out of office* is on.'

I ushered him inside and led him down the hallway, very aware this was the first time he'd crossed the threshold. I could see him taking in our small living and kitchen area – the orangey pine floors covered in faded Turkish rugs and reclaimed furniture, the walls featuring both hairline cracks that were starting to widen and my collection of colourful prints.

The house was the cleanest and tidiest it had been since Hazel was born. Over the last four days, whenever Hazel was happy rolling around on the floor, I'd stress-cleaned. I'd transferred mountains of clean laundry into cupboards, vacuumed and mopped the floors and wiped off the ring around the bath. I'd sorted, scrubbed and shopped. Although, now viewing it through his eyes, I could see it was still a minor bombsight – plastic baby paraphernalia everywhere and dried Weet-Bix cemented to the side of the table.

'Here's the guide, as promised.' I handed him an exercise book entitled 'An idiot's guide to looking after Hazel Harper'.

We'd meant to do a proper catch-up/induction/training session over the weekend, but Will had got stuck in the office tying up loose ends at work before he went on leave. So, here we were.

'And I'd be the eponymous idiot?'

'If the shoe fits!'

Will flicked through it, his eyes darting over the pages. 'Okay.' He snapped the book shut.

'Right. Milk's in the fridge. Her food's in the fridge. And the bottles are all in this box. And her dummies. Oh, and the baby first-aid stuff is here ...'

I reached up to the high cupboard above the stove for the kit Camille had bought me and put it on the table. He seemed perturbed.

'Oh, don't worry – I've never needed it for Hazel. Only stolen a Band-Aid for myself,' I said.

'No, it's not that. It's ... the zip on your pants is broken,' he said.

'Not broken. Just temporarily out of action,' I said, not meeting his eyes as I yanked my top down over the waistband of my pants, which was fastened together with an elastic hair tie. I knew, without checking, that the gap revealed a pair of pre-pregnancy transparent and lacy undies.

My simmering nerves ratcheted up to boiling point. I couldn't do it. This was a terrible idea. Will might be an efficient, exacting perfectionist but I couldn't leave Hazel with a man who knew absolutely nothing about babies. Who didn't even like them.

'You know how to apply Sudocrem, right? And how to adjust the thermostat so the temperature's right for the sleep suit TOG rating? And ...'

I saw a flash of panic break through his usual impenetrable mask. I was right – he was out of his depth.

Hazel, who'd been happily watching us from her highchair, suddenly squawked. We both moved to pick her up at the same time.

'Let me. Please,' Will said.

Reluctantly, I stepped aside and watched him gingerly unbuckle the straps and lift her up. She lunged for his glasses and he let her pull them off his face. He jiggled her up and down and she gurgled happily.

'Right, Hazel. We have forty-five minutes to get to know each other before your morning nap!' He spoke to her in a silly voice, which made her smile.

How the hell had he already memorised the schedule? He'd only flicked through my notes.

'I have a photographic memory,' he said with a shrug, as if reading my thoughts. 'Now let's do some tummy time. To help with your motor development.'

I involuntarily smiled. I had a sudden vision of Will buying and thumbing through a new copy of *Baby Love*, highlighting key paragraphs and making detailed notes. I almost felt sorry for him thinking that being in charge of a a baby was a situation where a textbook would give him all the answers. A book couldn't explain why Hazel suddenly made tiger noises when I put her down for a nap.

Or that mandarins gave her nappy rash. Or that 'Baa Baa Black Sheep' sung on an endless loop could sometimes keep her happy during the witching hours.

But a flair for silly voices, a commitment to my schedule and the knowledge that he'd done some research was a reassuring triumvirate. I felt the knot of anxiety, which had become increasingly tighter all weekend, loosen just enough.

'Go! This arrangement is useless if you don't actually go to work,' he said.

'Right,' I said. This was the part where I was meant to leave him with my baby, my world.

I leaned in to kiss Hazel goodbye, very aware she was still in Will's arms. I kissed her head, inhaling her intoxicating smell. And I inadvertently smelled Will, too – a mix of fresh laundry, ground coffee and woody cologne.

I gave Hazel one more kiss then I left her with Will, wondering how the combination of Johnson's baby shampoo and whatever no doubt expensive aftershave he wore, could be so reassuring.

Late afternoon, my phone pinged at my desk. It was a notification from Hazel's baby monitor app – it had picked up movement.

I'd promised myself I wouldn't check the monitor today, because I didn't believe in employers spying on their employees. Not that Will was my employee, exactly.

Another notification pinged. Okay, I wasn't going to spy on Will – I just wanted a glimpse of Hazel. I missed her so much it felt like a physical ache. I was like an addict craving a hit. I clicked.

My screen filled with a live video stream of our bedroom. Hazel was lying on her change mat screaming her head off.

'Ba, ba, ba, ba, bum, bum, bum, bum,' I heard Will singing. Was it ... 'Ode to Joy'? Had the man never heard of 'Twinkle, Twinkle'.

Hazel's wails intensified. Even though the video was black and white, I could tell that her face was bright red.

'Pick her up and cuddle her, you idiot!' I said to my phone. Monica gave me a pointed look from across the room.

'How about we agree that if I change your nappy you stop crying. Okay?' He sounded wrung out and frustrated.

I watched him struggle with the press studs on her bodysuit, then fumble to put on a clean nappy back to front as Hazel's cries reached a crescendo.

My heart felt like it had been mashed into a puree, as I watched helplessly until Will finally picked her up and they left the bedroom.

I stared at the video feed of our now empty bedroom for a few seconds then messaged Sofia.

Zoe Harper: Disaster! Dick Next Door as manny a total mistake.

Sofia Vass: Is Hazel okay?

Zoe Harper: She's fine. For now.

Sofia Vass: What happened?

Zoe Harper: The guy can't work out how to change a nappy. And he's letting her scream!

Sofia Vass: Eek!

Zoe Harper: I think I had this fantasy that he was going to be the male equivalent of a young Julie Andrews. A magical manny who'd teach Hazel how to sing and make her new clothes out of his curtains.

Sofia Vass: I think Dick Next Door is more of a Mr Banks/ Captain Von Trapp vibe, TBH.

Zoe Harper: I know. Which is fine. Love them both, by the end. But I can't let Hazel be his human guinea pig.

Sofia Vass: What are you going to do?

I held my fingers over the screen for a moment.

Zoe Harper: End it.

It was almost five. I'd leave on the dot, race home to rescue Hazel, then tell Will it wasn't going to work out. He could return to lawyering tomorrow and tell his boss I'd wanted to stay at home a bit longer – people changed their plans all the time. After a whole day with a baby, he'd probably be relieved.

Sofia Vass: Follow your gut.

Zoe Harper: Yep. Now I just need to work out how to break up with my fake boyfriend.

CHAPTER 7

I arrived home, mentally steeling myself for my first-ever breakup where I was the one doing the dumping. Not that Adam had had the decency to have a proper grown-up conversation and properly call it quits – he'd just begun to spend more nights at his apartment, gone on endless work trips and weekends away with The Boyz and taken days to reply to my messages. And by the time he told me he didn't want to marry me or have children, there was almost no relationship to end.

I tiptoed down the hallway, overriding an urge to fling open our bedroom door and run to Hazel's cot. If the past six months had taught me anything it was that getting a baby to sleep was real work.

Will was standing at the sink rinsing bottles.

'Hi, I'm home,' I said softly, as I gently shut the living-room door behind me. I felt like an interloper in my own home. 'How'd it go?'

'Good,' he said as he slowly dried his hands on a tea towel, then carefully hung it across the rail. 'Obviously, it was a steep learning curve. But she's fed and clean and napping. And we didn't end up at the Royal Children's.'

'That's an exceedingly low KPI.'

Will shrugged. 'Hazel's fine, but there's something I want to talk about.' He seemed cagey.

My hackles went up. I knew this tone – it was the one you used before you had an awkward conversation with your boss – it was the same hesitant, apologetic tone I'd used when I'd told Monica I was pregnant and would be taking maternity leave. He was going to quit.

'I knew you couldn't hack it. God – one day with a baby and you're fleeing back to the shiny world of the city!' I spoke before I could stop myself. It was as if all the angst and worry that had been building up for the last couple of hours had escaped the pressure valve.

What was I doing? This situation was perfect. If Will wanted to quit, I wouldn't have to fire him. I just needed to shut my mouth.

'How did you know I was going to quit?'

'Because looking after a baby all day on your own is exhausting. And monotonous. And no one gives you gold stars.'

'But you think I shouldn't quit?'

I paused for a second. This was the exact opening to say, 'Of course you should quit, I won't have anyone caring for my baby who's not completely invested. Go back to living your prestigious, corporate-ladder-climbing life. We'll be fine.'

'First, we made an agreement and by bailing on us you'd make our lives very difficult. And second, you already seem less like you're on the edge of a nervous breakdown. I'm going to be honest ...' I said, instead.

'... because you're normally so coy,' he supplied.

'You were grey with exhaustion. I'm sure you were on the edge of burnout. You already look less like the walking dead and it's only been a day.'

I braced, waiting for him to return my serve. Whenever I'd said even the most innocuously critical thing to Adam, he hadn't taken it well. He had a hair-trigger temper and would huff and puff until I'd retracted the statement and showered him in effusive compliments.

Will seemed taken aback.

'What do you mean?' The question wasn't defensive, more genuinely confused.

'Well ...' I said, in a slightly gentler voice. 'Before today, you seemed constantly wrecked. You worked all hours of the day and night, and you never slept. Your vibe was a bit ... zombie.'

He considered this for a moment. Was this really news to him?

'Being a lawyer is a full-on job,' he said. 'I was just working hard. I'm fine.'

'But you need a break,' I pushed him. 'You need some balance, some fun in your life!'

'I didn't need time off. I needed an edge to make partner.' He stared calmly at me. 'And the dad-who-took-parental-leave card was it. Anyway, I'm not going to quit.'

'You're not?' I asked, suddenly wrong-footed.

He carefully began to place the rinsed bottles in the base of the steriliser I'd forgotten to show him how to use.

'Today was hard. I was slightly in over my head. Nappies don't come with instruction manuals, though they should. The book said I'd be able to tell what her different cries meant, but apparently, I'm cry tone-deaf. And I used her bath thermometer to measure the temperature of her milk because I was worried about scalding her.'

'So, you do want to quit?' I asked again.

He stared at me like I was a moron. 'My whole life has been full of things that are hard. And I've worked it out, pushed through. I've never quit something because it's tough. I spent a year working for a partner who regularly threw things at her juniors. I don't quit. I don't let people down. Ever. I won't leave you.'

Everyone leaves, my brain screamed. *Everyone leaves you.*

'Everyone quits things,' I said, instead.

'I haven't.'

'What do you mean. You must have quit something.'

'Never. If I sign up for something I see it through. All the way.'

'Would you quit your job if they didn't make you partner?'

For a moment, his face filled with panic. It was the first time I'd seen anything other than supreme confidence radiate from him.

'You'll make partner,' I said. 'I was joking. Of course you will.'

He put down the steriliser then rested both hands on the kitchen table.

'I believe in commitment. And sticking to things. Staying the course – even, especially, during the lonely, shit bits. Being Hazel's carer is going to have some of those. Bring it on.' He gave me a searching look. 'Do you want me to quit?'

I paused for a second too long. He snapped the steriliser lid into place.

'Good. Then I'll see you tomorrow at eight-thirty.' And before I could reply he was already walking down the hallway.

I didn't feel angry anymore – more disarmed. And I realised that I hadn't asked him what he wanted to talk about.

A few hours later, once I'd smothered Hazel in hugs and inhaled my sanctioned glass of wine, I picked up my phone.

What did you actually want to talk about? I typed, and then pressed 'send' before I could overthink it.

Before you went off the deep end? he wrote back, almost instantly. Clearly, day one of our arrangement hadn't broken his phone addiction. Or directness.

Zoe Harper: Don't believe you've never quit anything. A sport?

Will Flemming: No. I joined Little Aths when I was a kid. Still run every day.

Zoe Harper: I've quit enough for both of us. Tennis, golf, cycling.

My finger hovered over the 'send' button as I reread my message. As I'd typed them out, I realised that each of the sports was a passion of an ex-boyfriend – high school, university, Adam.

I deleted the message.

Three dots appeared on the screen.

Will Flemming: I was going to ask if there's a day each week where you know you won't be working late? I thought I might sign up for a regular gym class. But no worries if not/you need the flexibility etc. Just an idea. Thought I might try to do some things while I have a bit more time. But totally fine if it doesn't suit.

I stared at the message for a moment. Will was always so sure of himself. But he'd appeared so hesitant this afternoon. And his message was full of disclaimers. Was this really what put him on edge – ring-fencing an evening for himself? It was hardly a big ask. Particularly not after I'd asked him to be my fake boyfriend. But then again, I'd never seen him arrive home from work during daylight hours. Maybe this was a huge deal to him.

Zoe Harper: Of course. Any night. You don't have to ask!

Will Flemming: Thnks.

I laughed, startling Hazel, who was lying against me feeding. Was his message a joke, or a brush-off? Was it possible he was funny, or did he just have a major problem with vowels?

I left WhatsApp and opened another message thread.

Sofia Vass: How'd it go?

Zoe Harper: I didn't do it. You know how Camille asked whether I trusted a stranger with Hazel? Well, Will might be an arsehole, but I believe he's going to try really hard to look after her.

I pressed 'send'.

As Hazel finished her feed and I scooped her up to begin our bedtime routine, I saw the kitchen light snap on in Will's house. I'd thought after so many years of living next door to him and our long-running feud, I'd known everything about his life, that I'd had the measure of him. But tonight, I'd glimpsed a side of him I'd never seen before – a glimmer of self-awareness, maybe a trace of a sense of humour.

I didn't know the guy next door. And given he was now my daughter's manny, the person apart from me she'd be spending most of her waking hours with, and my fake boyfriend, I needed to find out.

CHAPTER 8

The next day, I got home from work on time, determined to be both civil and sane. Hazel and I had been running seriously behind schedule in the morning, and so Will and I barely had a chance to talk before I raced out the door. And, using a reserve of self-control I didn't know I possessed, I'd refrained from checking the monitor all day. Even when I missed Hazel so much I had to go to the bathroom with my phone to watch videos of her.

But this evening, I was determined to begin project 'Get to Know Will'.

Will was kneeling in the playpen, tidying up Hazel's books.

'Honey, I'm home!' I trilled, then instantly felt like an idiot. 'I mean, hi.'

Will responded by holding up the book he was about to add to a neat stack (probably now arranged by the Dewey Decimal System). It was *My Farm* – one of Hazel's favourites. I could recite it from memory – a truly useless party trick. 'Have you noticed how many children's books are about farmyard animals?'

'Um, no,' I said, as I surreptitiously pulled out the two plastic bags of milk I'd pumped earlier out of my bag. 'But what's wrong with that?'

'These books form part of the education for the child's life ahead,' he said. 'How many kids these days are going to spend their lives toiling in the fields? Maybe two hundred years ago that was the norm. But now, we live in a developed economy. There's a reason why they no longer teach sickle skills at school.'

'So what, we should have books about smart phones and AI?' I asked, as I shoved the two sachets behind an almost empty container of Häagen-Dazs.

'Exactly.'

'Old MacDonald had a spreadsheet, e-i-e-i-iPhone!' I broke out into song, then felt instantly self-conscious, again.

'Old MacDonald's farm would have been acquired by Monsanto. I'm just saying that an early appreciation for say, binary code, would be more helpful than knowing that a cow goes moo and a pig goes oink,' he said, as he swung his long legs over the top of the playpen walls.

'How did today go?' I asked, trying to play it a bit cool but desperate to know.

'I wrote it all down. I thought you might feel more comfortable if you knew exactly what the two of us had got up to,' he said. He passed me a new notebook that was sitting on the clean kitchen table. *Hazel's Days* was written on the front in marker.

I suppressed a smile – I wasn't the only one who'd resolved to try my hardest today.

'You don't have to record everything,' I said, as I opened it up, though I secretly loved the idea that I would know every detail.

'I'm a lawyer. I'm used to keeping time sheets. If I don't write it down, I feel no sense of achievement,' he said.

I looked up to check if he was joking. He wasn't. I bit my tongue to stop myself saying something catty. We were on the same team now – Hazel's team – but old habits were hard to break.

'We did have one slight hiccup over lunch. She didn't want to eat much,' he said.

'Really?' I was surprised. I'd left an ice-cube tray full of pureed sweet potato, which Hazel normally inhaled.

'I think she found it a bit …' he searched for a word. 'Cold.'

'Cold?' I echoed, confused. 'How long did you microwave it for?'

He stared at me for a moment, then bit his lip. 'I was meant to heat it, wasn't I?'

He'd served her a puree ice block. I nodded as I tried to suppress a wave of laughter surging through me. I couldn't laugh in his face – not at an honest mistake.

'I thought it was a … nutritious icy pole,' he said. Then his lips twitched, and I realised he was trying to hold it together, too.

I broke first, doubling over, making cackling noises, as quietly as I could. Will held onto the table, convulsing with silent laughter.

We finally caught each other's eyes and lost it again.

'I'm sorry,' Will said, when he could finally speak. 'I promise I never make mistakes.'

I stared at him for a moment, through the tears of laughter, trying to work out if he was serious. What kind of person never made mistakes?

Once our hysteria died down, a heavy silence filled the kitchen.

'I better go. There's a lasagne if you want it. I thought you might not have the energy to cook,' Will said.

'Thanks,' I said, not knowing what else to say. I knew how to handle irritated and irritating Will. But I didn't know what to do with this version – the Will who laughed and who, apparently, could be quietly thoughtful.

'And thanks for today. Seriously, for the first time since I've been back at work, I was able to mostly focus on the job,' I said. 'How'd you find it? Bit different from your normal Tuesday?'

'Yep, very different. And physically more exhausting, for sure. But honestly, it was nice to …' He paused. '… See the world through a child's, well through Hazel's, eyes. We went to the park and she spent half an hour watching a tree, just smiling. I lay next to her and wondered when did we stop noticing trees, you know?'

I did know. I loved seeing the world afresh through her eyes – all of it new and magical.

'It's really weird to have an evening ahead of me with nothing to do. I can't even remember the last time this happened.' He sounded a bit freaked out.

'Stay and have some lasagne? If you don't mind eating dinner while it's still light,' I said, before I could stop myself.

'Are you sure?' He sounded surprised. He'd probably expected himself to say no.

'I need to give Hazel peanut butter to try. But I didn't want to do it on my own in case she reacts. So, you'd be doing me a favour, anyway.'

He nodded. It was another transaction – he got dinner and I had someone to crisis-manage alongside me in the event of anaphylaxis.

'The lasagne's in the fridge. I typically eat mine cold, but you probably want it heated up?' he offered.

I laughed again. I would never have guessed that beneath Will's brusque, corporate facade was the ability to be self-deprecating.

'I'm crazy like that. Wineglasses are in the top left-hand cupboard,' I said, as I turned on the oven then grabbed an already open bottle of white wine from the fridge.

Will pulled down two wineglasses and filled them.

'Warning. You could probably dress a salad with this stuff,' I said.

'I thought wine came in a box until I was a teenager. Anything in a bottle still feels fancy to me.'

I felt wrong-footed again. I'd had him pegged as a private-school boy who grew up in a house with a cellar. Or at least a wine fridge. Evidently not.

He raised his glass. 'To Hazel.'

I clinked his glass with mine and took a large gulp.

His phone rang, and he checked the caller ID. 'Work,' he said, his strained, guarded expression returning. 'I should get this.'

'Should you?' I asked. 'I mean, are they meant to be calling you during parental leave?'

His finger wavered over the 'answer' button, itching to press it. I got the impression he had never knowingly missed a work call.

'Ring them back later. Tell them you were busy with bath and bedtime,' I said.

He slowly put his phone on the table and turned it over. 'Have you had much help until now? Is your mum close by?' he asked.

'She lives two hours away,' I said, a bit too sharply.

'Where?' He was looking at me, but his fingers were inching across the table towards his phone, almost as if they were playing a game of What's the Time, Mr Wolf.

'I swear, the hours you work are a human rights violation. I don't know how you do it,' I said.

'I just do it.' The strain on his face was now joined by the familiar overlay of irritation.

'Sorry,' I said, meaning it. 'I didn't mean to sound so judgey. I hate it when people say to me, "I don't know how you do it." It really annoys me. Since Hazel, people say it to me all the time and what they really mean is, "I wouldn't have chosen to be a mum on my own."'

Not that my baby and Will's corporate overlords were exactly comparable. And, in my defence, Will did work too hard.

'Thanks. And it's not forever,' he said, still unconsciously stroking his phone. 'I'm up for partner this year and it's just how it works. You kill yourself for a few years, and then you've made it.'

I got the sense that he didn't quite believe his own line. And I'd seen what happened when Camille made partner – you earned more money, but the hours stayed long and the pressure increased.

'I feel the same about Hazel starting primary school,' I said lightly.

He laughed, breaking the pensive mood.

I topped up our glasses, which had been drained already. I knew I shouldn't have any more, but I couldn't handle this conversational rollercoaster without one. I was confident it's what Beyoncé would do.

'We should have done this earlier. Had a drink together. But after you reported me to the council for having ...' He held up his hands to make quote marks. '"A dangerous and unsightly premises" after I put up Halloween decorations, I wasn't really feeling a whole lot of neighbourly good will.'

I had done that. Sofia and I had got drunk and giggly one night and made a joke-complaint to the council citing the jack-o-lanterns and cobwebs hanging from the lacework on his verandah as a 'dangerous descent into Americanisation' and 'unsightly in the most vulgar way'. We'd found it very funny at the time.

'Don't worry, I got a very sternly worded email from the council about time wasting,' I said. Okay, so maybe the blame for our animosity hadn't sat entirely at his feet.

'Fair enough,' he said in a matter-of-fact voice, but his lip twitched.

'Although, Halloween is a stupid American tradition.'

'In my defence, it was my ex-girlfriend who bought the decorations. She did her MBA at Stanford and returned with a love of all "The Holidays",' he said.

Ex-girlfriend. I guessed he was single now – he hadn't mentioned anyone. And what kind of woman wanted her boyfriend pretending to be in a relationship with another woman? But it made sense that this was his type – an overachiever with a prestigious degree who was no doubt now scaling the dizzying heights of something terrifying, like management consulting.

'When did you guys break up?' I couldn't help asking.

'A few years ago.'

'Are you seeing anyone at the moment?'

He shook his head. 'No. I don't really have time for … all that. I went on the apps for a while, but I never actually had time to reply to the messages or go on the dates.'

'Maybe now you've got a bit of time up your sleeve, you can reinstall them?'

'No,' he said. 'I've sworn off relationships until …' He didn't finish his sentence, but I knew what it would be – until he made partner.

I took another sip of wine to stop myself from asking more questions. I knew I had to stop – Will looked as if I was asking him to give a detailed history of his prostate exams.

'So, how's it all going? Being a mum?' he asked, clearly keen to move the conversation away from his love life. But he'd gone big with his question.

'We have our moments. But we're bumbling through, you know.' I gave him my standard-issue answer, one I'd worked up to sound self-deprecating but also in control.

'And how are you really?' he asked. His expression wasn't judgemental. It was the bemused look of someone who knew they hadn't been told the truth.

I took a deep breath. 'It's been bloody hard,' I admitted. 'I wanted this so much. I chose to have her, knowing I'd be on my own. And I love her more than anything, I feel I have to qualify everything with that. But I miss my old life so much. I miss being able to do whatever I want. I miss being stupid with my money, and fitting into my old clothes, and not being covered in milk. I miss sleep! And my brain hurts from paying constant attention to everything. And I just feel so guilty the whole time. And on my own, there's just no break. Ever. It never stops. And it's quite lonely.'

All the things I'd felt but not said for the past six months tumbled out of me. What was it about Will that completely obliterated my filter, my need to keep up a front?

I waited for him to offer a platitude. 'It'll get better', or 'I'm sure everyone feels like that', or 'Have more wine'.

'I'm sorry. That's a lot,' he said. 'Feeling lonely is really shit.'

He spoke like he knew what he was talking about. Although, Will was so self-contained it was hard to imagine him needing someone.

Turning away from him, I pulled the lasagne out of the oven. I scooped enormous, steaming slices onto two plates, while Will set the table that at some point during the day had transformed from a dumping point for Hazel's detritus into a place you could actually eat on.

We sat down opposite each other, and I raised my glass again.

'To The Arrangement,' I said. When he clinked his glass against mine, it felt significant – the domestic equivalent of a white flag being waved. As if we'd reached, at least for now, a truce.

I took a forkful and groaned. 'This is amazing! It's like a proper rich ragu, but cheesy.'

Will took a bite and raised an approving eyebrow. 'Okay, that is bloody good.'

'I want to eat this every meal for the rest of my life. Where'd you get it?'

'I took Hazel on a walk to the Prahran Market. It's so close to us, but I hadn't been there in years. The firm has a chef, and they cook dinner for us every night. Or they pay for takeaway if we're working late.'

I'd seen the parade of delivery people on bikes turning up next door. I'd assumed that food was just another part of his life he'd happily streamlined – the culinary equivalent of his underwear subscription. But across the table, I could see how much he was enjoying a meal that hadn't come from a paper bag.

'I get it. I actually can't remember the last time I had a proper dinner. Something that wasn't microwaved or mostly came from a tin or a jar. Which is crazy, because I love food. But I guess, something had to give.'

'Maybe over the next few months we attempt to occasionally eat properly again?' Will suggested.

'Should we add in an additional term in the contract?' I teased. 'The Carer and The Mother agree for the duration of The Arrangement to eat food that, one, is delicious and, two, isn't left on our doorstep.'

'We're not touching the contract. I've completed hostile takeovers that had less heavily negotiated documents.'

'I guess I just have a natural talent for it. Ipso facto.'

He smiled, and I took a large gulp of wine. I needed it. Because I realised that over the course of our conversation, my deeply held belief that Dick Next Door was fundamentally an arsehole with no redeeming features, was being challenged. One of the axes of my, admittedly small, world had shifted.

CHAPTER 9

Notification: Will Flemming has changed the name of the chat to 'Hazel's Days'.

Will Flemming: Hazel's learned to hit the rattle on her play gym.

Zoe Harper: The elephant one?

Will Flemming: Yes.

Zoe Harper: I knew she had it in for him.

Will Flemming: I reckon in a few months I can get her started on a mini-violin.

Zoe Harper: Stop trying to hothouse my daughter. Maybe she's a beautiful dummy!

Will Flemming: No. I'm calling it – she's a genius. I reckon I can teach her to say 'Will' before the end of The Arrangement.

Zoe Harper: If 'Will' is her first word I will exact revenge. I'll sign you up to be Santa at the street party this year.

Will Flemming: You have an evil mind.

A month later, I was in the office hiding from Monica when my phone pinged. It was a photo from Will.

Apparently, he'd bought Hazel a pair of mini-sunglasses. They were objectively ridiculous but also the cutest thing I'd ever seen. When he'd started buying stuff for Hazel, I'd felt uneasy and protested. But he enjoyed spoiling her. His easy generosity had been another surprise.

You spent your hard-earned money on a product called Babiators?! I messaged back.

I zoomed in. Hazel looked like she'd been dressed by a Kardashian. Was she pouting for the camera? We'd decided that one of her key personality traits was attitude. She always knew what she wanted to play with (our car keys and phones) and her determination to learn to crawl was impressive (and definitely not a quality from my portion of her genetics).

We'd slowly got into the habit of texting throughout the day, replacing his detailed, handwritten time sheets with a thread that pinged every hour with messages and photos.

In the reflective lens, I could see Will pulling a goofy face to make her smile.

I'd learned a lot about Will over the past few weeks. He woke up at the exact same time every day (6.15 am) and went for a long run. He had a tailor who embroidered his initials (WAF) into the lining of all his jackets. His photographic memory meant he could recite passages from books and movies. He loved good food as much as I did. And he was a classical music aficionado and pianist extraordinaire, I'd discovered, who'd almost gone to a conservatorium but in the end chose to study maths and law.

Could you please turn up your music, I think it's helping settle Hazel, I'd messaged him last night.

There'd been a pause in the music and then my phone had flashed.

I can't turn it up – it's me playing!

Don't believe you. Though I did.

The gentle tinkling suddenly had switched to an exuberant rendition of 'Baby Shark'.

Okay! Point made – I'm impressed! Something soothing, jukebox.

He'd switched back to Brahms' 'Lullaby' and within seconds Hazel's eyes were fluttering shut.

I'd closed my eyes for a moment, letting the music wash over me. Next door, his hands would be running up and down the smooth white keys, gently but with confidence, the tips of his fingers vibrating as he applied pressure. I'd smiled. Over the past month, our truce had stayed in place. We'd become, as I'd proudly told Sofia, friends.

'There you are!' Monica sniffed me out in the kitchen. 'We've got access to the Park Street place at five – does that work for you?'

Of course it didn't, which she knew.

'I can make it work,' I said. It wasn't Will's gym class tonight – he wouldn't mind staying a bit later.

She gave me one of her reptilian smiles and tapped her pointy nails on the bench. 'I shouldn't be saying this, but …' She paused for effect. 'A new senior role is being created – senior copywriter, covering our prestige properties. And, well, let's just say – you haven't let the baby get in the way of your performance. If you keep it up, it should be yours!' she said sotto voce.

'Wow!' I said, genuinely surprised. I had pretty low expectations for my career post-Hazel. I knew that the reality for lots of mothers was that our careers were like a game of musical chairs – when the baby appeared, the music stopped and that's where we stayed. And that we were lucky to even have a chair – I'd heard too many horror stories about women being made redundant while on maternity leave to take my job for granted. I felt grateful most days that I had a job that had let me go part-time for a while.

But a promotion would be a dream come true. Well, the pay rise would be. Rather than just treading water, I could begin to save – to build a bigger buffer between me and Hazel, and the big, bad world. And maybe one day I could even buy one of the properties I wrote about, a small apartment maybe – somewhere we'd never have to leave.

'I can't tell you how many people turn up after maternity leave and … just. Don't. Perform.' She emphasised these last three words, with three bangs of her fist on the bench. 'They're always running off to grab their kids from care, or taking sick days to look after them, or spend half the day on the phone to the sitter. But not you!'

She chuckled conspiratorially. And I joined in, fully aware that I was betraying my sisterhood of working parents. And knowing that Will and The Arrangement were the only reasons that I was able to turn up to work every day and actually focus on what I was paid to do.

Still, the promise of a promotion on the horizon was good news, and by the time I got home I was feeling buoyant. We'd continued to have 'allergy dinners' as we called them, where we'd have a glass of wine and Hazel would try something new (I've bought a bottle of Chablis and I thought Hazel could try strawberries, Will had messaged earlier in the day). And we'd warm up something from the market, both inhaling food that wasn't microwaved or toast.

But my smile froze when I found Will sitting on my front doorstep, waiting for me.

'She's fine,' he said, before I could speak. 'Fast asleep.'

'What's wrong?' I asked.

'Nothing's wrong, exactly,' he said. 'But I had a call from work today.'

My heart began to beat faster, and my palms felt slippery. Had someone found out what we'd done?

'What did they want?'

'Every year, the partners at my firm go on a big conference. They pick somewhere nice and they all take their families. It's a bit of a junket,' he said.

'So … you're not a partner yet,' I said, not following.

'Well, they've invited me to come along to present on a panel,' he said. 'The presentation. The whole weekend. It's a test, a final hurdle, to see if I fit in.'

Suddenly it clicked. 'And you need to take your family along?'

'It would look really strange if I didn't. Especially when I'm on leave for my family. It's only a long weekend.'

'No way!'

'Technically, under the contract, you agreed to "publicly do all things consistent with being in a personal and co-parenting relationship with The Carer",' he quoted from memory, a trick I usually found deeply impressive but right now was infuriating.

'Screw the contract. You know what our deal is. We agreed that we'd be a couple on a piece of paper. On one piece of paper for your work. It's a totally different thing to do it in person. Go without us. You don't need us there to talk about the law!' I said.

'The panel they want me to be a part of is called …' He paused for a moment, unable to meet my glare. '"Having it all: Balancing Families and the Firm".'

I involuntarily guffawed in disbelief. 'Seriously! But you don't have it all – a family or balance! No way!'

'If I say no it'll be game over for partnership. This is my chance,' he said, in a quieter voice.

I instinctively knew he wasn't bluffing. And I also knew that what he was asking us to do was impossible. There was no way I could spend a weekend with his colleagues pretending to be one big, happy family, pretending to be in a relationship, in love with Will. We'd agreed that we'd bend the truth on one little form to one faceless HR person. Nothing more.

'Please, Zoe,' he said. 'I really need your help.'

'Zo!' I looked up and saw Sofia walking down our street, well waddling, really.

'I better go,' Will said, standing up. But Sofia was already descending upon us, moving at a speed that belied her size.

'Don't worry. That's Sofia, my best friend. She knows what's going on,' I said, relieved that this conversation had been interrupted. Surely, Will could see that there was no other answer than a hard no.

Sofia who, unlike me, managed to not resemble a farmer in a pair of overalls that covered her now impressive bump on her tiny body, leaned in and gave me a kiss.

'Sof, this is Will,' I said.

'At last, I properly meet Dick Next Door,' Sofia said, eyes wide open, as if he wasn't there. I winced. I hadn't exactly filled him in on his historical nickname.

'Nice to meet you, too, Sofia. I've heard a lot about you,' Will said smoothly.

'Come inside!' I said, deliberately not turning towards Will because I knew his expression would be one of mock outrage.

'So, Will. I'm thinking of hiring a nanny for this one,' she said.

'She's not. Her mum's going to look after the baby,' I said.

Sofia ignored me, all her attention focused on Will. 'Any tips on who I should be hiring? Do you think a law degree is a prerequisite?'

'I think a graduate degree is essential,' Will said, not missing a beat. 'But personally, I'd go for a doctor over a lawyer. Better in an emergency.'

Sofia burst out laughing.

'I was just asking Zoe if she and Hazel wanted to come along to my work conference,' he said. I was surprised he wanted to continue this conversation in front of another person, someone who was in my camp. Maybe he thought that given Sofia seemed to have warmed to him, that he had an ally in her.

'Oh, where is it?' Sofia asked.

'Cabarita Beach in northern New South Wales. Just before the Queensland border,' he said. 'It's not really a work-work thing. It's mostly fun activities and big meals.'

When he'd mentioned a conference, I'd imagined a grey conference room in a cold regional town and lots of mass catered sandwiches with curling edges (which had been the defining features of every work trip I'd ever been on). Clearly, things were a bit more upmarket at law firms.

'But we'd have to pretend I'm your … girlfriend,' I said. 'Or partner. Or whatever.'

'It's not like you'll ever have to see any of them again after the conference,' Sofia said.

'Exactly,' Will said. 'You help me out by enjoying a fun few days in the sun with Hazel. She'll have a ball.'

She would too.

'This winter's gone on forever. You've had an enormous year and been a superwoman on your own. But you deserve a break. Let a big law firm spoil you and Hazel for a few days,' Sofia said. 'It's a free holiday that's just fallen into your lap.'

They both looked expectantly at me.

'I'll think about it,' I relented.

'Thank you,' Will said. He didn't push it any further – he knew when to rest his case and leave the jury, or in this case juror, to reach their verdict.

'Dick Next Door is way more gorgeous than I'd remembered. Maybe it's because we never saw him smile?' Sofia said, after he'd barely shut the door. 'If you went on this trip you could seduce him! Holiday flings never count.'

'Not in a million years is there going to be a fling. Or anything!'

'If they think you're a couple, there'll only be one bed. Everyone knows what happens in romances when there's only one bed.' She wiggled her left eyebrow at me and grinned.

'Yet another reason to say no.'

'Agree to disagree.'

'So, what's going on with you?' I asked, keen to change the subject.

'It's almost baby-shower o'clock. I wanted to spitball ideas.'

'You want a baby shower?' I asked. Which was clearly the wrong thing to say. Sofia's forehead creased.

'It's going to be ironic. Obviously,' she said. 'But you have to celebrate all the things, right?'

''Course. Can I help?' I tried not to sound terrified. I was still recovering from helping Sofia plan her medieval-themed thirtieth (everyone else had interpreted the theme as sexy princess or wench – I had only regrets about my plague rat costume).

'That would be great,' she said, now smiling. 'I thought maybe you could organise the games. Not to take seriously … but just for a laugh.'

'Can do. Leave it with me,' I promised. I added ironic baby-shower games to my mental to-do list.

'And maybe we could do a gender reveal at the party? Ironic, too, of course.'

'But you want it to be a surprise, don't you?'

'I think it's silly to place so much emphasis on gender, when it's a construct,' Sofia debated with herself aloud. 'But it would be such a powerful moment at the party. And I saw these fun-coloured smoke cannons online.'

'Mmm.'

'Do you think it's possible to rent storks for an afternoon?' she added.

'How's the baby doing?' I asked, as if her question was rhetorical, which it definitely wasn't. I moved the conversation along before Sofia could have any more visions. 'What size is it?'

'It's the size of a lop-eared rabbit,' she said. Then she sighed, her energy morphing from upbeat and excited to a bit defeated. 'It's doing okay in there. The doctor told me at our last check-up that the baby's in breech. If he doesn't flip around in time my doctor wants me to have a C-section.'

'Sorry, Sof,' I said, genuinely sad that she was having to weather yet another disappointment. After a few rounds of IVF to get pregnant, she had a strong vision for her birth. A C-section with a spinal tap was the opposite of what she had in mind.

'It's okay. You just think these big moments are going to be … a certain way. You know?' she said, with a surreptitious sniff. I did. 'I better go. I have a hypno-birthing class around the corner from here. Morgs will be waiting for me.'

'I'll make sure you have the best baby shower ever,' I promised, as she hauled herself up.

Morgan was outside in the car. He gave me a big wave – I'd known him since our uni days, when he'd fallen hard for Sofia. Before they drove off, I saw him lean over and kiss her on the cheek and then feel the bump. His face split into a grin. The baby must have kicked.

I paused on the doorstep and mulled over what Will had asked. He had weathered some Hazel-related storms of late without much complaint – a fractious day after her vaccinations, a dicey moment when I'd forgotten to buy nappies, extra hours when Monica asked me to work late and on my non-working days. If spending a few days in the sun meant so much to him, maybe this would be a good way to say thank you.

And like Sofia said, we'd never have to see any of his colleagues after the weekend was over.

'*I promise I won't leave you guys!*' That's what Will had said. He'd committed to this arrangement, gone all in. It was probably only fair that I did the same for him.

I pulled out my phone.

Zoe Harper: Okay, fine. We're in.

Will Flemming: THANK YOU!

He wrote back almost instantly. Then he sent a row of smiling faces. Usually, his messages were a masterclass in restraint – I'd never seen him use caps lock or an emoji.

Will Flemming: Leave it all with me. I promise it'll be fine.

CHAPTER 10

Subject: Rules for Trip – Draft 4
From: William.Flemming@flemming.com
To: Zoe.Harper@gmail.com

Rules for Work Conference

1. Zoe gets hotel bed. Will will have access to one (1) pillow and blanket.
2. Zoe gets free mini-shampoos, conditioners, lotions etc. Will can have the shaving set.
3. Will gets the aisle seat on the plane. But will have to change Hazel's nappy (if required).
4. All chocolates left on pillows (if any) will be equally split between Zoe and Will.
5. Zoe will refrain from using any embarrassing nicknames for Will when playing the role of his girlfriend (including but not limited to: 'sweetheart', 'my love').
6. Zoe will only bring one suitcase. It's three days.
7. Even though it's a work event, Will will try to have fun.

Two weeks later, I found myself on Cabarita Beach, Hazel napping on a towel next to me, while Will sat in a dark conference room with a bunch of other lawyers.

We weren't staying at a drab, functional business hotel, like I'd expected, but the kind where you could have a proper holiday. There were pools dotted around the place and bright, airy rooms overlooking a long stretch of beach. The sun was high in the sky and blazing, and Melbourne's unrelenting, endless winter felt like a world away.

Hazel and I had spent the morning on a section of the beach dotted with jauntily striped cabanas, each furnished with a pair of lounge chairs and a retro beach trolley filled with ice and drinks.

I licked chilli-and-lime marinade off my fingers. Tanned waiters from the hotel had been circling our cabanas all morning offering up plates of delicious seafood and elaborate mocktails. All these partners and their families were attending this thing under the guise of 'work'. It was a total rort. But as a beneficiary, I wasn't complaining.

Today, the scheduled activity for the first official morning of the conference had been ominously called 'Family Activity Time'. Unlike Camille, who lived for organised fun, I dreaded any activities that required participation. We'd been allocated to a session called 'Beach Fun!'. The exclamation mark made me nervous, it implied vigorous volleyball sessions or maybe competitive sandcastle building.

But I'd been wrong. Our morning had been organised by someone, maybe a parent themselves, who actually knew what parents with babies wanted to do in their down time – which was very little.

I felt a rush of warmth towards Will. While he was stuck inside networking with his colleagues, we were out here enjoying paradise.

As I watched the other mothers (and they were all mothers – the partners of Will's firm being overwhelmingly men), who'd been surprisingly good company, pack up for the morning, I saw Will walking along the sand searching for us. I waved him over.

'I was worried I'd missed you guys,' he said, once he'd jogged to our cabana.

'She fell asleep. And you know my life philosophy is "don't wake a sleeping baby",' I said, as Hazel began to stir next to me.

'Should we take her for a swim?'

'Sure. I'll just …' But before I could finish, Will had unbuttoned his white linen shirt, revealing the stomach of an action hero. '… pop her hat on,' I managed to get out.

I turned away from him and riffled through my bag, pretending to search for Hazel's hat, which I knew was on the end of the lounge. When I finally looked back up, I knew my cheeks were flushed, and hoped he'd just think I was a bit hot. Clearly, it had been far too long since I'd been around a half-dressed man – my body didn't know how to react normally anymore.

'It's not here!' I announced.

Will was now holding Hazel against his abs, which were unexpectedly defined. Had this been hiding beneath his shirts the whole time? Or was this the end product of the gym classes he'd finally had time for over the last six weeks? I forced my eyes to move up to his face, very aware I was staring at him as if he were a sculpture.

'I better put some sunscreen on,' he said.

'I've got some,' I squeaked, riffling through my bag again and pulling out the bottle. I passed it to him and took Hazel.

He squirted cream into his hands and began to rub it onto his arms, which were surprisingly golden and muscular. He moved on to his torso, which seemed to ripple as he rubbed his hands over it. His chest was covered with dark hair that tapered off as it reached his navy swim shorts.

Will was a nerdy genius. Weren't guys like him meant to wear unflattering rashies and bucket hats with a drawstring? Prescription goggles, at least. Maybe some zinc.

'Could you do my back?' he asked.

Was this part of our relationship role play? A chance to really commit to our parts.

I took my time offering Hazel a long drink from her sippy cup. Finally, I stood up. Of course, this was part of the act – Will didn't half-arse anything.

'Sure,' I said. I could play along – pretend to be the caring girlfriend while people from the firm were watching. Placing Hazel on the towel, I took the bottle from him and started with his shoulders, rubbing in the cream until it melted into his skin.

'Don't miss anywhere.'

'You're lucky I'm not drawing a picture of a penis that will burn onto you!' I said, then instantly regretted mentioning a penis while my hands were nestled under his shoulder blades.

As I worked my way down his body, rubbing cream into the small of his back and hips, I felt a bit woozy. It was a hot day – had I drunk enough water in this heat?

I gave Will a gentle slap on his shoulder. 'There you go!'

He turned around as I kneeled down to pick up Hazel. Wow, his abs were right there in my face, now all glistening and coconut scented. I stood up.

'Do you want me to do you?' he asked.

'That's okay – I'll keep my shirt on.' I hadn't been touched by a man in forever. I wasn't convinced that I wouldn't spontaneously combust, even if it was just Will.

As we walked down to the water, I could feel the gaze of the other mums on me. I knew that at events like this, everyone was silently calibrating the health of their own relationship against those around them.

'Do you think we look like we're together?' I whispered to Will.

He offered me the hand that wasn't holding Hazel. I took it, noticing for the first time that he had nice forearms.

'We can up the ante on the love charade,' he whispered and gave my hand a squeeze.

A charade. That was exactly what this weekend was. And something I needed to keep front of mind. Sometimes I wasn't great at separating the pretend from the real. I had a tendency to believe stories, versions of stories, that weren't quite true. And, of course, this weekend was all a front – I had to be convincing for Will's sake, but make sure I didn't get caught up in it all.

When we reached the surf, I came to. I stopped caring what anyone thought. I was here for Hazel. And her sheer joy blocked out the rest of the world.

Will dunked Hazel's chubby legs in the water, and she burst into a fit of giggles. Then he lifted her up onto his shoulders, and her laughs became louder. Her hysterical cackles were a better sound than anything a musician could ever create, even Will. And every time she laughed we laughed too, and then she'd laugh again.

'You're the sea queen. Survey your kingdom!' he said, in a deep, silly voice, clearly one Hazel was used to and found hilarious. 'Let's vanquish the sea monster!'

He kicked up his leg, splashing me. I squealed and kicked a spray of water towards him.

'Oh, that's me, is it? The monster!' I said, pulling a silly face at Hazel.

'Let's get her!' he said, as he slowly jogged towards me in the shallow surf. Hazel, still sitting up on his broad shoulders, giggled with glee as I pretended to run away from them. When he reached me, he wrapped the arm not supporting Hazel around me, and pulled me in close.

I stood for a moment in his arms, the gently rolling waves beating against our calves. His skin was warm and wet. I could feel his heart beating rapidly from exertion. And smell his deodorant, something much spicier than mine – a completely masculine smell. His hand was on my shirt, which now wet, was transparent and clinging to me.

I looked up. To check if Hazel was okay, of course. But our eyes locked en route.

I didn't move. And neither did he.

Then Hazel squealed, and we both turned towards her. She was impatient for more horsing around, and so we continued to chase each other in the shallows. And as I readjusted my bathers, I sent a silent thank you to Hazel, and the universe, for saving me from such a potentially awkward moment.

CHAPTER 11

Those few minutes in the surf occupied my thoughts for the rest of the afternoon. Clearly, after a morning of being pampered, my mind had been suggestible. Against a backdrop of sun, sand and sea, I'd been primed for flights of fancy.

And honestly, his body hadn't helped – it should have come with a warning sign. I'd been ripe to conjure up a fantastical scene, a Mills & Boon moment. The more I thought about it, the more I was convinced that all of it had been in my head. We'd only been so close in the surf because I was a prop in his game to make Hazel laugh – I was the sea monster.

Publicly playing the role of Will's fake girlfriend had obviously already messed with my head; I'd got a bit too method. For the rest of the weekend, I had to remember who I really was – Hazel's mum and Will's friend.

Will had conference sessions for the rest of the day. With a free afternoon, I'd taken Hazel for a long walk in her carrier. By the time we'd made it back to the hotel, she'd fallen asleep against me. I checked my watch. Will's panel session was on now – the one we'd come all this way for.

Only the lawyers were meant to attend and I knew that Will would be mortified if he saw me there, but I couldn't help myself. I needed to hear what he said about The Arrangement.

The foyer to the hotel's ballroom, the epicentre of the conference, was abandoned, but I could hear the muffled sounds of voices booming through microphones on the other side of the doors. I slowly opened one and snuck into the darkened room.

There were three people on the panel, two women and Will, all sitting in a row on the stage. Will was in the middle wearing chinos, a white linen shirt with his sleeves rolled up and tan loafers – which I knew all had been bought especially for the trip.

The trio were being interviewed by an older man, who managed to pull off by sheer charisma a bald head, protruding ears and a loud Hawaiian shirt. You could tell he was that guy, the one a bit more emotionally intelligent than the rest, who was wheeled out to moderate every seminar on a 'tricky' topic – like anything involving women.

'What has surprised you about being a working parent?' the moderator asked the woman sitting on Will's right.

She had the look of a working mum – one whose preening time was now confined to basic hygiene only. You could tell she'd never been fashion forward, but her ability to even tangentially keep abreast of trends had come to a standstill with her first pregnancy. Her resort wear was Birkenstocks and a singlet, one strap of which had been stretched out, presumably by a toddler. There was an aura of both patience, cultivated by having offspring, and a sense of impatience, borne from never having enough hours in the day.

'I think for me it was realising how ruthless I had to become about my time. That I'd never be able to tick everything off my to-do list like I did before kids,' she said. 'And that I had to let go of guilt. But that one's a work in progress.'

'What about you, Will?' The moderator moved down the panel.

'I get to use the good parking spots at the supermarket, which is handy.'

I could tell he'd rehearsed this line. That, like his outfit, his opening gambit had been carefully selected. I knew that he wanted to come across to this crowd as Will the Good Bloke, Will the Relatable. The audience tittered.

I felt a sting of annoyance. This was what he had taken from spending time with my daughter. Better parks.

'Will, you're currently on parental leave – the first senior male lawyer to take advantage of our new policy, which the partnership is really excited about,' the moderator said. 'Do you think it's important for men to have access to paid paternity leave?'

'I do. Returning to work after maternity leave is full on. I don't want to speak for you guys …' Will gestured at the women sitting either side of him, '… but Hazel's mum, Zoe, returned to work a little over a month ago. And it's a tough enough gig to be a working mum with a young baby without worrying about complicated childcare arrangements. Particularly at the start, when rebuilding your confidence is so crucial.'

I stood in the shadows at the back of the room, waiting for the cynical part of my brain to begin its director's commentary. Except … none came.

'Hazel doesn't always sleep through the night, so Zoe often starts the day running on empty. And she's still breastfeeding, so she has to express at work and then hide the milk in a paper bag in the office fridge so all her colleagues don't freak out.'

I did do that. I must have told Will after a glass or two.

'I used to do that, too!' the woman on Will's right interjected. 'And prayed no one would walk into my office when I was expressing. Well, mainly that John wouldn't barge in with one of his "urgent" client questions.'

There were some appreciative laughs in the audience.

'Tell us about your experience of paternity leave,' the moderator asked Will.

I felt a sudden clench in my stomach. Up until now, pretending that we were a couple had felt very administrative. But this felt more like a proper lie shared with an entire ballroom of lawyers. But I reminded myself that no one, except for Sofia, Will and me, knew for sure that Will wasn't my boyfriend. The circle of trust was tight and trustworthy.

'I have a newfound respect for stay-at-home parents. It's bloody exhausting – physically. And often mundane and unrelenting. And Hazel's dirty nappies are surely in breach of the Human Rights Charter.'

The room tittered again. He'd stolen that line from me.

My stomach tightened once more. Had I imagined our nascent friendship over the last few weeks? Did Will hate our arrangement? Was he gritting his teeth on the days he had to spend with Hazel, dreaming of his four-day weekend? Or partnership promotion, more likely.

'But it's also been the most incredible experience. The moments of joy that punctuate the long days are the best thing I've ever felt in my life. And with all due respect to your kids, Hazel is objectively the best baby in the whole world – she's amazing.'

The audience properly laughed now. The two female lawyers on stage were looking at Will with soft eyes. He'd articulated, possibly mansplained, what they felt but probably would be penalised for saying out loud, particularly in this context.

Maybe Will had known he'd win over the room by waxing lyrical about Hazel. No man was ever penalised for declaring his love for his kids, was he? Will was smart and never did anything without careful strategic thinking. Had he worked up these lines for maximum effect?

'It's great to see another side to you, Will!' the moderator said. 'That feels like a great thought to end this session on.'

I snuck out of the room before any lights were turned on.

I was dressed and settling Hazel into her travel cot for the night, when Will returned from his final session of the day.

'The bathroom's all yours,' I said, grateful we'd been allocated a room with a small, separate living area, so the carefully negotiated one-bed situation had become less of a crisis.

'Thanks,' he said, without looking up – he was glued to his phone, back in work mode.

Hazel, exhausted from the sun and sea, fell asleep after only a few lullabies. So, while I waited for Will to get ready, I touched up my makeup and readjusted the dress, a concoction of expensively draped blue silk I'd rented, with one eye on the bathroom door.

Would people believe I was the girlfriend of a successful corporate lawyer? I didn't have any proper jewellery or subtle highlights or pouty lips. But I'd picked up some sun today, and for the first time in a long time, I presented less like a human zombie and more like my old self. Which was good because I felt nervous about this dinner. For the next few hours, we'd be on show – under the scrutiny of people with high IQs and analytical minds.

I took a deep breath to steady myself. I just needed to remember that tonight I was playing a role, that the evening was all a performance.

Will emerged dressed. I hadn't seen him in his work clothes since The Arrangement had begun. And while I was sure this was one of his old suits, he seemed different in it now. Tonight, it was more like something to wear than a corporate coat of armour.

'You look dapper,' I said lightly. The ends of his hair were still damp and I could smell both the expensive hotel shampoo and his woody cologne.

'You look great,' he said.

'It's insulting how shocked you sound!'

'Yes, my intention was to shatter your confidence before you meet a room full of strangers.'

I did a twirl. 'Would you believe I'm the kind of woman who spends all day doing boring yet urgent things on Excel, and then does reformer Pilates after work? That's the vibe I was going for. I think that's your type.'

He laughed. 'One – that's so not my type. And two – just be yourself. Except yourself who's madly in love with me.'

'That's why I needed a backstory – to make my performance believable.'

The conference paid-for babysitter arrived.

'We're going to be late – let's go,' he said.

We walked together to the hotel restaurant, like the couple we were pretending to be.

'Wow! This is weird! I haven't been out at night without Hazel since she was born. I want to run to the room and hide. But I also want to do rounds of shots!' I said, as we reached the marble-coated hotel lobby. I struggled to articulate the rush of emotions I'd felt since the room door had clicked shut behind us and it had hit me that I was going to be out after the sun set. Will stopped in his tracks.

'Remember when I said to be yourself tonight?' he asked.

'Five seconds ago?'

'I know you need to let off some steam. But maybe not … tonight,' he said, an expression of genuine concern on his face.

'I'm not going to make a fool of myself. Or you.' Ebullience was usurped by irritation.

'You forget – I met you before you were a mum. And I know you can … embrace a night out.'

'Sorry that my Saturday nights weren't all Scrabble and tea like yours,' I said, now feeling quite huffy.

He took a deep breath to stop himself from making the retort I knew he'd quite like to make.

'I'm just a bit … nervous,' he finally admitted, running his hands through his freshly washed hair. 'We're all on show tonight. And this is …'

'… really important to you.'

'Remember the day that you accosted me in the cafe and asked me to take paternity leave?'

'I wouldn't use the word "accosted" …'

'That afternoon, I overheard Robert talking to one of the other senior partners at the firm. About me. They basically said that no one knew the law better and no one had higher billables, but … I'd never make partner because I was more robot than human.'

I could tell that even now, weeks later, these words still stung.

'I promise I'm not going to use your work dinner to defrost my deep-frozen wild side,' I said in a prim voice. 'I get it. Our job tonight is to show these idiots that you're not just Will the Genius, but Will the Guy Who's Just Like Them.'

He laughed and visibly relaxed, and I realised he was properly worked up. I'd never seen him in a real-life social setting, in a crowd of people. Since The Arrangement had begun, we'd mainly existed in a bubble of just the three of us.

'Remember the final rule of the trip – please promise me you'll try to have a bit of fun tonight?' I added. I might not have a fancy law degree or work in a Collins Street skyscraper in the Paris end of the city, but I knew how to get on with people at a party. And I was good at marketing things. Sure, it was normally real estate. But Will was the human equivalent of the houses that I loved to write about – the ones that were hidden treasures, but because they needed a coat of paint, or were filled with hideous furniture, were overlooked.

Now my night had a purpose other than maintaining our lie – it was my job to show these people the side of Will that I'd seen over the last six weeks. Sure Will was a bit socially awkward and prickly, but he wasn't a robot. Beneath his composed, controlled exterior that gave away nothing, was a genuinely good guy.

'Promise. I always have fun with you,' he said, visibly relieved, then he offered me his hand.

I felt the nerves in my own stomach settle down as his strong hand wrapped around my smaller one. 'Then let's go, sweetheart,' I said. He shot me a look.

And so, with both of us now slightly calmer, we walked into the restaurant together.

CHAPTER 12

Dinner was in the hotel restaurant that the firm had booked out for the night. It overlooked the beach, and as it was a balmy evening, the sliding doors had been left open so that you could hear the waves crashing on the beach and smell a hint of salt and seaweed mixed with expensive perfume and aftershave.

It was a beautiful scene – large reclaimed wooden tables were filled with flickering tall candles and elegant vases of fashionable native foliage. The room was already thronging. Will stood at the entrance like a deer caught in headlights. I could tell he was more nervous than he'd even admitted.

'Zoe!'

Kate, my new conference friend, spotted us and beckoned us over to her table. Will, still visibly overwhelmed by the packed room, raised a questioning eyebrow.

'Follow me,' I said. Will nodded, clearly grateful that I'd taken charge.

'We met this morning in the cafe when I snuck down to feed Hazel because I'm so considerate and wanted you to sleep in,' I explained in a low voice as I led Will through the crowd to the table. 'She was feeding her son, Freddie. He threw up, I handed her some wipes and we became instant friends. We spent most of this morning gossiping on the beach!'

'Right.'

'Did you know her husband, Nick, ran a conference call while she was in active labour?'

'I didn't know Nick had a baby, so no.'

When we reached Kate's table, she pointed at two empty blue-and-white wicker chairs.

'I saved you two spots. I want to sit next to someone I can actually have a proper chat with, so I don't spend the whole night in a conversation about cross-border M & A, just nodding and wishing I was at home watching *Love Island*.'

I refused to look at Will, whose expression would be blank but whose eyes would be flashing with mirth. I noticed Robert, Will's boss, also sitting at this table. A spark of panic shot through me. Now the pressure was really on to give a convincing performance as a couple.

I thanked Kate as I sat down next to her, Will on my other side.

'I caught you two holding hands,' Kate said.

'We'd just made up after a fight in the lobby,' I said. 'Will was worried I'd go a bit nuts tonight. I haven't been out since Hazel was born.'

Kate's head shot back in laughter. She pulled on the arm of the man next to her, interrupting his conversation. 'Nick, listen to this. Zoe and Will had the same fight we did,' Kate said. 'Nick read me the riot act in the hotel room – I'm on my best behaviour, too.'

'Great minds think alike, Will,' Nick said, pivoting his chair around to join our conversation. Beneath his thick, black-rimmed glasses, I could see that his eyes were marked with the panda rings of exhaustion that used to mar Will's face. I guessed he was only in his early forties, but his hair had already begun to grey. He tipped his beer bottle towards Will. 'Now I hear you have a new daughter?'

I could almost hear the cogs in Will's mind whirring, searching for an answer that wasn't a bald lie.

'Hazel's seven months old, so pretty new.'

'I got to meet their new baby this morning. Freddie. He's divine. He's a few months younger than Hazel and made her seem like a giant.'

'Congratulations! How's it all going?' Will asked, sounding a bit stilted. I guessed he didn't normally have these types of conversations with his colleagues.

'Freddie's great,' Nick said, his face properly lighting up. 'We're not getting much sleep. It's a different type of all-nighter, isn't it?'

'It is,' Will said, with an appreciative chuckle. I exhaled – he was warming up. 'Some nights I wonder which is harder – finalising a DD report through the night, or pushing Hazel up and down the street in her pram in the early hours trying to get her to sleep.'

'What pram do you have?'

'Zoe chose Hazel's pram,' he said. 'But if I was going to pick again, Bugaboo Fox – no question.'

'No way, mate,' Nick replied. 'It's all about American design – the specs on the UPPAbaby are, well it's the Ferrari of prams.'

They were off.

I turned to Kate, who entertained me with an upbeat monologue on how all the lawyers here had met their partners. A surprising number had met in the office, and Kate, who worked in the firm's recruiting team, knew every salacious Christmas party or late-night office tryst story, and wasn't afraid to share it.

'And how did you two meet?' she finally asked, with the expression of a woman who was ready to listen intently then package up the story to share around. 'Obviously not in the office.'

'No,' I said with a high-pitched laugh, trying to buy time. I gave Will, still deep in conversation with Nick, a small kick under the table.

'Kate just asked me how we met,' I said, when he caught my wide eyes.

'Ah,' he said.

'We had no idea you even had a personal life,' Nick said with a deep chuckle. 'I thought we'd buried you in too many deals for that. But clearly, you're a man who can juggle it all.'

'He can. He's pretty amazing like that,' I said. 'He really can keep all the plates spinning at once. Nothing seems to faze him.'

I wondered if I was laying it on too thickly. But Nick seemed impressed, and Will had relaxed into the night and it didn't seem like he wanted to kill me.

'Tell us your story!' Kate said, evidently not going to let go of this line of questioning.

'Well, Zoe and I have lived next door to each other for … forever,' Will began. I let out a silent sigh of relief, glad not to have to conjure up the fictional tale myself. 'And we got off to a bad start.'

'What do you mean?' Kate asked, both her body and wineglass tilted towards us.

'Zoe would have these parties at her house all the time. And she'd forget to take her bin out, run out of room and then dump all her empty bottles in mine.'

'I knew I liked you,' Kate said with a smile.

'And then he made a noise complaint about my thirtieth birthday party,' I said.

Will's eyes narrowed, confused. 'No, I didn't.'

'Yes, you did! You called the police and they shut my party, my thirtieth, down,' I said.

'I did come over and asked you to turn the music down. Your friends told me it was your birthday and invited me in. But I said I couldn't – I was working through the weekend on New York hours for Project Bear,' he added for Nick, who nodded appreciatively. 'It must have been someone else on the street. I wasn't going to ruin a big birthday party. I just couldn't hear the call I was on.'

For years, I'd been furious at him for doing just that. It was the next morning that we'd come up with the nickname Dick Next Door.

'Right. I didn't know that.'

'Surprises for everyone in this story,' Kate said, which was an understatement. The three of us waited for Will to continue.

'But even though we were ostensibly enemies, I couldn't help being fascinated by the girl next door,' he said. 'She was this whirlwind who was always rushing off somewhere with her friends, always laughing, always in bright clothes, always having fun. And I always secretly wanted to get to know her properly.'

He was doing a convincing job of pulling together a romantic story. Now Nick was also leaning towards us.

'But she had a boyfriend,' he continued. 'Then one day Zoe was running late for work, her car had been blocked in and her day was imploding – so I took my chance. I offered to give her a lift. And later, she popped around to say thank you. We were both now single. And the rest is history.' He put his hand on top of mine then turned to me. Did he want to end the performance with an intimate gaze? Or was he gauging my reaction?

I pulled my leg, which I realised was still resting against his calf under the table, away. Holding hands in front of Nick and Kate was a nice touch – a perfect flourish to make Will's tale more believable. But they didn't have X-ray vision – they couldn't see our legs touching under the table.

The rest of the evening, which I'd expected to be stilted and hard work, turned out to be quite fun. Kate and I gave each other regular permission to have another glass of wine, while Will was ensconced in a conversation with most of the lawyers at our table.

While we attacked dinner, Will and I both salivating over the perfectly grilled seafood, Robert gave a short speech.

'As managing partner, it's my honour to welcome my fellow partners to our conference. And this weekend, we've also extended an invitation to some of our most senior lawyers – the future of our firm.'

As Robert delivered this line, I could have sworn he turned towards our table and gave Will a small smile.

That had to bode well. I glanced at Will and saw he'd also noticed and was trying to hide his pleasure by taking a small sip of his red wine. I gave him another gentle kick under the table, but this time I made sure I didn't accidentally leave my leg too close to his.

When all the food had been cleared, most people began to gear up for serious networking, moving from table to table, full drinks in hand.

'Do you mind if ...?' Will asked.

'Go!' I said.

I stayed at the table for a moment, before deciding to head outside for some fresh air. Kate had gone upstairs to feed Freddie. And I was beginning to feel a bit light-headed, and aware that I was in danger of breaking my promise to Will not to overdo it.

The restaurant overlooked the beach, and so very carefully, unused to wearing even low heels after such a long break, I walked towards the sand.

I sat down, closed my eyes and felt the light breeze on my skin. Maybe it was the wine, maybe it was the beach, but right now I felt like myself again, as though the core of me that I'd been before Hazel had survived the journey.

CHAPTER 13

'Hey.'

I looked up and saw Will walking towards me. I'd been on the beach for a while, but I hadn't realised it had been search-for-me long.

'Hi,' I said, as he sat down next to me on the sand. He took off his jacket and gave it to me.

'I'm fine.'

'You're shivering and I'm hot,' he said.

I accepted it and gratefully wrapped it around my shoulders. After sitting for so long in my flimsy dress, the silk lining felt like an indulgent hug.

'Shouldn't you be in there working the room?' I asked.

'I've kissed enough arses for one night. And I just agreed to play Santa at the firm's Christmas party. So, I'm going to quit while I'm behind.'

'Karma's a bitch,' I said, with a shrug. 'I think Nick likes you. And Robert.'

'Actually, Nick and Robert like *you*.'

I raised a surprised eyebrow.

'Nick's never given me the time of day before tonight. Most of the partners on our table haven't. Unless they needed something done urgently.'

I'd wondered about that. I'd got the sense that tonight

we'd sat at a table of heavy hitters – that Kate had invited us into the inner sanctum.

'Well, once you've talked to someone about cracked nipples, you're pretty much friends,' I said, and then immediately regretted mentioning my nipples.

'You know I'm not great in big groups, at parties,' he said. 'But you're an expert at it. And some of your social magic rubbed off onto me, and those guys at our table stopped seeing me as a workhorse. They saw me as a real person with a life. And they wanted to get to know me.'

He spoke as if all of this was a revelation. What did they teach people at Oxford?

'Did you always want this? The big, fancy corporate life? Long hours, nice suits, corner office?' I asked, glad the beach was so dark and Will couldn't see my cheeks flush. I knew he was drunk on the high of a successful night. As soon as he came back down to earth, when tonight's performance was over, his snarky wit would return fully intact.

He considered the question for a moment. I continued to stare straight ahead, towards the dark, crashing waves.

'I got a scholarship to one of the best boys' schools in Melbourne. And if you were smart they didn't ask you what you wanted to do with your life, it was "medicine or law?". And … blood makes me feel nauseous.'

'Did you like school?'

'I loved the learning part. But otherwise, I hated it,' he said, without hesitation, his words laced with bitterness.

'Why?'

'I know it's hard to imagine, but I didn't always have this amazing sense of style.' I laughed. 'Picture me as a teenager – skinny, braces, thick glasses, acne, jeans and runners.'

'So I'm going to need to see a photo of this.'

'I was a nerd with no mates. At a school with a toxic masculinity problem, guess which instrument I played in the school orchestra?'

'The bassoon?'

'Worse.'

'The triangle?'

He turned to me and even in the dark I could see his expression of mock outrage. 'The piccolo,' he said.

'Wow! Although, you know what they say … the smaller the instrument, the bigger the …'

The memory of Will in the surf, his wet board shorts clinging to his body, flashed unbidden through my mind.

'Brain,' I finished, my voice a bit too high-pitched.

Will laughed. 'Story checks out. The double bass player was barely literate, though his dad was CEO of a mining company, so it didn't really matter.' More indignation cut through his joking tone.

'How did you end up playing the piccolo?'

'I thought the flute was too masculine.'

'No, seriously?'

'My mum's a music teacher. I pestered her to teach me something when I was little and I guess she thought a small instrument was a good idea for a tiny kid.'

So, he'd inherited her passion, and talent, too.

'You'd be a great teacher. Seriously, you've explained heaps of boring things to me but made them interesting.'

'I'm trying to work out if that's a compliment.'

I laughed again.

'I was embarrassed by my parents when I was at school,' he said, his voice steady but now much quieter. 'All my classmates' parents were businessmen or surgeons or …' He trailed off.

Partners at law firms; I could basically hear his unfinished thought.

'Mine were both teachers and I was ashamed of how normal they were.'

'You were a teenager. Everyone's embarrassed by their parents at that age. And you don't feel like that anymore.'

'No, now I just feel angry. At how the school and the other parents looked down on them.' He paused for a moment. 'At how I judged my own parents.'

Before I could stop myself, I grabbed his hand and squeezed it.

'What are your parents like?' he asked, a note of hesitancy in his voice.

I pulled my hand back and sat on it. 'Okay, here's the story. My dad left when I was five. On my first day of school, actually. I went off in the morning in my too-big dress and legionnaire hat thinking we were one big, happy family, and by the time I got home he'd moved out. I told you I don't like first days. That's why.

'Mum was devastated. Dad moved interstate to live with the woman he'd fallen in love with, and so Mum raised us on her own.'

I let the whole sorry tale pour out of me, then swallowed to try to dislodge the frog in my throat.

'That must have been really … rough,' Will said. For the first time, he properly turned to face me, but I couldn't bring myself to meet his eyes.

'It was,' I said, staring at the moon's reflection dancing on the gentle waves. I shrugged. 'After Dad left, Mum just … wasn't there anymore. I mean, she had to work heaps so she wasn't home much. But she also just became this self-contained unit. *Never rely on anyone!* It practically became our family motto after Dad left, Mum said it so often. Camille nailed the brief, of course. Became everything Mum wanted her to be – a trailblazer at work. And she does heaps of pro bono work helping women leaving shitty marriages.'

I took a deep breath, letting the fresh air fill my lungs. I was surprised by how much I'd told Will. It had all just sort of poured out of me.

'I always disappointed her, jumping from serious boyfriend to serious boyfriend, clinging to them like a limpet. But after Adam left me, I realised that Mum was right.'

'About what?'

'That women just get hurt when they let men in. That I needed to break my pattern of co-dependency,' I said, with an involuntary sigh. 'When I decided to have a baby on my own, I thought I'd never have to rely on anyone ever again. But look at me. Hazel's not even one and I have a fake boyfriend to help with childcare. Mum would die if she found out.'

I tried to sound like I was joking, but Will didn't laugh.

'Has she helped you out much?' he asked, even though he'd been around us long enough to know the answer.

'Mum moved to Bendigo as soon as I finished school. She was offered a better job,' I said. 'She's visited a grand total of twice.'

Last time she'd visited, Hazel had been four months old. She'd walked in the door and asked me what I was cooking for lunch ('Peanut butter toast?'), and things had gone downhill from there.

'I'm sorry,' Will said, putting his arm around me. I stiffened for a moment then let my head fall onto his broad shoulder.

'Hazel is the best thing that's ever happened in my life. But I'm the worst thing that ever happened to theirs. Dad left the minute I was old enough to go to school. And Mum did the same as soon as I went to uni.'

We sat in silence for a moment. I waited for the wave of shame, the one I normally felt when I talked about my parents and how little they were interested in my life or Hazel, to wash over me.

'You're an amazing mum,' Will said, before it did. 'I think the main job of being a parent is to make sure your kid feels loved. And Hazel will never spend a single second of her life wondering if she's loved. You're her whole world.'

I meant to say thank you, but instead, I burst into tears. Not cute glistening tears gliding down my cheeks. But ugly, heaving sobs, the ones that choke up your throat and puff up your eyes.

He put both of his arms around me and I sank wordlessly into his neck. As my chest heaved, he pulled me in tighter until my sobs subsided and my breathing returned to normal.

'And,' he said, pausing as I wiped my sleeve – well, his expensive woollen sleeve, really – across my wet face, then looked up at him. I knew my skin would be covered in red patches and that my eyes would be bloodshot slits. I could see all the makeup I'd carefully applied covering his white lapel.

'That stuff I said at dinner. About wanting to properly get to know you for ages. That was true,' he said.

My whole body felt as if it had been electrocuted and that all my senses were suddenly enhanced, like a hero in a Marvel film. I could smell the hint of the coconut sunscreen I'd rubbed on his back this morning, and I could see the green flecks in his eyes.

Upstairs in the hotel, a few minutes away from this beach, was a king-sized bed – one made up with crisp sheets, the type that felt cool against hot bodies. The type to get tangled up in.

And next to that bed, in a travel cot, was Hazel.

I'd drunk more tonight than I had in a year. Will and I had just got caught up in our made-up story – we'd played the part of being together too well.

I stood up, pulled off Will's jacket and brushed the sand from my dress.

'I told the babysitter I'd be back by midnight,' I said.

CHAPTER 14

'What are you doing here?' Camille said by way of greeting, when she found us sheltered from a downpour on her doorstep at 7.45 am on a freezing, storming Monday morning. She grabbed Hazel, only her head visible in a padded puffer jacket, out of my arms for a cuddle. I used my sleeve to mop up the stream of dribble cascading out of the corner of Hazel's mouth and heading straight for Camille's beautifully tailored suit lapel.

'A hiccup with childcare, so I've taken leave,' I said, as I peeled off my sodden raincoat. It was sort of the truth. I'd messaged Will to tell him I was feeling a bit under the weather so would stay home with Hazel. 'I thought I'd pop by and say hello.'

Camille gave me a searching look. 'It's chaos inside, but come in and have some breakfast.'

I followed her through the modern house – all clean lines, blond wood and edges, punctuated by the primary colours of toddler bikes, scooters and balls.

I kissed Remy and Arti, who, judging from the brown rings around their mouths had used the few minutes away from their mum's eagle eyes to hoe into a jar of Nutella.

In a single movement, Camille cut two slices from a loaf of artisanal grainy bread, popped them in her gleaming Alessi toaster and pulled one of the twin's old highchairs to the table for Hazel.

'Mum called me this morning,' Camille said, as she began to unload the dishwasher, while ignoring the twins competing for Hazel's attention. 'She's coming to visit.'

'When?' I asked, unable to hide the petulance in my voice. Of course she'd called Camille first. I tried to remember the last time Mum had called me. I couldn't.

'Father's Day.'

'Are you serious?' I replied, my voice now somewhere between a high-pitched whine and an angry yelp.

'It's not a big deal,' Camille said, now stuffing papers into her backpack.

But it was a big deal. After Dad left, Mum turned Father's Day into Mother's Day #2 each year because, she'd say, '*I'm doing the work of two parents!*' She seemed to enjoy the day, almost revelled in it, but I'd always hated it.

'It's typical Mum,' I said. 'Not interested in helping her single-mother daughter with her new baby. But there'll be bells on for lunch. To celebrate herself!'

'I'm sure the main reason she's coming is to spend time with Hazel,' Camille said with a weary sigh. 'This doesn't need to spark an existential crisis.'

'How can you never have them?' I asked.

What I really meant was, 'How can you not care?' It was the question I'd wondered since we were both teenagers. She didn't seem to hold a grudge against either of our parents.

'Because I don't have time to navel gaze!' she snapped. 'I have a terrifying mortgage to pay. And a husband who needs attention. And toddler twins.'

On cue, Ed appeared in the kitchen in gym gear. 'Hi, Zo,' he said and gave me a kiss on the cheek.

'Do you think you could drop off the twins this morning?' Camille asked.

'I've got a PT session. I'd be late,' he said, checking the time on his smart watch.

'They're fed, dressed and their bags are packed. If you leave now you'll be fine,' Camille said, a dangerous edge to her voice. Ed must have noticed it, too. He sighed.

'Fine. Come on, kids. Let's go,' Ed said.

Camille showered each of the twins in goodbye kisses and hugs but barely acknowledged Ed. They disappeared out the door in a noisy blur.

'Is everything okay?' I asked tentatively. Camille was always harried, but this morning she seemed more strung out than usual.

She ran her hand through her dark, blow-waved straight hair. 'It's all just … a lot at the moment,' she said. 'Everyone in Melbourne's decided now is the time for an acrimonious divorce. And to hire me. Which is great, for me, not them. And last night, I was working in the study and popped into the living room to say hi to the kids. And Remy saw me and said, "Mummy, you should be working" and marched me back to my office and closed the door on me. I didn't know whether to be impressed or disturbed!'

I'd never seen her as bad as this – she was wound up like a coil. One that I was slightly worried might snap.

'I couldn't do what you do on your worst day, on my best day.'

'Most days I'm the first to leave the office and the twins are the last to be picked up from their room,' she said.

'Could Ed do some of the pick-ups? Give you a bit of breathing room?' I suggested gently.

'He's busy, too. And travelling all the time,' she said.

'Could he … travel less?'

'I just feel like I'm doing everything badly,' she said, with a sniff she quickly tried to restrain. 'I feel like I'm letting down everyone. Every day. And it's just not tenable.'

'Could you book in a holiday? Take a few days off and have some fun with the kids? Drop a few balls at work? Have a date night with Ed? I can babysit the twins whenever you need a break,' I brainstormed out loud.

Camille stared at me like I was speaking a foreign language.

'This parent thing is just …' I tried again, searching for something to say that might cheer her up. 'Really, bloody hard.'

She nodded her head and blinked a few times.

'And I read somewhere that it's way harder for really smart people,' I added, and she involuntarily smiled.

'I need to get to work,' Camille said, stuffing the last few papers into her backpack and standing up. The window for vulnerability had closed. Camille was even efficient when it came to her life crises.

'I had a weird moment with my next-door neighbour,' I blurted out.

Camille sat back down.

'Promise you'll keep everything I tell you now a secret?' I asked.

'I promise.' And I knew she would – she wasn't a gossip (otherwise I'd know far more about celebrity divorces than I did). I knew Will wouldn't necessarily love the idea of me telling Camille about The Arrangement. But when it came to secrets, she was a vault. And I needed her advice.

'So, my neighbour Will,' I began.

'The guy who shut down your thirtieth?'

'That may have been fake news.'

'Your nemesis?'

'Yep, him. Well, we olive-branched. And he's a senior lawyer trying to make partner at his firm. And Robert, his boss, your old boss, thought he was Hazel's dad when Will dropped us off at your childcare centre that morning. And encouraged him to take paternity leave. Said it would help him make partner. So he did.'

'I'm not following.'

'You know how I said a neighbour was babysitting Hazel while I worked?'

I could see her putting the pieces together.

'No. You two didn't!' Her eyes were wide open.

'We did.' I felt like my heart was going to skip a beat.

'But he's not Hazel's father,' she said.

'Will said his work's policy covers co-parents.'

'But he's not that, either!'

'Well, as far as they're concerned we are. We've told them we've been in a relationship for a while. And that Will's been raising Hazel,' I said.

Camille blinked at me a few times, for once at a loss for words. 'He's committing fraud,' she said finally. 'And you've helped him.'

'His firm wanted men to take paternity leave. They're thrilled he did it. And no one's ever going to know.'

'Except I know. I have a duty to the court. Now that I know, I should report him to the Law Institute.'

'You won't, will you?'

She didn't answer for a moment. Had I got it wrong? Was she going to blow up everything? My heart began to thump.

'No,' she said. 'I promised I wouldn't.' But I could tell how uncomfortable she was being on the wrong side of the ethical line. Unlike me, she saw the world in black and white – there was truth and there were lies, and she had no time for any grey in the middle.

'There's more,' I said.

'How?' Camille's eyes were almost popping.

'When we began The Arrangement, we couldn't stand each other. But we became friends. Then this weekend, we went on a trip. And I feel like something might have changed between us. There was a moment on a beach after a lot of wine, late on Saturday night. And now I'm a bit confused about what to do.'

'Hence the turn-up-on-our-doorstep-at-dawn scenario?'

I nodded. 'What do I do?'

'Have you spoken to him?'

'Not about this,' I said. After the beach, we hadn't been alone again, and by the time we finally got home, all I'd wanted to do was to put Hazel to bed and collapse in a heap.

'Then you talk to him. You make it crystal clear that nothing can happen,' she said, as if it was the most obvious thing in the world. 'You tell him that it's not the right time in your life to be shacking up with the next-door neighbour.'

'But what if it was nothing and I imagined it all? I don't want to make a complete idiot of myself,' I added.

'It never hurts to set clear boundaries. In any circumstances.'

That's why I'd really come here rather than Sofia's. Because I knew that Camille, who always faced up to things, would make me do the same.

She paused and rearranged her angular face into an expression I knew too well – concern. I braced.

'You have to remember, Zo, that it's not just about you anymore. It's about Hazel. What's best for her. You've got to be really careful about who you let in.'

I could feel my cheeks burning, like I'd been slapped. My hackles stood on end. Was Camille implying that I was, or could become, a negligent mother, unable to put her daughter before her hormones?

I deflated. She wasn't. She was just telling me the other thing I'd needed to hear out loud. Whatever decisions I made about my life, Hazel was now the priority. The only priority.

I couldn't avoid Will. I still needed his help with Hazel for the next six weeks. And so, as much as I desperately wanted to avoid it, I needed to talk to him about what had happened, or more to the point what didn't happen over the weekend.

Not that it would be an issue. Will did everything to the highest standard – he probably had been determined to be the best fake boyfriend in the world in front of his colleagues, and become too invested in his performance.

And I wasn't exactly the biggest catch – a single mother, perpetually exhausted. I was almost certain that his perspective was the same as mine – that what had happened over the weekend was just the two of us believing our own lie, fuelled by free booze and a bit too much sun.

At the end of the day, Will was Hazel's manny three days a week. And she loved him. The Arrangement was working. Without it our family, Hazel and I, couldn't stay afloat until I'd worked out a new plan. Will and I could be friends – that was all.

I had to stay in control of the situation. What I needed was Will's help, nothing more. And in six weeks' time, we could sensibly disentangle our lives. I could carefully transition Hazel from Will's care to whatever friendly daycare I'd begged or bribed our way into. I made a mental note to up the frequency of my regular calls to our local childcare centres to check if Hazel had crept up any waiting lists.

'It's not even a question. Now's not the time for a new relationship. Particularly with someone where things are already so … messy,' Camille said, sisterly concern giving way to sisterly judgement.

'Nothing will happen with him. If there was even anything there at all,' I promised and Camille nodded, knowing I meant it.

'I have one more question,' I said. 'How do you add something to a contract?'

'How is that relevant?'

'Will and I signed a contract about our arrangement,' I said.

'Show me,' Camille said wearily.

I pulled up the email and handed her my phone. Her well-practised eyes darted over it.

'Jesus. He put this all in writing. And I thought he was supposed to be a smart guy.'

'We wanted, we want, to have clear boundaries,' I said. 'But as you say, they could be … clearer.'

'There's a variation clause. You'd need another contract to vary this one,' she said.

'So, we'd need to sign another contract?'

'It's more like a sub-contract that amends the first one,' she said, shrugging on her trench coat. 'And speaking of contracts – I'm now late for work.'

CHAPTER 15

Contract to Tweak The Contract

between

William Flemming

and

Zoe Harper

Recitals: The purpose of this extra part of the contract between Will Flemming and Zoe Harper ('The Contract') is to be extra-crystal clear about a few things to do with The Arrangement.

Section 9 – Relationship between The Carer and The Mother

The Carer and The Mother agree that their relationship will be strictly platonic ('Friendship'). The relationship between The Carer and The Mother will not be physical.

I spent the day at Camille's house, leaving just before I knew she'd arrive home with the twins. As we pulled into our street, I saw Will standing in front of his house, the garage door open. I'd geed myself up to speak to him this evening, but I felt robbed of the few extra minutes I needed to steel my nerves. My heart began to race as I parked.

'Feeling better?' Will asked with a wry smile.

'Turns out I'm fine – confused allergies with a cold. Do you have time to talk?'

'I don't.'

I felt a sting of irritation. I was trying to be a grown-up here. The last thing I needed was Will at his prickliest.

'We should talk.'

'No, I really don't have time. I'm late for a birthday-drinks thing.'

My heart sank. I knew that if I didn't talk to Will now I'd never work myself up to do it again, that it was entirely possible I'd move houses, maybe countries, in the middle of the night to avoid having this conversation.

'I'll give you a lift.'

He climbed into the passenger seat and typed a Hawthorn address into my maps app. I immediately regretted inviting him into a small, confined space to have this conversation. Although, at least we didn't have to make eye contact.

'I might be totally overreacting, but I think we should talk about the weekend,' I said, as soon as he shut his door. I ignored the urge to turn on the child locks.

I glanced at him. His expression gave away nothing. It was the one he used when he was working – the mask.

'I feel like we possibly got a bit carried away with the pretending-to-be-together thing. But …'

'… now we're back home with no one watching us, we can drop the charade. Just be friends,' he said, finishing my sentence.

'Oh great. That's what I was going to say. Except in your preferred language – legalese. Open my drafts folder in my emails.'

Will raised an eyebrow at my command, picked up my phone off the dashboard and scanned my new clause. He burst out laughing.

'You've drafted a "no sex" clause.'

'It's actually broader than that. It's a no any-bases clause.' I wondered if it was possible to die of embarrassment?

'I don't think we need a contractual provision to prevent any bases being reached,' he said.

I exhaled. I'd got worked up for no reason. Will felt exactly how I did.

'I never thought I'd hear you turn down the opportunity to put something in writing,' I said. 'But hey, I'm just trying to do what you taught me – to cover all my bases.'

'To avoid getting to any bases?'

'Exactly,' I said, concentrating hard on the road ahead, knowing my cheeks were now bright red. 'So, you're happy to sign it?'

'I have some issues with signing something of this quality,' he said.

'I know you're not used to seeing such a high calibre of writing and creative flair.'

'But yes, I'll sign it.'

'Great,' I said.

Mortification aside, the conversation had gone better than I could have imagined. In fact, Will had been the one to say that we were just friends before I had.

We drove for the next few minutes in silence.

'This is the one,' Will finally spoke. My Yaris had wheezed its way up a hill, where at the top mature oaks guarded white Victorian mansions, which no doubt had sweeping views over the Yarra River and the city skyline. I pulled up in front of the house Will had pointed at. At work, we called these types of houses 'stately', which meant imposing and enormous. It had a tower with a flagpole.

'This is where your drinks are? This is where the guy who doesn't like parties, parties?'

Will laughed, and the tension that had built up in the car dissipated. 'My dad's sister married a very rich man. And this is their house.' There was a note of barely disguised contempt in his voice when he mentioned his uncle.

'You're not the biggest fan?'

'Uncle Duncan is a total moron. And his two sons have about one brain cell between them. But Duncan inherited his dad's company and has managed not to fritter away the entire fortune. Yet …'

I'd never heard him speak with so much disdain.

'Why do you care? You know you're a million times better than some trust-fund trolls!'

'You don't get it. At the school I went to, at my firm, they're made for people who grew up in places like this.' Will's mask had now slipped. He gestured towards his uncle's house, which I could see even from the street was replete with a tennis court and swimming pool.

'They grew up in the right suburb. They barrack for the right football team. And everything is just … easier for them.'

I knew what he meant. He could have been describing Adam, who'd been brought up with a silver spoon in his mouth yet made it clear when we were dating that he truly believed he'd earned his prestigious job, giving no weight to the privilege that had given him an enormous leg up.

'And they treat my parents like yokels because they don't have MCC memberships and black AMEXs. And ever since I was a kid, they've treated me like I was some freak because I enjoyed reading and not footy.'

I'd never seen this side of Will. He was normally so calm and in control, so self-assured. But now I saw the undercurrent of anger, righteous fury even, that bubbled beneath the surface.

I pulled my keys out of the ignition and opened my door. 'Well, Hazel and I are going in for a drink.'

Surprise cut through his stormy face. 'You're going to go into my family party, and meet my parents, without me?' Will asked, attempting to call my bluff.

I began to unbuckle a very sleepy Hazel from her seat. Shit – I really hadn't thought this through. And apparently, I'd just agreed to meet Will's parents. But I couldn't stand the idea of a bunch of snobby idiots making Will feel bad about himself.

And, slightly less altruistically, I was desperate to find out more about Will and his family. And the source of the enormous chip on his shoulder.

'Yep. It's the kind of thing friends do.' I pulled Hazel onto my hip. 'And it would be really weird if you didn't follow me.'

CHAPTER 16

The inside of the house was even more opulent than the facade – all heavy oak furniture, silk curtains and green marble.

Genetically blessed twenty-somethings in crisp white shirts and black aprons scuttled around the formal living room, handing around glasses of champagne and offering up platters of tiny canapés to the crowd of well-heeled, well-preserved white people.

'Darling, you're here! John, he came.' A short woman, with a wiry grey bob, wearing a bright-red tunic dress, nudged the man next to her. The couple, surely Will's parents, seemed beyond thrilled (and a little bit surprised) to see him.

Will's mum enveloped him in a hug. 'He left work early to see us. I told you he would, John.'

Will's dad gave him a friendly pat on the arm. So, Will's height came from his dad. John was a tall man who I guessed had spent his life unsuccessfully trying to fade into the background. And he was every inch the maths teacher Will had told me he was, from his thick glasses to the sensible black orthopaedic runners on his feet.

Will gave his parents a big bear hug each. His mum's eyes twinkled with happiness.

'Mum, Dad, this is my neighbour Zoe and her daughter, Hazel. She gave me a lift, so I invited her in for a drink,' he said. 'Zoe, these are my parents – Helen and John.'

'It's so nice to meet you! Thanks for teaching Will to play the piano. It's the only thing that settles Hazel some nights. We can hear it when both of our windows are open.'

Will shot me a look, though it was more bemused than annoyed. John didn't smile, but I saw his eyes, chestnut like Will's, watching intently as I rambled on.

'You still play?' Helen asked Will, clearly pleased.

He sort of grunted a yes, like a petulant schoolboy, and I suppressed a giggle. It was quite fun to see this teenage version of Will.

'Can I have a cuddle?' Helen asked, arms already outstretched. 'She's the cutest little thing. How old? She's so alert. And Hazel – what a cute name.'

Will's reserved manner evidently came from his father. I handed Hazel over, and Helen jiggled her up and down on her hip. I felt a pang of … longing, really. Hazel hadn't even been old enough to hold her own head up the last time Mum had visited.

Adam's parents had been nothing like mine – they'd been much younger, glamorous, far more urbane. But Will's were familiar – ordinary people you wouldn't look at twice if you passed them on the street. And they were completely lovely.

Hazel grizzled.

'She's probably hungry.'

'It's her dinnertime.'

Will and I spoke over each other. I saw Helen's eyes narrow, not suspiciously, just a bit confused. We'd clearly become so used to pretending to be a couple that we'd forgotten how to not play our parts.

'Little munchkin,' Helen said as I took Hazel from her.

'The prodigal son has arrived!' We were interrupted by a man, who I guessed was Uncle Duncan. He strolled towards our group wielding a bottle of champagne. The word *slimy* sprang to mind. His silver-grey hair was slicked back and even the material of his suit jacket was shiny. He was trailed by two younger versions of himself, replete with matching jackets and hairdos. They stood either side of him, a step behind, like his henchmen, but I guessed they were his sons.

'Incorrect use of the expression,' Will muttered under his breath as the men shook hands. 'Thanks for having us. This is my friend Zoe and her daughter, Hazel. Zoe, my uncle Duncan and my cousins, Malcolm and Mark.'

'Let me top everyone up. No wine from a box tonight!' Duncan said as he refilled Helen's and John's glasses to the brim. They smiled politely. Will's expression was thunderous – he clearly wanted to throttle the man. 'And we need to get you two a drink. You pay top dollar for caterers and they hide in the kitchen eating all your food!'

I could see why Will couldn't stand his uncle.

'How's the paper pushing going, Will? Still dotting i's and crossing t's for people like me?'

'Will's on the verge of becoming one of the youngest partners at his firm.' It came out before I could stop myself. And it was true – Kate had told me.

'It'll be nice that all your hard work has paid off,' Helen said. I could tell she wanted to sound supportive, but she didn't have her son's ability to mask her emotions.

Duncan seemed put out. 'Mark just got his boat licence, because I bought a new boat,' he announced, apropos of nothing. 'And I've just promoted Malcolm to be my COO.'

'Congratulations, boys. Very exciting!' Helen said and seemed to actually mean it.

'You finally got a girlfriend, Twinklefingers!' Mark, the cousin who presented as slightly less dopey than the other, said to Will. He turned to me. 'We called him Twinklefingers at school because he played the piano.'

'So clever!' I said, but he missed the sarcasm. So Will had gone to school with Tweedledum and Tweedledee. I got the sense that these guys and their cronies would have ruled the playground and made life pretty miserable for people like Will.

'No, Will's not my boyfriend. But I am his neighbour and see the girls Will does date coming and going from his house. It's a parade of Amazonian goddesses. Most of them could be models.'

I wondered if I'd gone too far. But the gormless trio were now staring at Will, slack-jawed, impressed. Helen looked surprised and John's face gave nothing away (I now definitely knew where Will's expressions came from).

I avoided meeting Will's eyes. I knew he'd want to kill me.

'This is where you're all hiding!' A bottle-blonde who'd modelled her face on an Instagram filter toddled towards us in sky-high heels. I suspected whatever family resemblance had existed between her and Will's dad had long been obliterated by a celebrity plastic surgeon or five.

'Lovely dress, Helen,' she said, her expression showing she meant the exact opposite. 'One of your clever op-shop finds?'

'Happy birthday, Tracey,' Helen said, either not clocking or ignoring the slight. 'Yes, it is.'

I could see why Will had dreaded this event. His extended family was vile – condescending, rude and stupid. And if this was how they behaved in front of an outsider, I dreaded to think what they were like when they weren't on their best behaviour.

Hazel began to whine, so I bounced her a few times. Suddenly, my leg felt warm. I looked down. Vomit covered the bottom of my dress. Green vomit.

'Do you think she's having a reaction to something?' Will asked.

'The last thing she ate was my zucchini frittata,' I said.

'In her defence, that's made me gag,' he said.

Hazel retched again and a spray of emerald vomit splattered over Will's aunt's stilettos. And the apricot carpet. And she was suddenly very pale. I felt a pang of fear. Hazel was many things, but she wasn't a big vomiter.

Under normal circumstances, I would have felt embarrassed and begun rushing for some towels and soda water while I apologised profusely. When I saw Tracey's face, working against the injectables to convey horror, this ordinarily would have ratcheted up to mortification.

I glanced at Will and he now also looked concerned.

'We should get her home,' he said. I nodded.

Will flagged down a waiter and grabbed the linen serving cloth from their arm then handed it to me. I mopped up as much as I could off Hazel, noticing Tracey's eyes narrow again. But right now, I didn't care what she thought. I just wanted to get home.

'I'm going to drive them,' Will said.

'Of course, darling,' Helen said.

I didn't protest. For once, I was happy for Will to drive if it meant I got to sit in the back seat and keep an eye on Hazel.

I knew there were things I was meant to say – thank you, goodbye. But I just turned and followed Will out of the room and the house.

As I buckled Hazel into the car, she threw up again.

'It's okay, my muffin,' I soothed her. 'We'll be home soon.'

Even more colour had drained from her face.

'Should we go straight to the doctor?' I asked Will, who was hovering behind me. 'The hospital?'

'It's your call,' he said, his voice steady. 'Maybe we should ring the nurses' hotline while we drive? Ask someone medical what they think?'

He'd already keyed the number, one I knew by heart because I'd called it so often, into his phone. I pressed the 'dial' key as I clambered into the back seat next to Hazel.

A nurse, with a reassuringly calm voice, answered the call before we'd even made it to the end of the street.

'Oh, hi,' I said. 'I have an almost eight-month-old daughter and she's just started throwing up nonstop. And she's really pale. What should I do?' I asked, holding Hazel's tiny fingers in mine, possibly a bit too tightly.

'The nurse said it's probably a tummy bug. The key thing is to keep her hydrated until she feels better,' I relayed to Will as soon as I'd hung up. 'They said I should take her to a doctor if she has a temperature.'

'That's good to know. So, what do you want to do?'

I appreciated that he was deferring to me. I was wobbly and I knew that if he weighed in I could be easily swayed. But I also knew, deep in my gut, that I could do this, handle it. That I knew what was best for Hazel. That I could look after her.

'I think we should take her home. We can always go into the ED if things get worse overnight.'

As I was undressing Hazel, gently as if she was a newborn again, Will appeared in our bedroom with the baby thermometer. He pulled off its cap and popped it under Hazel's chubby left arm. We both watched the numbers climb up, as intently as if they were lottery numbers being called. It beeped.

'Thirty-six-point-five,' he said.

'That's normal range. Good. Great.' I breathed a sigh of relief. 'And Camille messaged me. The twins picked up gastro at daycare, so they must have passed it on to her this morning. At least we know what it is.'

I gave Hazel a bath and then sat on the couch, holding her close to me until she fell asleep.

'I should put her in her cot, but I'm worried she'll choke on her vomit or something.'

'We'll keep checking on her,' Will said.

I put Hazel down. Dosed up on baby Panadol, she stayed asleep.

'If you want to have a shower, or whatever, I can keep an eye on her,' Will offered when I returned to the kitchen.

I knew I should say no. It had only been a few hours since we'd agreed to keep things strictly platonic between us. But on the other hand, I smelled awful. And it wasn't like he'd be in the shower with me.

I stripped off and let the scalding hot water wash over me, grateful that Will was here. I knew that once he left and I was alone I wouldn't be able to let myself leave Hazel for a moment.

As my skin turned pink, I suddenly felt a wave of nausea pass through me. I turned off the spray, pulled a towel around me and made it to the toilet just in time to heave.

CHAPTER 17

I remained clutching the toilet bowl until I was empty and shivering.

There was a gentle knock on the door.

'Are you okay in there?' Will asked softly.

My stomach knotted again and I leaned over the bowl. I waited for a few more seconds, flushed the toilet and then stood up. My legs felt wobbly, but I wanted to check on Hazel.

I emerged from the bathroom in my dressing gown.

'Get out of here while you still can!' I croaked, as I checked Hazel's monitor. She was still asleep. 'This is the house of the plague.'

'I'm getting supplies.'

I didn't argue. I was too weak.

I was back in the bathroom when Will returned. He could have been gone for five minutes, he could have been gone for five days – time had lost all meaning. I heard him shuffle about the kitchen over the truly horrifying gurgles my stomach was now making.

Please put earphones in, I messaged him (I'd brought my phone to the bathroom so I could watch Hazel sleep on the monitor while I was chained to the toilet).

My phone pinged. He'd sent me the pooh emoji. I stared at my phone and burst out laughing. Then my stomach cramped and I groaned. My phone pinged again.

Do you need anything?

New body? I typed back. My head pounded and the room felt like it was a million degrees.

Then Hazel began to cry. I hauled myself up from the bathroom floor and jogged to the bedroom, but Will had got there first. He was holding Hazel up to his shoulder, slowly rubbing her.

'It's okay, Hazelnut. We're here.'

'Is she okay?'

'She's thrown up again. I think we should try to get more liquid into her.'

'Yep.' I took Hazel from him. She was still pale and floppy and looked so helpless and small in her sleep suit. 'Hey, both of us are really contagious. You should go home or you'll get it.'

My stomach lurched again, making a symphony of gurgles.

'Go!' Will said. 'I'll give her a bottle.'

'No, I can feed her,' I said, wincing. It felt like there was a knife in my stomach.

'Zoe. Let me help.'

'You didn't sign up for … this! This wasn't our deal.'

'I'm not here to fulfil my contractual obligations. Right now forget the contract. I need you to stop being a stubborn idiot and go throw up.'

I wanted to protest, but I wasn't sure what would come out of my mouth, literally. I handed Hazel to him and sprinted to the bathroom.

*

I lost track of time after that. I'd been in such a rush to see Hazel that I hadn't noticed that Will had transformed the living room into a recuperation station. He'd set up a camping mattress on the floor ('so you don't wake up Hazel during the night') with a tactically placed bucket next to it. And the kitchen counter was filled with lemonade and crackers.

Will changed her, her bedding, gave her a bottle, and by the time I'd emerged from the bathroom (again) got her to sleep.

'She drank some of the milk. And she had a bit more colour in her cheeks,' he updated me before I could ask.

I exhaled. 'I hate this so much, the poor thing. I never should have taken her to Camille's house. It's all my fault.'

'Don't be stupid. All kids get sick and guilt's not a helpful emotion. Lie down.'

He'd made up the mattress with sheets he must have brought from next door. Resting on a bed so close to Will was exactly the type of thing I wasn't meant to be doing. But it looked as enticing as a hotel-room king-sized bed. And now that I was pretty sure there was nothing left in my system, I felt weak and desperate to be horizontal.

I collapsed on it. The sheets smelled of Will – like the laundry powder he used. And they were cool against my burning skin.

'You can go. It's late. I've got it from here,' I said.

'Are you going to go to sleep?' he asked.

I shook my head, knowing that even though my body craved nothing more than deep sleep, I wouldn't be able to.

'Then it'll be like old times. Both of us up in the middle of the night.'

The next few hours passed like a stop-motion film. Will lay on the couch and I curled up on the mattress. We rested in front of a series of black-and-white movies he'd put on (of course Will liked old movies). Outside rain bucketed down, landing heavily on the metal roof. Howling wind shook the windows, and through the sheer curtains I could see lightning streak across the sky.

At intervals, I'd lurch up and make a dash for the bathroom. And when Hazel woke up, we'd both spring into action – taking her temperature, offering her milk, changing her.

Just before the sun rose, as the storm finally calmed down, we lay next to each other in silence. My stomach had given me a window of respite. Hazel had slept for a few hours in a row, and Will hadn't left. Although we were in my living room, the space where we'd spent most of our time together, it felt like we were somewhere else – like the middle of the wilderness.

'Thanks for coming in to the party with me,' Will said.

'I think your aunt and uncle were thrilled we showed up.'

'I literally can't think of anyone more deserving of vomit-strewn carpet.'

I laughed, then groaned as my stomach curdled.

'You okay?'

'Yes. No. I don't know. I mean, I'm nauseous, but I'll be fine if you distract me,' I said.

'I could play the piccolo for you?'

'Please, God, no,' I said, trying not to laugh again. 'Your parents are divine.'

'They're great.'

'Did you ever tell them how bad things were at school?'

I could feel him stiffen next to me.

'They're teachers. I'm sure they worked it out.'

'You can be quite good at hiding your feelings, you know. You do this sort of unreadable face.'

'I know I can … shut down,' he admitted. 'I probably learned how to do it when things got really bad at school.'

'Don't worry, I've become pretty good at deciphering it,' I said. 'The upper right-hand side of your lip twitches when you want to laugh. And your eyes glint when you're angry, or find something funny but don't want to admit it.'

'You should run negotiations. You're an expert at reading people.'

'It's a byproduct of being a lifelong people pleaser,' I said. 'It's weird because before I got to know you, you were the one person I didn't try to win over.'

'Why?'

'I don't know,' I said. 'Maybe because I needed someone who I could just … be the worst version of myself with. And you were there right next door. And the stakes felt low. I didn't think I'd ever really get to know you.'

'I like the worst version of you,' Will said. 'Actually, I think the version where you say exactly what you think without a filter might be the best version.'

'Your parents' faces lit up when they saw you. I thought your mum was going to explode with happiness when you arrived,' I said quickly.

We fell into another silence.

'I didn't tell them that I was getting bullied ... God, I don't think I've ever said that out loud. I didn't tell them I was getting bullied at school because they were so proud of my scholarship. And I knew that if I told them they'd make a big fuss. I didn't want to let them down.'

'I know I only met them for a few minutes, but I got the sense that the only thing they care about is your happiness. Not some fancy school or ...' Law firm. I left the sentence dangling.

'Now you know my darkest secrets. What're yours?' Will asked.

'You're in my house all day. You know everything about my life.'

But I knew that he didn't know my darkest, deepest secret. No one did. I didn't let myself think about it. My mind flashed to the night it had happened ... a whir of drunken snippets.

He glanced at me from the couch, and I could tell that he knew there was something I wasn't telling him, something I was withholding.

'Okay. I'll tell you something really embarrassing,' I said.

'You don't have to.'

'That's okay,' I said. 'You told me the piccolo story. It's mutually assured destruction.'

'Fair point,' he said.

'So, I secretly booked my wedding to Adam, but he never proposed to me.' I buried my face under the doona.

'I'm confused,' he said.

I pulled the doona back down. 'I knew Adam had bought an engagement ring. I saw it by mistake. And one day, I was bored at work and called Adam's favourite winery to check their availability. They said that there was a two-year waiting list for Saturday weddings, and did I want to lock in a date now because otherwise we'd probably miss out? They said women did it all the time when they knew a proposal was coming. So, I did it – I had a time and a date for our wedding. I paid a deposit and everything. I thought Adam would be thrilled when I told him after he proposed. Except … he never gave me the ring. He broke up with me instead.'

'I'm sorry that happened,' Will said. 'And for what it's worth, I don't think you should be embarrassed about taking your life by the balls. Or the whatever.'

'I mean, I've booked a wedding and no one's ever proposed to me. That's pretty embarrassing.' I croaked out a laugh.

'Okay, it's tragic,' he said. I play-hit him with a weak arm. 'But that's not what I'm talking about. It's really impressive that you wanted to have a kid. And you did it your way.'

A silence fell between us. If there was ever a moment served up to tell him the truth, the whole truth, this was it. And I was tempted. Except I couldn't. I could barely admit it to myself.

Hazel began to wail. We both jumped up and raced towards her cries.

'She feels hot,' I said, holding my hand against Hazel's forehead. Will already had the thermometer out. We watched the numbers rise again.

'It's gone up – thirty-eight degrees.'

'I want to take her to a doctor.'

CHAPTER 18

'Mate. Sorry to call you so early in the morning ...'

Before I could ask him what he was doing, Will had pulled his phone out of his pocket and was speaking to someone. He walked out of the room and I was too preoccupied with soothing Hazel to eavesdrop.

'My best friend's a paediatrician. He'll be here in ten,' he said when he returned.

'You have friends?' I replied before I could stop myself. 'Sorry. I didn't mean it like that. Thank you – that's amazing.'

The idea of leaving the house with both Hazel and a bucket on zero sleep felt gargantuan.

'Of course I have friends. I just don't spend hours a day messaging and calling them like you do with Sofia.'

Will's best friend, Charlie, was as cheery as Will was reserved. Since Hazel was born, I'd noticed that paediatricians had a particular energy to them – they sort of bounced around with exuberance and wore lots of colour. Charlie didn't disprove my rule.

'So, you're the sick muppet,' he said, distracting her with a plastic monkey attached to his stethoscope. 'Now I'm just going to take your temperature.'

I held Hazel, who was far quieter and stiller than usual,

on my knee while Charlie took her temperature using an ear thermometer.

'It's a bit high. Is she drinking?'

'We've been giving her milk throughout the night. She's had some, but a lot's come up again.'

'Do you have Hydralyte?'

I shook my head.

'She's old enough to have some. On your bike, Flemming,' he told Will. 'Get some baby Nurofen, too. She can have that with Panadol.'

'That's okay, I can go,' I protested.

'She's sick, too. Hasn't been able to keep anything down all night,' Will said, picking up his wallet from the table.

It was only when Will had left and Charlie and I were alone with Hazel that I realised what it looked like. Will had obviously slept over. His stuff was everywhere, and I was in my pyjamas.

'Will's my next-door neighbour. He saw that Hazel wasn't well, so he helped out last night. It's just me and her.'

'Will's told me all about you. It's nice to finally meet you.'

Will had told his friend about me?

'Sorry to get you out of bed so early. The nurse said to see a doctor if her temperature went up, and it did. And Will just … called you.'

'No problem,' he said, and I could tell he was the kind of person who genuinely didn't mind. 'Will's helped out our college gang with lots of legal stuff.'

'Is Hazel going to be okay?'

'Babies get sick really quickly. But they also bounce back fast. If you can keep her hydrated over the next twenty-four hours she should be okay. You might find she's a bit quieter than usual. And her sleep might regress.'

Relief flooded my body. Hazel was going to be okay.

'And she won't be able to go to childcare this week,' he added.

'Oh, she doesn't …' Then I stopped myself. Charlie was from Will's real life. I guessed he didn't know about The Arrangement, couldn't know about The Arrangement.

'I think Hazel will be fine. I'm more worried about you. You've clearly been hit hard and I suspect you'll need an IV drip to get some fluids into you. I'd like you to go get checked out by the ED.'

I almost laughed, because the concept was ludicrous. If I took another day off work Monica would kill me. And my to-do list was a million items long. Sofia's baby shower was next weekend and I needed to sort out all the games and I wanted to buy her the perfect present. After a weekend away, neither of us had any clean clothes. And there was no food in the fridge.

'I haven't thrown up in … almost an hour. Soon, I'll be able to get some water into me and I'll be fine.'

'I'm serious. I'm guessing before you got sick you were run-down. Is there someone who can watch her while you get checked out? I'm sure Will wouldn't mind.'

Deep down I knew that Charlie was right – I wasn't at my best. I hadn't slept in two days. And did I eat anything yesterday? Or drink something that wasn't coffee?

But I couldn't ask Will for more help. Not after everything he'd already done. Not when he'd been up all night. But Camille and Ed were out – they'd be in their own seventh circle of hell with the twins right now. And I couldn't ask Sofia to be near an infectious baby while pregnant.

'I'll call my mum,' I said, with as much conviction as I could muster.

I went into the bedroom, scrolled down my contacts until I reached 'Mum' and pressed 'dial'. I knew she'd pick up – unlike everyone my age, she wasn't afraid of a phone call.

'It's early, Zoe.'

'Sorry. Did I wake you up?'

'No, you know I'm always up early,' she said, a bit defensively.

'So Hazel and I have gastro. And a doctor thinks I might need a drip. And … I was wondering if you might be able to come and help us out today?'

With every word, my stomach twisted. Did I need the bathroom? Or did I need this conversation to be over?

There was a long pause on the other end of the line.

'Is Hazel okay?'

'She's not great, but the doctor thinks she'll be fine in a day or so.'

'That's good.' There was another long pause. I could imagine her padding around her kitchen, straightening her canisters filled with different types of tea bags and lining up the tea towels hanging from the oven.

'You know I'm a two-hour drive away … Have you tried lemonade? You girls always passed on your bugs to me. And I found that I could always soldier on if I had lemonade on hand. Camille's sick, too. Must be going around. She's going to work from home today. She's bought lemonade, too.'

When I'd been lying on the bathroom floor overnight, gut churning and worried about Hazel, I thought I couldn't feel worse. And a few minutes earlier, I'd thought my mouth couldn't feel drier. I'd been wrong.

'Good idea. I'll try that,' I said, as if I hadn't spent the night throwing up the few sips of Will's lemonade that I'd been able to get down.

Will had arrived back while I'd been on the phone, with what appeared to be half the chemist.

'I'll drive you to the ED now. And I can watch Hazel,' he said.

'That's okay. My mum's going to drive up to help. She'll meet me at the hospital.' The lie came out before I could stop it. It was bad enough that Will literally had seen me at my lowest point last night. I couldn't handle any more pity.

'Fine, but I'm driving you.'

I was too weak to protest. After thanking Charlie profusely, we all clambered into my car. Will drove us to the hospital in silence. The mood had changed as the sun rose. Overnight, we'd been running on pure adrenaline. And when Will and I had lain in the dark living room together, it had felt like a teenage sleepover, where you could safely whisper secrets in the middle of the night.

But now, in the harsh light of day, I felt truly horrendous. My mouth was salty and my ribs hurt from heaving. And the conversation with Mum kept reverberating around my head. I must have been delusional to have made that phone call and expected a different answer. What had I been thinking? I'd known that I was on my own. I'd just lost all sense of reality along with the contents of my stomach.

Will insisted on coming into the hospital. No amount of assuring him we'd be okay would dissuade him. He waited on the hard plastic bucket seats until a doctor, one who looked too young to grow facial hair, finally saw us. After he examined me, he agreed with Charlie's assessment.

'We're going to admit you. Dad can come through, too,' the fresh-faced doctor told us.

We were led into a small room that smelled of antiseptic and was shielded from the hustle and bustle of the hospital by a flimsy green curtain on a rail. Another doctor inserted the drip. I held it together until the three of us were left alone and I'd fed Hazel to sleep. Then salty tears, not unlike the saline being put into me, escaped in a steady trickle.

'I'm sorry,' I said, pawing at my eyes with my free hand. 'Thanks for being here. I lied – my mum's not coming.'

'I know,' he said simply.

'I did ask her, but she was busy. She takes her job really seriously. And … she did it all on her own, so she thinks I should just … be able to handle it.'

'She didn't do the baby years on her own. And anyway, she should have come.'

'She was never going to come. I'm not the kind of person people come for. I'm the kind of person they leave.'

'That's not true.'

'No. It really is. My dad left as soon as I started school. My mum left as soon as I finished school. Adam left as soon as I told him I wanted a baby.'

Was there truth serum in this drip?

'On the day I had the procedure to conceive Hazel, it was in a room just like this. And I knew exactly what I wanted and why I was doing it. But I remember lying on the hospital bed and imagining that being a sole parent, well, that days like today when the shit totally hit the fan would be … really bloody hard and lonely.'

Where had my filter gone? I never talked about that day. I didn't even like to think about it.

'So, thank you for making it less bloody hard and lonely.'

'It's …' Will searched for the end of his sentence. '… almost nine. You probably should let work know you won't be in today.'

I exhaled. We were moving back into more familiar territory – practicalities.

'My phone's in my bag. Would you mind?'

Will was already up. He went to hand it to me, but Hazel was asleep in my arms and we both knew that the slightest twitch could wake her.

'Why don't you dictate?'

'Okay. My password's three-one-eight-one.'

Will raised an eyebrow at my use of our postcode but said nothing.

'My boss's name is Monica. Could you please message her and say, "I'm so, so sorry, but I've ended up in hospital so won't be able to come into work today. I'm sure I'll be fine tomorrow. Please call me if you need me – I've got my phone on me."'

Will tapped away. '*Monica. I need to take a day of personal leave today and am unlikely to be back at work until next week.*

I'll give you a call when I'm able to discuss urgent deliverables. Zoe,' he read out his draft.

'That's not how dictation works.'

'You don't owe it to her to give her the details.'

This would be news to Monica.

'And you don't need to apologise for ending up in hospital. I refuse to let you use the word "sorry". Your boss walks all over you!'

'How often do you take sick days?'

'I should take more,' he said sanctimoniously. 'You know, I've actually listened to some of the stuff you've said about my work-life balance.'

I suppressed a smile. My lips cracked. 'Work's not that bad. I have a new work best friend who keeps me sane,' I said. 'And they're doing a family day at the zoo on Saturday.'

'Because that's what parents really want – to spend their weekends wrangling their kids in front of their colleagues, while protecting them from lions,' he said.

'Pot kettle black – we just spent a long weekend with your colleagues!'

'Then I owe you help at your work thing?'

Was it a genuine offer? Did Will really want to spend his Saturday at my inevitably dire work event? And did I want him there? It would be easier wrangling Hazel with another pair of hands. But there was no way I was doing the fake-relationship routine again.

'I guess you can leverage off me for a free ticket to the butterfly enclosure,' I said. 'But we go as friends. Obviously.'

We were interrupted by a paediatrician who'd been called down to the ED to do an exam of Hazel. He was even younger than the doctor who had treated me and took Hazel's medical history as if his final qualification depended on it, running through his checklist in painstaking detail.

Hazel, just awake but still floppy in my arms, sneezed. Was she warm enough? Was she also coming down with a cold? The doctor glanced up from his clipboard.

'Any significant issues of asthma or allergies on Hazel's maternal side?'

'No,' I said. I couldn't fault my parents' genetic history.

'And on the paternal side?' Doogie Howser MD turned to Will.

'I don't know,' I said. 'He's not Hazel's dad. There's no father.'

'But surely, the clinic gave you a full medical history of the donor?' Will, who until this point had been silent, asked.

'They did, yeah,' I said. 'But I don't remember the details. My brain's not working this morning. Nothing significant, I don't think, or I wouldn't have picked him.'

I focused on the doctor, who was furiously transcribing every word I said, but out of the corner of my eye I could see Will give me a strange look. And my stomach, which had given me a temporary moment of respite, began to churn again.

CHAPTER 19

'She lives. And, quelle surprise, just in time for a party!' Monica greeted me, acting as if she'd made a joke rather than a dig at me. I wondered if she'd chosen today's picnic spot outside the hyena enclosure because she felt a particular affinity with the species?

On Saturday morning, the horrors of gastro behind us, the three of us had driven across the city to Melbourne Zoo for the company's annual family morning. A trestle table, bookended by banners with the company's logo, was filled with finger food. My colleagues with kids looked like they'd been awake for too many hours; the ones without like they'd just rolled out of bed.

'Are you guys okay?' Kajal asked with genuine concern.

'Hazel bounced back. I haven't eaten in a week, but the silver lining is I now fit into my old pre-baby clothes again,' I said lightly. 'This is Hazel, my daughter. And this is my friend Will, who's helping me out today.'

'Nice to meet you, Will!' Kajal extended her hand, which was perfectly manicured with pastel rainbow tips. She probably had been out all night but still was a vision in a pale-yellow slip dress and lilac jumper.

'Ah, Zoe's work wife,' Will said, taking Kajal's hand.

'I like to think of us as office soulmates,' she said, as they slowly shook hands. He laughed, his face lighting up.

'Your eyes met over the photocopier and it was love at first sight,' he said.

'Exactly,' she replied, with a giggle as she ran her hand through her perfectly curled hair.

'And this is Monica,' I said.

'I've also heard a lot about you, Monica,' Will said evenly as he turned away from Kajal and shook Monica's hand.

'And yet I've heard nothing about you,' she replied.

'I'm sure Zoe's just being the consummate professional – very focused at work. Strict boundaries,' he said.

Monica shrugged her bony shoulders, which were on display in a hideous knitted top with cut-outs. 'Have you been here with Hazel yet? On one of your many days off?' Monica asked.

'We're lucky if we get as far as the supermarket,' I said, with a forced laugh. 'And I don't think she's old enough to properly appreciate it yet. A sparrow's just as impressive as a giraffe, at her age.'

'And Zoe ends up working on a lot of her non-working days,' Will added.

'Not that Will's an expert on balance,' I interjected.

'We're a very family-friendly company,' Monica said, an edge to her voice. She might have a skin as thick as the rhinoceroses, which were chomping on their morning tea a few metres away from us, but she was hyper-attuned to criticism. 'We do an event like this annually. This year, there's a face painter.'

'Much more fun than a flexible work policy,' Will said.

'We might ...' I performed a dramatic sniff of Hazel's bottom. 'Yep, we definitely need to change Hazel's nappy.' Monica's nose wrinkled with disgust. I gave Will a meaningful glare to make it clear he should follow us.

'What the hell are you doing?' I snapped in a whisper, as soon as we reached the edge of the work group.

'Being myself?' he replied.

'Okay, but can you not?' I asked. 'That's my boss.'

'I know you think it's your job to keep everyone happy, but you can call out bad behaviour.'

'No, I can't! She's the woman who signs my paycheques. Which buys Hazel a roof over her head and the required amount of mashed-up food and nappies. It's literally my job to keep her happy. So, please, stop making career-limiting comments.'

'The only one limiting your career is you. You can do better than this. You know you're bored shitless by this job.'

'You don't get it. An interesting, stimulating job, working for someone without sociopathic tendencies – that's a privilege. One for people like you.'

'No, it's not. You're allowed to want more. You know you need more,' he said.

'So, that's why you offered to come today – to be my protector? To force my hand by screwing around with my job?'

'No, I came because I wanted to say thank you for everything you did at my work conference and repay the favour.'

'Well, consider the debt well and truly repaid after all your help this week. We're square. Just don't go into debt pissing off my boss,' I said. 'Go visit the meerkats or something.'

Will did not go to visit the meerkats. Kajal made a beeline for him, but at least he stayed away from Monica. I spent the morning switching between networking with colleagues and silently fuming. I'd practically tap-danced in front of his superiors, and he'd been the rudest, prickliest version of himself to mine.

And where did he get off lecturing me about my job satisfaction, when his job had led to burnout? And yes, I was critical of his work, but in private, like a normal person.

I saw Kajal throw her head back as Will made her laugh. Oh, so now Will could be charming and hilarious.

An hour later, I stomped up a small flight of stairs to the wooden platform where Will and Kajal were showing Hazel the giraffes and effectively hiding from our colleagues.

'Sorry to interrupt. We should probably go soon,' I said.

It was an unusually warm late-winter day, the sun was beginning to bite and I didn't want Hazel to be outside too long after her tough week.

I noticed that they'd had matching butterflies painted on their cheekbones. How had Kajal convinced Will to do that? I regretted the full tiger number I'd let the face painter plaster onto me, which was upsetting Hazel.

I wondered what I would think if, like Kajal, I'd met Will today for the first time. He was relaxed (except when near Monica), and appeared self-assured in chinos and a shirt with sleeves rolled up, revealing his tanned forearms. His floppy hair was glossy in the sun, and since he'd relaxed his shaving schedule, his stubble accentuated his strong jawline.

'Okay,' Will said. 'It's been lovely to meet you, Kajal.'

'Thanks for saving me from the morning from hell,' she said. 'I might do a runner, too.'

'Do you want a lift?' Will offered.

'That would be great, if you don't mind,' Kajal said, with a winning smile.

Great, now we wouldn't get home in time for Hazel's afternoon nap and she'd fall asleep in the car instead of her cot and I wouldn't get a proper break all day.

I felt the remnants of my good will towards Will, like my tiger face paint, melting away.

After I fed Hazel dinner, I drove to Camille's house. She'd insisted on having Hazel for a sleepover when she'd found out that we'd caught the twins' bug and ended up in hospital. It wasn't her fault, but she was adamant.

'Stay for a wine?' Camille asked. I agreed, mostly because I was surprised that Camille, who barely ever drank, wanted one herself.

While I settled Hazel into the twins' old travel cot, Camille poured half a bottle into each of our glasses.

'How was your work thing?' she asked.

'Total nightmare!' I inhaled an enormous slug of wine. 'My boss was a cow, as per. And then Will niggled away at her …'

I realised as soon as I mentioned Will that I'd made a mistake.

'Will was there?' An arched eyebrow flew up.

'He offered to come help with Hazel, after the week we've had. As a friend. Don't worry, we made that very clear. And honestly, after today, I'm not sure we're even that.'

I realised I wasn't just irritated, but was angry at Will – for believing that he had a right to turn up and interfere with the gossamer-fine world I'd built up around Hazel and me. I'd told him that I wanted to do things alone, so where did he get off intruding, uninvited.

'I've been thinking about what you told me the other day. About Will taking leave,' Camille said.

'Please, let's talk about something else, anything else,' I said.

'Fine.' She held up her hands, uncharacteristically letting something go. 'But I do want to talk about it.'

I took another gulp of wine, instantly feeling its warm kick. I hadn't eaten much today, so it would go straight to my head. But for once, it didn't matter. I'd fed Hazel and pumped enough for her morning feed.

'I thought I'd do a big Greek lamb for Father's Day. Mum loves my lamb,' Camille said.

'Okay, not that, either!' I said. The last thing I wanted to talk about was bloody Father's Day. Or fathers. Or Mum. Not tonight.

'Did you like Adam?' The question popped into my mind out of nowhere. Well, not nowhere. He always snuck into my thoughts unbidden, despite my best efforts to permanently delete him.

'I thought he was your type,' she said.

'What does that mean?'

'Well, all of the guys you dated were a version of Adam.'

'I don't have a type!'

Camille seemed surprised. 'You totally have a type,' she said. 'We all have a type. I like guys who are super-smart, hyper-ambitious and charming.'

'That's Ed! The only guy you've ever dated! One person doesn't make a pattern.'

'What can I say? I know what I want and I'm efficient.' She shrugged.

'So, what's my type?' I asked.

'You like guys who are ...' she paused, clearly working up some diplomatic language. 'Who need you. I mean, they're all smart, successful guys, but they were all ... I don't want to use the word *damaged* ...'

'You just did!'

'And you would take on their interests, mould yourself to fit in with their lives, as if you were trying to be their perfect fit,' she said.

I drained my glass.

'Are you driving home?' Camille asked.

'I'll walk.'

'Mum told me you called her. Asked for a hand.'

'Mine was hooked up to saline – I literally needed another hand,' I said. 'The doctor said the bug hit me hard because I was so run-down.'

'I'm sorry that I was ... otherwise indisposed that day. I had to turn off my camera during a huge mediation to throw up in my office bin.'

I failed to suppress a snort of laughter. 'Didn't you try lemonade?'

Camille laughed darkly. Despite her assassination of my dating history, it was nice to see her like this, letting her hair down a bit. And any acknowledgement that Mum was less than perfect made me feel less like I was crazy to expect – to want – more.

'Do you ever wish that Mum was around? Helped us out a bit?' I asked, taking advantage of this rare opening.

'We're grown-ups. She gets to live her own life now.' Camille's voice was measured.

'You can tell me what you really think.'

'I just did!'

'You don't always have to give me the perfect answer.'

I knew how much Camille loved Arti, that she'd do anything for her daughter. Didn't Camille ever wonder why Mum didn't seem to feel the same way about us?

'I know you're in a bad mood, and mad at the world tonight. But don't take it out on me, okay,' she snapped.

'Sorry,' I said, taken aback. Camille's composure almost never slipped. I didn't think I'd seen her like this since she was a teenager studying for her final exams.

'No, I'm sorry. I didn't mean that. I'm just really tired. Ed's in Hong Kong. I'm just …' She didn't finish her thought.

'Are you sure you want Hazel tonight? I could stay here – you could go see a movie or something?' I offered.

'Don't be silly. I'm fine,' she said, but I wasn't convinced.

'You're doing an incredible job. Arti's the smartest, most curious kid I've ever seen – a mini you. And Remy's so sweet and adorable, you just want to eat him up.'

She fluttered her hands as if batting away my compliments. 'Go – sleep while you can!'

*

As I left Camille's house, part of me wanted to scoop up Hazel and take her home. But she was sound asleep, and I'd be back when she woke up.

I walked from Camille's salubrious suburb to my own, passing gaggles of hens' parties dressed up and heading to bars, pumping restaurants and couples en route to date night. I felt like Dorothy arriving in Oz – I'd forgotten the world could be so bright and shiny. And that people made plans at night.

Finally, I reached the front of my own empty house. I'd hoped the walk home would help me shake off all the emotions swilling around me. I did feel exhausted. The week had begun with an emotional crisis, ended with a hideous work event, with a nice sandwich of gastro and extreme dehydration in the middle. But I also felt as if I'd never be able to sleep again.

As I settled on the couch with another glass of wine, trying to remember how I used to spend my free time, there was a knock on the door. Even before I opened it, I knew it would be Will.

'I wanted to say sorry for slightly overstepping today,' he said.

'I missed that. What did you say?'

'You heard. Don't milk it. Contrition isn't a natural state for me,' he said in a low voice.

'You don't need to whisper, Hazel's at Camille's for the night.'

'Wow. Are you going to sleep for twenty hours?'

'I thought that's what I'd want to do. But I think I just want to get out into the real world.'

'I'm going out tonight. You could come?'

'Where are you going?'

'Surprise.'

'You want me to use my one night off, possibly ever, to go somewhere random with the guy who honestly, I'm considering relegating back to enemy status?'

'Get your stuff,' he said.

'Fine,' I agreed. It's not like I had any better offers – since I'd been pregnant, I'd barely been out and I'd dropped off all the group message threads organising fun nights. And I knew Sofia, my go-to choice, was spending the evening with her new dance-class BFFs, crafting costumes for their concert. So, that left me with Will.

I was sure that Will was going to take me to a fancy restaurant, but we drove down Chapel Street and along Toorak Road, past a dozen bustling restaurants with linen tablecloths, without stopping. Finally, still giving nothing away, Will parked in a tree-lined side street near The Tan.

'If your secret plan is a late-night run, I'm out,' I said. A pack of fruit bats swooped overhead.

'Yes, I thought I'd spring some twilight interval training on you.' He pulled a picnic rug out of his boot.

It turned out Will's big night out was a free concert at the Music Bowl in the Kings Domain.

'The Melbourne Symphony Orchestra do one concert here every year. Tonight, they're doing film scores,' he said, unable to disguise the excitement in his voice.

The sloping lawn, which overlooked the sunken stage, was heaving with people – a jigsaw of blankets and picnics across the grass. And there were people our age here – lots of them, though it wasn't an edgy crowd – there was lots of linen and loafers.

'It's popular!' I said.

'I'm not the only non-retiree in the city who likes classical music.'

'Who knew?'

'I'll get us drinks.'

'Now, that's music to my ears.'

Will returned with a bottle of wine and two burgers, just as the orchestra finished their warm-up. The sun was slowly setting, washing the sky with an apricot glaze. The evening was still and balmy – after an uncharacteristically sane and warm Melbourne day. Tomorrow would no doubt be freezing – but tonight for the first time in months you didn't need a coat.

The city's silver skyscrapers sat in the distance behind the bowl's swooping roof. I could see Will's building – one of the tallest – a burnished orange in the sunset. This spot, on the edge of the city, was probably the meeting point between our two worlds – Will's corporate tower and our inner-city suburban, domestic life.

As we finished inhaling our burgers filled with salty bacon, dripping cheese and smoky meat and washed them down with a pinot, the conductor came out and everyone clapped. And then it began.

I recognised the music but couldn't place it. I knew Will could tell me all about it, but I didn't want to interrupt him. For once, he seemed entirely present as he let the music lap over him. As the first note had struck up, all traces of worry and stress had melted from his face. He was transported. I'd never seen him like this – so free, so full, so content.

He closed his eyes, completely unselfconscious, his long, dark eyelashes resting behind his glasses. The only sign that he was awake was one finger gently tapping against his thigh, just where his navy linen shorts met his tanned olive skin.

When the piece ended, his eyes fluttered open. He smiled, as if he'd been having a magical dream.

'Lie down. Close your eyes,' he said. 'Use me as a pillow.'

I slowly leaned back and rested my head on his linen-covered stomach, as the next piece of music began. With each gentle inhale and exhale, we rose and fell together, my breathing moving in time with his. I could smell the red wine on his breath, or was that mine?

The music began to swell, and suddenly it felt like I wasn't breathing at all, the corners of my eyes tingling. I sat up and dabbed them.

'You okay?' Will was now sitting too and watching me with concern.

'Orchestras are very emotionally manipulative,' I whispered.

He smiled, and we gazed at each other, my eyes slightly foggy, his bright and alive.

'It's Morricone. "The Love Theme",' he whispered.

When the music reached a crescendo, I could feel all of me tingle, as if each instrument had ignited a different part of my body. I raised my chin, then moved my head slightly forward, towards Will.

He paused for a moment, but not long enough for me to move again, to retreat. And then he leaned forward and kissed me. I kissed him back, slowly, feeling calm and safe. Maybe it was the wine, or that I was just wrung out after an enormous week. But my brain, normally whirring and overactive, finally slowed down.

He tasted like peppery red wine. His slightly gravelly chin brushed against mine, and I let out an inadvertent whimper. Feeling his mouth pull into a smile, I nipped his lips with my teeth. He groaned and it was my turn to smile.

'Oh shit,' I said.

'I know,' he said.

I traced the faint outline of the butterfly, the remnants of the face paint he'd tried but failed to fully scrub off, on his right cheekbone with my index finger.

'That feels good,' he said, his voice rougher and lower than usual.

'That's good.' My voice didn't sound like my own, either.

I knew I should pull away. Except, right now, I didn't want to think. I just wanted to kiss him. And so I leaned back in, and we kissed through cinema's greatest scores, until the last note had been played and the sun had set.

We packed up our rug, then walked across the dark park under the canopy of the fig trees, now a playground for possums, to Will's car.

'Do you need more real-world time?' he asked me.

'Nothing about tonight has felt real,' I said with a smile.

He gently pressed me against the car and kissed me again. 'Home?' he asked, when we finally pulled away from each other.

I paused before answering. What did he mean? His house or mine? Alone or together?

'Or another drink first?' he asked.

'Will anything be open?' There was no moon tonight, just a blanket of stars across the inky sky. It felt like the middle of the night. I pulled my phone out of my bag to check the time and froze. There were missed calls from Camille.

I stepped away from Will, onto the footpath, and I pressed 'dial', my heart racing. I could hear Hazel's cries before Camille said anything. All the headiness of the last few hours drained out of me, evaporated.

'Oh you're awake. Sorry. I didn't want to disturb you, but she woke up. I tried to calm her down, but …'

'I'm on my way,' I said, without looking at Will.

CHAPTER 20

Subject: Extra part of The Contract
From: Zoe.Harper@gmail.com
To: William.Flemming@flemming.com

Hi Will,

I realised that I hadn't counter-signed our 'no bases' clause – whoops. All done and officially part of The Contract now ☺

Best, Zoe

Subject: Re: Extra part of The Contract
From: William.Flemming@flemming.com
To: Zoe.Harper@gmail.com

Received. See you tomorrow morning.

W

I met Sofia at Prahran Pool, for a fortuitously timed catch-up to plan her impending baby shower, the next morning. While we waited, Hazel rolled around on the grass next to the open aqua water. It was still early for a Sunday morning and the only other swimmers were the regulars, pumping their lean, tanned bodies up and down the lanes.

Sofia arrived in an electric-yellow tracksuit that made her bump look like the sun. By contrast, I'd tried to dress as the night sky during a lunar eclipse. To get here, I'd practically sprinted past Will's house, Hazel's pram rattling, hoping my black dress (the only one I owned) and enormous Jackie O–style sunglasses rendered me invisible.

'Thanks for meeting me here. The water's the only place I forget I'm a mini elephant,' she said.

'You're a vision!' I said.

'Want to see my dance routine?'

''Course.'

She set up her phone, and Elton John crooning 'Rocket Man' blared.

'Okay, so imagine that I'm in a nude body suit. Except the part around my belly is cut out. And my bump is painted to look like Earth,' she said.

'Uh-huh. Yep, I'm seeing it.'

'And all the other dancers are dressed as sexy space people – think silver lingerie and helmets,' she said. 'And they're dancing around me, dreaming of coming back home.'

'Love the literal interpretation.'

Sofia danced around the lawn by the pool – leaping and bending – arms, legs and bump moving wildly. Hazel was transfixed.

The lifeguards and swimmers around the pool, who'd stopped what they were doing to watch Sofia's performance, and I clapped when she finished. She bowed to her adoring crowd, not a bit self-conscious.

'Amazing. Out of this world. You're going to be a star,' I said, as she sat on her towel, out of breath.

'What's news with you?' she asked.

'Will and I kissed last night,' I said.

'Yay!'

'No, not yay,' I said.

'Okay, I reserve my level of yayness until I hear the whole story.'

I ran her through our day – the zoo, the fight, the surprise concert, the strange effect the music had had on me.

'Is he a good kisser?' Sofia asked.

'That's not the point.'

'That's a yes.'

'Like … unexpectedly amazing. We made out for hours.'

'Hours?'

'Yep – basically through the entire concert.'

We both giggled, like we were schoolgirls again.

'I shouldn't be laughing, it's not funny,' I groaned.

'Why don't you go for it? See what happens?'

'I missed all these calls from Camille while I was acting like a teenager. Hazel was distraught. And I wasn't there for her.'

I held my baby, who was mauling a cheesymite scroll, close to me. By the time Will had dropped me off at Camille's house, Hazel had stopped crying, but she'd been puffy-eyed and had clung to me.

'I promised when I decided to have her on my own that it would be just the two of us. I made a vow to her. I'm not going to let her down because I got overpowered by … Beethoven.'

'What if Will feels differently?'

'He doesn't.'

I showed Sofia the messages Will had sent me first thing this morning. Sorry (again) about yesterday. All of it.

Then another one, a few minutes later. Don't worry about The Arrangement – business as usual tomorrow morning. Let's forget yesterday.

'Are you going to reply?' Sofia asked.

'I'll just say that I agree. That we should forget all about last night, that it was a blip.'

'Are you sure that's what you want?'

'It's what he wants. And it's what I want. It was a lapse of judgement for both of us,' I said. 'Now that you're up to date on that situation, can we talk about your baby shower? And more specifically, your vision for the games.'

'Oh, just keep it light. Like nothing too traditional. Just fun stuff, you know?'

I really didn't know. 'Do you have anything specific in mind?'

'No – I trust you completely, you're the creative genius,' she said. 'Oh, and here's the gender for the fun reveal. Don't open it now – I'll be able to read your expression!'

She handed me a sealed envelope. I hadn't realised she'd been serious about the gender reveal being a feature of the party. Or that I'd be in charge of organising it.

This morning, I'd been determined to nut out the details of the games for next weekend together, but clearly Sofia's input was going to be limited to a high-level brief. And now, with no games sorted, I also had a light, non-traditional and fun gender reveal to add to the list.

*

'What did she say?'

Kajal found me at my desk during Wednesday's lunchbreak, in a Google doom spiral, frantically searching for baby-shower game inspiration.

'What did who say?' I asked, glancing up from my computer.

'I assumed you were looking like you'd lost the will to live because of something Monica said.'

'Good guess. But for once, no.'

'A parcel arrived for you.' Kajal handed it to me.

I opened up the padded envelope and recoiled. It was a packet of tiny plastic dolls. 'Jesus! Have you ever seen anything creepier?' I asked.

Why the hell had I ordered a pack of mini-babies? Oh yes, it was for a game called 'Break the Waters' I'd read about online. You froze mini-babies into ice cubes and put them into everyone's drinks. The first person to notice theirs had melted yelled out, 'My waters have broken' and won. It must have seemed like a fun idea at the time, in the throes of gastro when I was severely dehydrated and sleep deprived. Now I just wanted to wave some incense over these mini-devil children and set them free.

'Wow! What are they for?' Kajal asked.

'I'm organising games for a baby shower this weekend. And I am … totally screwed.'

My phone lit up.

Sofia Vass: Good news! Baby's done a somersault so now in right position – natural birth back on! More to celebrate at party!

Sofia Vass: Also I'm going to wear a flower crown on Saturday. My vibe is going to be edgy fertility goddess!

I took a deep breath, knowing that it wasn't the end of the world if I did a half-baked job. There'd be a room filled with all the people who loved her, and surely that was the most important thing to Sofia.

But I also knew how much this day meant to her. It had taken her years to get to this point. Years of injections and clinics and hormones. But the scary part was over – the odds were good that she was going to have a healthy baby. And if she wanted to celebrate like a TikToker – well, I owed it to her to make that happen.

'I have three older sisters and I helped organise their baby showers,' Kajal said diplomatically. 'Maybe I could help?'

'Are you serious? That would be amazing!'

She clapped her hands together with glee.

'There's a twist – everything needs to be ironic,' I added.

'I prize nothing more than irony, except sarcasm,' she replied sincerely.

It turned out the cavalry had been sitting in our reception the whole time. She wasn't just our hilarious, straight-talking receptionist, but a baby-shower-saving angel.

In between phone calls and handing keys to clients, we brainstormed ideas, dreaming up ridiculous versions of the standard games. Kajal even offered to make a blue cake with purple icing for the gender reveal. We decided that if we decorated the cake with enough devil baby dolls, we were well into the realm of the ironic.

By the time I'd thanked Kajal a thousand times, I was starting to think the shower might actually be okay, fun even.

*

Three busy days later, I arrived early at Sofia and Morgan's art-deco apartment in St Kilda to help set up for the party. They lived a few streets back from the beach, and even though I couldn't see the water, I could smell the salt on the gentle breeze. It was still only August, but blue skied enough to feel like the type of Saturday to drink a chilled glass of wine with your friends mid-afternoon.

The place looked like a dream (albeit a fever dream). Every surface was covered with Morgan's sculptural floral pieces – pale-pink peonies and white orchids dyed bright blue were woven together. I examined one of the arrangements more closely.

'Are there … eggs in the flowers?' I asked.

'I wanted to work in a symbol of fertility,' Morgan said proudly.

'A deeply ironic one given my dodgy eggs caused so many issues in the first place,' Sofia said. 'What do you think?' She did a twirl in her pastel rainbow boiler suit and enormous floral crown, ribbons cascading down her back.

'Very midsummer chic,' I said.

'Exactly what I was going for.'

As I was getting the games paraphernalia out of my car, Camille's SUV pulled up behind me.

'You're here early!' I said, as she walked towards me.

'I thought I'd help you set up,' she said, a bit defensively. 'Well, it was either leave the house or murder my husband.'

'What did he do?' I tried to keep the surprise from my voice. I'd never heard Camille say anything negative about Ed out loud. Of course, I'd noticed the irritated expressions and the not-so-subtle impatient glares, but she'd never openly complained.

'It's more what he didn't do. Not a load of washing. Or preparing a meal for the twins. Or unloading a dishwasher. No – that would be a waste of his weekend, apparently.'

She slammed the car door shut, her flushed cheeks almost matching her red shift dress. She was like an angry thoroughbred – pointy features shiny and nostrils flaring.

'I have no social life, none. And I told him, weeks ago, that on this one Saturday I needed a few hours to come to this. And he forgot and organised a golf day, and then he had the audacity to be pissed off when I said his options were to organise a babysitter or stay home.'

'What did you do?'

'I just left. I just walked out the front door and left him with the twins.' She laughed, slightly maniacally. 'Anyway, I'm here now. Let's go help Sofia.'

Sofia and Morgan greeted Camille warmly, as if it wasn't strange that she'd turned up early and thrown herself into party prep.

'I'm going to defrost these a bit before they go in the oven,' Camille announced, holding up a box of spinach-and-cheese pastries. 'Where's your microwave?'

'We don't have one,' Sofia said.

Camille stared incredulously at her. 'Are you serious? My microwave's more helpful than my husband most days.'

I shot her a warning look from across the room.

'But to each their own,' she said. 'You do you.'

'I'll show you how to turn the oven on,' Sofia said.

'I'll do it.' Morgan jumped up. 'I want you to rest, to stay off your feet. Your only job today is to be celebrated.'

'You'll have to childproof this kitchen!' Camille said, her voice higher than normal.

'Not for a while, though,' Sofia said. 'The baby'll be an immobile blob for ages.'

'They'll be riffling through the knife drawer before you know it!'

'Hey, Camille, can you help me get some more stuff downstairs?' I called.

'I can help,' Morgan offered.

'If you could just keep an eye on Hazel that would be great.'

'What's going on?' I asked, when we reached the entrance of the apartment building. 'Are you okay?'

She brandished her phone at me. 'Jesus! Read this message from Ed. *Do they need lunch?* Do they need lunch? Well, it's lunchtime. So yes, Ed, they probably bloody need lunch!' Camille seemed like she was about to combust with rage.

'Give me your phone,' I demanded, and held out my hand. She reluctantly handed it over. She was almost as addicted to her phone as Will was.

'My favourite girls!' We were interrupted by Sofia's mum, holding two giant paper shopping bags. I snuck Camille's phone into my pocket.

Sofia's mum, Mary, was a tour de force – a single mum who ran her own dental practice, and worked even longer hours than our mum.

Where Sofia's innate sense of style had come from was a mystery – Mary, when not in her work scrubs, invariably wore boxy jackets in jewel colours, liberally applied blush and orthopaedic shoes. Today was no exception – she was resplendent in an orange blazer and tangerine trousers.

She gave us both a big hug. 'Where's little Hazel?' Mary asked, searching around as if I'd hidden her.

'Morgs is watching her upstairs.'

'I made this for her,' Mary said, pulling a knitted beanie out of one of her bags. It was cream with small flowers around the edge.

'It's beautiful, thank you!'

'I've taught myself to knit,' she said proudly, as she pulled a series of teeny cardigans, blankets and beanies from her bags. We admired the array with the requisite amount of enthusiasm.

I wasn't surprised that Mary had taught herself to make such beautiful things. What was surprising was that she had wanted to.

'When did you have time to make all this?' Camille asked.

'I've semi-retired,' Mary said. 'I'm going to babysit my grandchild when Sofia goes back to work.'

Mary, who'd worked every hour of Sofia's childhood, now seemed thrilled by the prospect of being a hands-on grandmother.

'I'm sure you can't keep your mum away from darling little Hazel!' Mary said.

I almost guffawed. 'She's still working a lot,' I said, a bit too sharply, not looking at Camille.

'Well, I'm sure you won't be able to keep her away for long,' Mary said. 'Being a grandmother is the greatest gift – all the fun bits of having a baby, without the real work.'

I felt jealousy's familiar sting. Sofia was in her thirties and had a mum who was reshaping her life for her baby. And mine wanted nothing to do with me.

'Mummy!' The three of us turned to see Arti barrel towards Camille, her ruler-straight fringe bobbing with each step. She was a confident jogger but hadn't quite nailed the stopping part. She tried to slow down, tripped and burst into tears.

'Darling. Does anything hurt?' Camille scooped up her daughter into a bear hug, while giving Ed, who was walking towards us holding Remy, a death stare.

'What are you doing here?' she asked.

'Aren't we all invited? Baby showers are family-friendly events, right?' Ed replied, almost convincingly. He'd evidently determined that he'd already had enough alone time with his kids.

'What a beautiful family,' Mary cooed, oblivious to the various layers of tension between us all.

'We should head up – make sure everything's ready,' I said, before Camille could reply.

CHAPTER 21

The party was, in spite of my worrying, a roaring success. All the groups from both of their lives – Sofia's journalist friends, Morgan's mates from art school, all the dancing astronauts who'd soon be pirouetting around Sofia's bump – coalesced into one chatty, mingling crowd.

Everyone loved the creepy baby ice cubes in their punch, and the version of Articulate that Kajal and I had dreamed up, where everyone had to invent fake meanings for baby names then guess which was the real one, had people crying with laughter.

Kajal had turned up with the cake, which was a triumph. She'd even made a batch of penis-shaped cookies to hand around after the reveal.

'They're cockies,' she said, lifting the Tupperware lid to show me.

'They're a thing of beauty,' I said.

'You know your friend Will. Is there something between you guys?' Kajal asked.

I wondered how invested she was in my answer. 'Nothing,' I replied firmly. 'We're just friendly neighbours.'

Which was true. In a few weeks' time, The Arrangement would end. And that's exactly what Will and I would be once more.

'I couldn't find him on social media. Do you think I could have his number? He's a cool guy. In like a fun, nerdy way, you know?' she said.

I nodded, as nonchalantly as I could. 'Yeah, of course.'

She stayed for a drink and I watched her effortlessly mingle with the dance crew. She and Will would be perfect together. She was thoughtful, outgoing and fun – his perfect ballast. And her life was simple – she'd never be a drag on his enormous ambitions for himself.

Just before it was cake time, I made a beeline for Sofia with my present. She was sitting on a chair covered in flowers, which was more like a floral throne. Mary sat next to her, beaming with happiness and helpfully entertaining Hazel, looking every inch the proud grandmother, while Morgan ran around the apartment, manically topping up drinks and handing around plates of food.

'I got you a little something,' I said, and handed her a giant box.

'Oh, Zo!' she exclaimed.

I waited with anticipation as she ripped open the wrapping paper. It was a small portable bassinet – like a pillow with a little indentation to pop the baby into. It meant the baby could sleep next to you on the couch, or in bed. It had cost a fortune, but I'd wanted to give Sofia something special.

'That's brilliant – thanks! Come see what Zoe got us!' she yelled across the room to Morgan, who was refilling the punch bowl. Camille, who'd been watching Morgan, turned towards us, too.

She rushed across the room, brimming with concern. 'You can't use that! They're not safe. No nests have been SIDS approved.'

'It's not like she's going to leave the baby alone in it,' I said. 'I would have killed for one when Hazel was little.'

'Yeah, well, you're good at telling yourself the version of facts that suits you best.'

The hum of conversations around the room fizzled out as Camille's now shrill voice rose.

'Let's … come with me,' I said.

I grabbed Camille's arm and marched her into Sofia and Morgan's bedroom, ignoring the eyes of the party following us out of the room.

'What is your problem?' I asked, as soon as I'd shut the door. 'Ever since you got here, you've been a total bitch to Sofia. I know she does things differently from you, but so what, she's your friend!'

'And I'm meant to just keep quiet about things that are dangerous,' she said. 'Or fraudulent.'

The tip of her nose was now white with anger. Was that what was making her so irate – what I'd told her about Will? I knew she wouldn't like it, but I didn't think telling her about us would send her off the deep end. Had she been stewing for two weeks and today it had all bubbled up and exploded?

'Forget what I told you the other day. Will and I have a deal that works for both of us. You don't need to worry about it.'

'Well, I do worry because now I'm implicated in your fraudulent activity.'

'It's not fraud. It's basically all true. We've just added some gloss. And everyone benefits.'

'Listen to yourself. You call it glossing over the truth. It's lying! And you don't even know you're doing it. You believe your own twisting and contorting of the truth. At least be honest to yourself – you've both lied to get ahead.'

'Okay, fine. I'm lying. We're lying to get ahead. But I'm doing it for Hazel. That's what parents do. They do whatever it takes to protect their kids.'

Seeing her eyes flashing with rage, I felt vindicated. There were so many times I'd been tempted to tell Camille secrets, like I'd done unthinkingly when we were both teenagers, and hadn't. But now, I knew I was right not to share some things with her, or anyone. Other people were unpredictable. Some things were better locked away, in the far corners of my mind, where I barely had to think about them myself.

'No, the job of parents is to teach values to their kids. And then role-model them,' Camille shot back.

'What are you role-modelling for Arti – how to run yourself into the ground by trying to be perfect?'

Camille took a step back like she'd been slapped.

'Sorry,' I said. 'I didn't mean that.' Although we both knew I did.

'One thing I can cross off the to-do list is helping you,' Camille said. Then she stormed out of the bedroom.

When I rejoined the party, I realised I'd missed the finale – the gender reveal. Sofia and Morgan were thrilled they were having a boy, and although I ate a slice of aqua cake and a cockie, both tasted like ashes in my mouth.

After most people had left, including a slightly perturbed Ed trying to wrangle two toddlers (Camille had apparently stormed out without saying a word to anyone), I tried to help clean up, but Sofia wouldn't let me. And Hazel, after missing her afternoon nap, was mutinous and wanted to be exclusively held.

'I'm going to drive you home. Then I'll get out of cleaning up, too,' Sofia said in a stage whisper. Morgan, wearing a pair of rubber gloves at the sink, smiled. We both knew he wouldn't have let Sofia do anything more strenuous than toddle off to bed for a nap.

'Could you hear us screeching at each other?' I asked Sofia, as Hazel ate leftover party food for dinner.

'My gender-reveal squeals were loud enough to cover any noise, human or otherwise,' she said.

'A boy!' I said. 'Good choice – girls are total bitches. Except Hazel, obviously.'

'Thanks so much for today. It was exactly what I wanted,' Sofia said. 'Now after you've fed her, you're going to have a rest and I'm going to put her to bed.'

I tried to protest, but she insisted.

Lying on the couch, feet up, I felt all my emotions percolate. I was jealous of Sofia – of the relationship she had with Mary. Of all the support she was about to get as a new mum. She wasn't at all worried about her life being upended – and it wouldn't be, not in the same way that mine had been.

I was irritated by Kajal. Not seriously, just on a shallow level – for being young and free in a way I never would be again.

But mostly, I was angry – angry that Camille had ruined a day I'd worked so hard to make special. I was angry that the present I'd spent hours agonising over was now tainted. I was angry that my sister, who had everything – a house she owned, a husband who loved her, a career with an upward trajectory – was doing such a good job at being negative. And critical of me.

Sure, maybe I'd overstepped. But she'd started it. Up until now, the only person I'd ever had a proper fight with was Will, in his past life as Dick Next Door. And where did she get off attacking me for my arrangement with Will? Of course having a fake boyfriend, lying, hadn't been my first choice. I'd been driven to it by necessity. What did she know about that?

As I silently fumed, I realised that Sofia had been ages. I crept to the bedroom and found Hazel fast asleep in her cot, and Sofia softly snoring in my bed. I carefully shut the door, deciding to go walk off my feelings around the block, while I could. My monitor would ping if Hazel woke up.

I made it a few metres down the street before I heard, 'Zo! Are you okay?'

Will was standing in the middle of the road shouting at me. He was in his gym shorts and sneakers, and was pulling a running shirt over his head. Did he usually sit around his house topless?

I waited for him to jog down the street.

'You just stormed past my window like you were competing in the Olympic walking event,' he said.

'I'm trying to walk off … mainly feelings of rage,' I said.

'Do you want to be alone or should I come?' he offered.

'Do you really want to be my human punching bag?' I asked.

'I've had years of training.'

A smile broke through my stormy mood. We began to walk together.

'So, I'm guessing the party wasn't a success?'

'It was, actually. But I had a fight with Camille. She arrived in a foul mood, and after picking at Sofia all afternoon, had a go at me. I'm talking full character assassination.' I didn't go into the details of Camille's attack, not wanting to tell Will that it was The Arrangement that had set her off.

We reached the end of our long street and wordlessly turned the corner of our block.

'Want my take on it?' he asked.

'I was mainly planning to vent at you, but sure.'

'Get over yourself,' he said.

I stopped in my tracks and glared at him. I realised he was slightly sweaty. His damp shirt clung to him, and he smelled like spicy deodorant and laundry dried in the sun.

'Did you seriously just tell me to get over myself?' I asked. 'There has to be something in the contract about you being this level of arseholeness.'

'You talk to me about your sister a lot. And you've been worried about her since The Arrangement began. From what you've told me, Camille's got a lot going on in her life. She does everything I do in my normal working life, plus most of the things I'm doing now for Hazel, except she has two of them. And she does it all at the same time.'

He began to walk again, and I begrudgingly followed him, while silently vowing to stop telling Will every passing thought I had. I probably had told him a lot about Camille. I'd told him a lot about everything.

'I think she's likely been unhappy for a long time, and you were the easiest person to get mad at, without actually having to confront the people and things that are making her miserable,' he said.

Without noticing, we'd finished the loop of the block and were in front of our houses again.

'Another block?' he asked.

It was tempting to keep walking, to keep talking. 'I better not. Sofia's with Hazel, but she'll want to go home.'

'Okay. Night, Zoe,' he said, and turned towards his house.

'Hey,' I said, one hand on my front gate. 'If the partner thing doesn't go well, I'm not sure life coaching is your backup career. "Get over yourself!"'

But as I crawled into bed next to Sofia, who was dead to the world and looked like she was going nowhere anytime soon, I realised that I no longer felt murderous.

Maybe it was exhaustion, or maybe it was sleeping next to someone after so many nights alone, but I fell into a dreamless sleep.

I awoke to Sofia gently shaking me. It was already light, but Hazel was still fast asleep in her cot, clasping her toy tiger and sucking on her dummy like Maggie Simpson.

'I need to show you something,' she whispered.

Bleary-eyed, I shut the kitchen door behind us, so we could talk without hushed voices.

Sofia was holding her phone, her expression grave.

'It's about Will.'

CHAPTER 22

'About Will?'

'I was lying in bed reading all the emails I've ignored during baby-shower prep. And that article I mentioned, the one about more corporate guys taking parental leave … well, I was copied in on a draft.'

'Okay, so …?' Why had Sofia woken me up to tell me about a random article?

'Well, I'll just read you a bit …' She clicked on her phone.

'*Some people were surprised that Managing Partner Robert Whittaker is the biggest champion of the firm's new parental-leave policy, which entitles all fathers to take up to three months of paid parental leave.*

'*"In my view it's these kinds of changes that will move the dial for both working fathers and mothers. I'm really proud that this year I encouraged Will Flemming, a senior lawyer in our team, to take three months of paid parental leave while his partner went back to work …"*'

My heart began to beat faster. There was going to be a news story about Will taking paternity leave to help out his family. When he didn't, in fact, have a family.

'*His partner, Zoe Harper, was a single mother who conceived her baby, Hazel, using a sperm donor. After Zoe and Will formed a relationship, Will began the process of adopting Hazel. "It speaks to the progressive nature of our firm that we support both men and families that are formed in all types of ways," said Whittaker.'*

'Is this for real?' I asked, my heart now pounding. 'I'm going to call Will. They must have done this without asking him. He'll be furious.'

'Wait ... there's more.'

I braced.

'*"I've loved the chance to take care of baby Hazel while my partner, Zoe, returns to paid work. I'm so grateful to the firm for having such a generous, forward-thinking policy," Flemming said.*'

'Wow.' My heart sank. Will knew about the article – he'd given a quote. One that specifically mentioned both me and Hazel. And then had kept it from me.

Our lie was going to be out in the world in black and white.

Everyone read Sofia's newspaper. Well, I didn't, but Camille did religiously, which meant she'd send it to Mum. At work, we put copies in our reception area, so there was every chance Monica and Kajal would see it. Adam read it every day. Surely, some of Will's friends did too.

'Hey, take a deep breath.'

'Doesn't he care at all about Hazel? Stuff stays online forever. If this article's printed it'll be the first thing that comes up when you search her name.' I took a few shallow breaths.

'Hey. Calm down. You're spinning out,' Sofia said. 'Honestly, I'm surprised he did this. It's a risky move. If anyone finds out what he's done, well can you imagine the headline – "Lawyer fakes being a dad for time off".

God, it's the kind of story I'd froth over. His career would be finished.'

'He cares about his career, about making partner so much, Sof. He's got the most enormous chip on his shoulder. He isn't rational when it comes to his job – it's like he's got blinkers on.'

'Does he care about his career more than his family and friends. And you guys?'

'Apparently he does,' I said. 'I bet his boss called him up and said, "They want to run an article about the firm and showcase you. It'd be great for your career – just the thing you need ahead of the partnership candidate meeting this week." And from his pinstriped prison, it probably seemed like a good idea. Maybe he didn't even think of us at all.'

I realised that there was another emotion gushing through me, bumping up against the churning panic. It was relief. My vow – to create a self-contained bubble of just Hazel and me, to not let anyone else in, to save all my love for Hazel – had been the correct one.

I'd been right to keep my distance, to put up boundaries, contractual boundaries, between Will and me. And, temporary lapse in judgement at the concert aside, it had been the only sensible decision.

'Did we know that Will had the body of a Greek god?' Sofia asked.

'What do you mean?'

'There's a photo they're planning to run with the story. Will doesn't have a top on and he's ripped as! You're gorgeous, too.'

'What? What photo?'

'You're all mucking around on a beach together. Hence the no-top situation.'

Now my heart began to properly race. That morning on the beach, the conference photographer must have been there. I hadn't noticed.

'Is Hazel in it?'

'Yeah, she's on Will's shoulders. She's really cute in her bathers.'

Panic swelled through me like a contraction. 'This article and the photo can't be published. Seriously, Sof, it can't run. Can you stop it?'

She gave me a searching look. I knew she thought I was overreacting, even for me.

'I can try. But if I get randomly involved it might … raise questions,' she said delicately. 'The best chance would be for Will's firm to get in touch with the writer directly. Ask him to edit out the bits with you guys. And it'll need to happen pretty fast so there's enough time to make the changes before tomorrow's edition goes to print.'

'What a mess.' I buried my head in my hands.

'Just go speak to him,' Sofia said gently.

'What if Will says no? Or his firm does? Or your colleague?'

'Then the story will run tomorrow. And we'll deal with it,' she said, as Hazel woke up and began to cry.

Her just-awake bright-blue eyes lit up when she saw me, and she reached out her chubby hands. There was a dummy ring still imprinted around her mouth and her wispy hair stood on end.

I picked her up and hugged her like we'd been apart for a year, not a night.

'Mama,' Hazel said.

I pulled her away from my chest and stared at her and then at Sofia.

'Did she just …?'

'She did!' she said, grinning. We both stared at her like she had just recited a Shakespearean soliloquy.

'Is that the first time?' Sofia asked.

'Mama,' Hazel said again.

'Yes, I'm your mama, my gorgeous baby,' I said, kissing her chubby cheeks.

Mama. That's what I was. Hazel's mum. Her world. Full stop. My most important job was to protect her.

'Mamamamamama,' she said again, enjoying her new party trick. Each time she said it, my resolve to stop this article, to protect her, grew.

Sofia offered to stay with Hazel while I went next door.

I printed out a copy of the article, skimmed the text and then stared at the black-and-white photo. A wave of nausea passed through me.

Galvanised, I charged over to Will's house.

He answered the door in a faded law-school T-shirt and navy shorts. His hair was fluffy and he looked about five years younger without his glasses on. And I really needed him not to be rocking a just-rolled-out-of-bed look right now.

'Are you okay?'

'I'm really not,' I said. 'They're publishing this tomorrow.' I handed him the printout. He read it at his usual supersonic speed, his face now serious.

'Shit,' he said then properly clocked my expression. 'Wait – you think I knew about this?'

'It literally has your words in it.'

'You work in marketing. You know things can be taken out of context,' he said.

It felt like we were the old Zoe and Will again, sparring over bin night. Except not in a good way. Back then, it had felt like a game. I'd felt a sense of release after we'd gone head to head. This just felt real.

'Something has to exist to be taken out of context,' I said.

'Why don't you ask for my side of the story?' He ran his hand through his bed hair – it stood on end.

'Fine. Tell me your side of the story.'

'I did give a quote. But it was for some stupid internal feedback on the parental-leave policy. Why would I think they'd use it for an article, let alone one in a national paper?'

I didn't reply.

'Did you really think I did this behind your back?'

I shrugged. 'Don't stare at me like that. Anyone would have thought the same thing that I did. Because your career is the thing you care most about in the world. You agreed to lie about being in a relationship to get ahead at work. We played happy families in another state for your career. So, don't try to make me feel like I'm the crazy one.'

'No, not everyone would have thought that,' Will said. 'Only someone who doesn't know how to trust anyone would think that.'

'This isn't about me. I don't need an unsolicited personality assessment right now,' I said.

'You just walked in here and accused me of deliberately scheming and hiding things from you. We're both the injured parties here. Some idiots in our communications team stuffed up and—'

'Not everyone in the world is an idiot except you, Will. I know that guys like you think that nothing is ever your fault, but please take some responsibility.'

'Guys like me?' he replied.

'Yes, guys like you.'

'What, you think I'm like Adam. That I'm going to screw you over, too. You do, don't you?'

We stared at each other. I could see again all the parts of Will that originally had repelled me – his stubbornness, his arrogance, his defensiveness.

'Well, haven't you screwed me over?'

He didn't reply, but his face became mask-like again.

'I don't want to be some poster girl for solo mums by choice. I never asked for that. All I wanted was a baby. And for the two of us to be left alone.'

'Is that what you want?' he asked. 'Because last night you didn't want to be alone.'

'Last night I was upset after a hectic day, and highly emotional,' I said. 'And that's not the point right now. This article, this photo can't run.'

'Can Sofia do anything?'

I exhaled. This was the Will I needed. The outcome-focused one.

'She thinks if she gets involved it'll seem a bit dodgy. She said it's best if your firm asks the journalist to edit out the parts that mention us. Do you think they'll do that?'

'I honestly don't know. The article gives the firm progressive brownie points. It's great PR. They'll like that,' he said with a shrug.

'And like you.'

'I'll fix it. I promise,' he said.

'We've made a lot of promises. And all we've done is break them,' I said, my voice flat and hard.

Will took a step away from me and pulled back his shoulders. 'I know it's easier for you to process all this by making me the villain. By once again turning me into Dick Next Door, some nameless corporate shark who doesn't care about anything except his job. But you can't just pick the story that makes it easier for you to ignore what's actually happening,' Will said. 'Someone has written an article that hasn't been published yet. Things happen. And when things happen you have to face up to them, rather than get emotional and build them into something they're not. You deal with them and normally they don't end up being the disaster you think they'll be.'

He spoke with the calm authority of someone who was paid a lot of money to be the voice of reason in a crisis.

'Great. Once you're finished talking in memes, can you call your boss?'

Even though his expression gave nothing away, I could see a flicker of hurt in his eyes.

Before she left, Sofia told me to try not to panic. I tried, as I squished Hazel's blueberries between my fingers (because according to Instagram, an unsquished one was deadly) and vigorously hand-mashed roasted sweet potato, but calmness was out of reach. Adrenaline coursed through me, my body unable to switch out of fight mode, my brain whirring.

At the end of the longest day in the world, as the sun began to set, I put Hazel to bed and checked my phone again. Still nothing. Surely, it was too late for anything to change now – the article replete with a photo of Will, Hazel and me was going to run tomorrow, our lie out there for everyone to see.

I poured a large glass of wine and drank half of it in a few sips.

Any update? I messaged Will, again.

I could see that this morning I'd felt embarrassed and betrayed, and I'd lashed out at Will. That I had leaped to casting him as the villain, when it had turned out that his side of the story had been reasonable.

Maybe Camille was right – perhaps I did have a tendency to make up my own version of events, to reach an unappealable verdict, before I'd heard all the evidence, or even asked to hear it. Maybe I did contort things in my mind.

I couldn't work things out with Will tonight, I wasn't sure I was ready to. Or that he'd want to speak to me either, possibly ever again. Not after the things we'd said to each other.

I checked my phone again. Nothing. No reply from Will. I finished my glass of wine as I did laps around the kitchen.

I had no control over the newspaper article. And I couldn't call Camille, the person I'd always relied on when my mind was racing down rabbit holes, when I was spiralling. She'd made it clear I hadn't met her sky-high standards and that she'd had enough of me.

I picked up my phone again. Still nothing.

I couldn't speak to Camille or Will. Camille hated me, and I'd alienated Will. But there was someone I could speak to. I could have the conversation I'd never had, with the person who'd been haunting me. I could face up to my past head-on, and find closure. That was something within my control right now.

Opening my phone, I typed his name, feeling the familiar sting of rejection and guilt.

Our message thread popped up. The last message he'd sent me was eight months ago. Congratulations on beautiful Hazel – she's perfect. x

I began a new one.

Hi Adam ...

After finishing the message, I pressed 'send'. I stared at the screen. What had I done? A few seconds later, my phone pinged. My already racing heart sped up. Had he already replied? No, it was Will.

I fixed it.

I let out a breath, one that I felt like I'd been holding all day.

Thanks, I wrote back.

Three greys dots flickered on my screen, then disappeared.

CHAPTER 23

Four days later, on an overcast Thursday, I weaved my way through a part of town I'd avoided for the past few years, on my way to Adam's apartment building. I stopped in my tracks, blocking the lunchtime crowd milling around the entrance to South Yarra station, as I felt an overwhelming urge to turn around and get straight back on a train to go home. What was I doing?

I'd impulsively messaged Adam, in the eye of the emotional storm the threat of the article had caused. I hadn't been thinking straight – I'd been all gut and no brain, drunk on a mixture of panic and white wine. I'd told him I wanted to catch up and he'd replied to my message, almost straightaway, and invited me around. We'd arranged to meet up on my next day off, and Sofia had offered to watch Hazel over her lunch break. But now that I was actually en route to see him, I had cold feet. Why had I thought this was a good idea?

I took a deep breath to steel myself then began to walk again. I needed to do this. I'd thought I'd known why he'd broken up with me after so many years together – that I'd wanted a wedding ring and a baby, and he hadn't. But now, after everything Camille and Will had said to me over the weekend, I was doubting everything I knew about, well, everything.

Things had been frosty between Will and me over the past few days, our conversation limited to logistics in the mornings and evenings. We hadn't talked about the article again, which had run in Sofia's paper without any mention of our fake relationship. And neither of us had broached our fight.

I reached Adam's building. He lived in a pocket of new high-rise apartment buildings with views over the Yarra River and Botanic Gardens. It wasn't the kind of place where families lived. In fact, it wasn't the kind of place where people in their thirties lived. This was a hub for twenty-somethings who wanted to spend their new corporate salaries on shiny apartments close to the city, who preferred a big, fancy gym in their building to a proper kitchen in their flat.

Adam lived on the top floor. It wouldn't take a very adept psychologist to wonder if this decision was linked to his height.

He buzzed me into the building. The foyer was lined with mirrors. It had only been two-and-a-bit years since I was last here, but those years had taken a toll. I leaned into the closest mirror. My skin was dry, my hair's most notable feature was its number of split ends and my eyes were bloodshot. I needed one of those sheet masks filled with plumping, rejuvenating serums, except for my whole body.

Adam was waiting by the lift on his floor. He looked exactly the same, better maybe. He was still in good shape, presumably from all his cycling, and his dark, slicked-back hair was as voluminous as always. He'd told me he was working from home today and was wearing his version of smart casual – a Ralph Lauren knitted jumper, navy chinos that I knew would have been tailored by P. Johnson and brown suede slip-on loafers. He was like a poster boy for the kind of guy Will hated.

He kissed me on the cheek and then led us into his apartment.

Seeing his place through fresh eyes, it was as if he'd specifically chosen each piece of furniture to be as baby unfriendly as possible – all glass and sharp edges, particularly now that Hazel was crawling and constantly on the move like a little tornado with no concept of personal safety.

He'd already arranged two glasses and a green bottle of mineral water on the low glass coffee table.

'Thanks for taking the time. I know you're busy,' I said. I knew I sounded stilted, as though I was meeting a client for the first time.

'It's fine – it was great to hear from you.' He filled up one of the glasses and handed it to me, then gestured for me to sit down on his white linen couch.

'I want to talk about us. About how … we ended.' I got straight to the point, channelling the voice on the meditation app I hadn't done in a year.

This was something I needed to do. I was here for information, like a relationship detective in pursuit of the answer to a very specific question – I wanted to know what had really happened at the end of our relationship.

'Oh. Right,' he said. 'Okay.'

'Those final years we were together, you knew I wanted to get married. You knew I wanted to have a baby.

And if you didn't want those things, why didn't you tell me? Why did you keep me … hanging?' I tried to keep my voice level as I asked the question I'd been rehearsing for the past four days. But despite my best efforts, I could hear the strain in my voice.

'Biology has given you more time to choose what you want from life. But you knew I didn't have that time. And instead, you … took those years, those fertile years, from me. You took away my chance to find another partner, one who actually wanted to have a baby with me. Someone who actually wanted … me. You limited my choices. And I want to know why.' I blinked hard, but I could feel unwanted tears welling up.

Adam stood and walked out of the room.

I took a deep breath. Of course he'd retreated from the tough conversation. I fought the instinct to leave. I was here for his side of the story.

He returned a few moments later with a bottle of wine and two glasses. 'I don't think water's going to cut it.'

I nodded. I didn't disagree. He did two generous pours and handed me one.

'To Hazel!' He raised his glass and I clinked mine weakly against his.

'The thing you said before. About taking those years from you. I'm really sorry about that,' he said.

I stared at him in surprise.

'I started seeing a therapist after we broke up.' He shrugged. 'I'm pretty addicted to it, actually. I knew you wanted to get married and have a kid. You weren't exactly subtle about it,' he said with a hollow laugh. He paused and I could tell he was about to say the thing he never thought he would get to say out loud. 'But I knew you didn't love me. And I didn't want to have a baby like that.'

Shock reverberated through me. Not because he was right – I hadn't loved Adam. But because he'd known it. And never said anything. I hadn't even known that I hadn't loved him until recently.

'So, why did you stay with me for so long?'

'Because … I always thought we had this … thing that made us work.'

'What thing?'

'Neither of us expected to be loved, so neither of us could get hurt. Again.'

All his bravado was gone. In front of me, was the vulnerable kid who'd had a miserable childhood. Whereas I'd had an absent father, his had been far too present. A bully who worshipped Adam's older, thuggish brothers and made it clear that his youngest son could never measure up.

Adam played with the stem of his glass. 'I did plan to propose. I always knew that I was batting above average with you. You're smart and gorgeous and funny—'

'Adam, I didn't come here to dig for compliments …'

'I know you don't think so, but it's true. I bought a ring because I wanted you to be my wife. I planned proposals – I booked Vue de Monde then a hot-air-balloon trip then a weekend in Port Douglas. But I found myself cancelling them all at the last minute. I thought maybe it was just nerves. It took me a long time to work out why I couldn't do it,' he said.

'Why?'

'Because I knew you didn't want to marry me,' he said. 'But you didn't want to be alone even more.'

I took a large sip of wine as I let his words sink in. 'I thought you left me because I'm the kind of person people leave. Because I'm … unlovable,' I said. 'And so … you didn't want a baby with someone like me.'

'That's not true at all. I really loved you, Zoe. And I want kids,' he said. 'I just don't think you're meant to have them with someone you didn't love. And you didn't love me.'

I was temporarily rendered speechless. Was that really the reason he hadn't wanted to have a baby with me?

'I just wish you'd figured all that out for yourself sooner. You almost robbed me of the one thing I've always wanted.'

'I know that. And I'm sorry. But I'm glad it all worked out,' he said.

'It all worked out,' I echoed, suddenly feeling a bit feverish. 'I better go.'

'Wait … before you leave, I want to give you something.'

He jogged towards the back of his apartment and I saw him disappear into his spare room (or as he called it – his Peloton den). He emerged carrying an enormous, garish, plastic play centre.

'I bought some stuff, some presents when Hazel was born. I just never got around to … dropping them off. Well, I didn't think you'd want to see me.'

'You really bought that for her?'

Adam put down the box. 'When she was born, I went to Baby Bunting to buy her a present. I ended up buying a trolley full of stuff. I don't know what I was thinking. It's not like I had any idea what she actually needed.'

'I mean, I wouldn't say that's necessarily an essential item,' I said. 'But she'll love it. It's like a pokies machine for babies.'

'I also bought her a motorised toy Jeep. Like she can drive it and everything,' he said and smiled for the first time since I'd arrived.

I couldn't help it – I burst out laughing. It was such an Adam thing to buy.

His smile became sheepish. 'It's pretty cool. It matches mine. Please take it – all of it. It's just gathering dust in the spare room.'

'Thanks, Adam. That's really sweet. But I got the train here today – I'll come grab it another time.'

I smiled gratefully, though I knew that I couldn't take any of it.

I'd thought my conversation with Adam would provide closure. But now I just felt even more confused. Adam had given me answers, just not the ones I'd been expecting.

So, it was a strange sort of relief when Will knocked on my door on Friday evening, as I was feeding Hazel dinner, yanking me out of my head and back into the real world.

He was holding a bottle of champagne and smiling. Gone was the reserved tone of the past week, where we'd barely spoken to each other. He seemed buoyant.

'Are we celebrating something?'

'Maybe.'

'You won the lottery? Inherited a house from a long-lost great-uncle? Won a Nobel Prize?'

He gave Hazel a kiss on her fluffy head and then pulled down two glasses from the cupboard.

I watched him, confused. Our interactions all week, since the article, had been overly polite – a masterclass in civility and no intimacy. And now he was acting like nothing had happened between us?

He popped the cork in one deft movement and filled two glasses. Then he handed me one and raised his. How many toasts were going to punctuate my emotional crisis?

'To Hazel. The newest student at Play on the Park.'

I held my glass midair, still confused. 'What do you mean?'

'Remember I took her on a tour a few weeks ago and really liked it. Well, I rang them today to check in. And they offered Hazel a place in the baby room. On the three days a week you work.'

Was he serious?

'But no one gets a place there. Not even Camille!'

'Well, we did!'

We. I'd done nothing. This was all him.

'Wow. That's incredible!' I said, genuinely thrilled. This had been the point of the whole arrangement – to buy us time to find a permanent spot for Hazel somewhere they'd really care for her. And it had worked.

'There's only one catch. They need to fill the spot straightaway. So, she'd have to start the week after next.'

Now it made sense why he was so happy. He wanted out, and he'd found his escape route. He must have spent the week doggedly ringing all the centres he'd seen. And he, unlike me, had succeeded. Of course he had. Guys like Will always got what they wanted.

In one week, The Arrangement would be over. In one week, Will would be out of our lives, weeks before we were contractually meant to go our separate ways. Will, true to his word, never quit anything. But he'd found an elegant exit.

I took a sip of champagne. It should have tasted like celebration – Will had sprung for some good stuff. But it left a sour taste in my mouth.

Although, of course we should be celebrating. This was great news. Hazel would spend the next few years being properly cared for, while I worked and supported us both. We'd become the self-contained duo that I'd dreamed of us being. No more relying on anyone else.

'Obviously, I'll look after Hazel next week. But I might need someone else to watch her for a few hours at some point.'

'Yeah, of course, that's fine. What are you up to?'

He tried but failed to hide a grin. 'Robert wants me to come in for a meeting next week.' The grin spread across his whole face, causing the green flecks in his eyes to dance behind his glasses. God, he was handsome when he smiled. I pushed the thought away. 'The partnership candidate meeting was last week. He said he had some news.'

I threw my arms around him before I could stop myself and danced up and down. Hazel tried to copy me from her highchair, flailing her arms in the air.

Will froze, and I realised it was the first time we'd touched since we'd kissed. Then Will, to my surprise, joined in – jumping up and down. For a moment, the three of us flung our arms around and squealed.

'Yay!' Hazel said, her face lighting up as she watched us.

'She just said "yay". And she's right. Yay! You did it! You bloody did it! Partner Will Flemming. It has a ring to it!'

He stopped dancing and stepped away from me. 'I don't actually know anything yet. All will be revealed next week.'

'You deserve it, Will. You've worked so hard for it. And it's what you want?' I hadn't meant to phrase it as a question.

'Thank you. It is.' And I could tell my question had brought him fully back down to earth, that the fizz that had overtaken us all after the champagne had been popped had dissipated.

'I should go, leave you guys to it,' he said. 'I just wanted to … tell you about Hazel's place. You're happy, right? Proper educators taking charge of her. No more hopeless corporate lawyer feeding her undefrosted mush.'

I smiled at the memory. That first day seemed like forever ago. Had it really only been two months since we'd begun this whole thing?

'Very happy. Ecstatic. Thank you!'

And I meant it. This was exactly what I'd wanted. And I was grateful for all Will's help over the past two months.

Except why, then, after he'd left and when Hazel had gone to sleep, did I burst into tears and cry into my pillow until my face felt like a wrung-out sponge?

On Sunday afternoon, I left our southside bubble and ventured forth to the inner north for Sofia's concert.

I'd been stuck for a babysitter – Camille and I hadn't talked since the baby shower and I hadn't wanted to ask any more favours of Will. So, when Kajal genuinely had offered I'd leaped at it.

Northcote Town Hall, the concert venue, was heaving with people and buzzing with school-play energy.

Break a leg! I messaged Sofia from the foyer.

She called me almost instantly.

'How did you know you were in labour?' she asked. I could hear a strain in her voice.

'I felt like I had period cramps but worse. Like an elastic band was tightening over my tummy.'

'I think I'm in labour,' she replied, and I heard her groan.

CHAPTER 24

'Wait right there. I'm coming!'

I managed to blag my way backstage – it turned out 'I have to get in – my friend's about to have a baby' was an effective line.

Sofia, in full hair and makeup, was surrounded. I recognised some people from the baby shower, though they were mostly covered in silver body paint and hair spray.

I pushed my way through the extraterrestrial crowd and kneeled beside her. 'We're going to call the hospital, and if they think you should come in I can take you.'

'But … the performance …' she said. 'I'm the focal point.'

'It'll be way more meta without you,' I said.

She nodded and then winced. I squeezed her hand through another contraction.

Once Sofia had told a nurse how far apart her contractions were, the hospital told us to come in. Sooner rather than later.

'Do you know where Morgs is sitting? He's not answering his phone, but I can go find him in the audience,' I offered.

'He's not here. He's doing a wedding today. They're paying him a fortune. It's in bloody Woop Woop.'

'Your mum?'

'At a conference, which means her phone's off.'

'The doula?'

'Holiday,' she said. 'The baby wasn't meant to be here for weeks.'

Right. So, Sofia and I were on our own.

'That's okay. I'm here,' I said, as Sofia and I slowly processed through the tunnel her dance troupe had created solemnly for her with their silver arms, out of the theatre.

We were whisked to a birth suite, where it was confirmed by a midwife that Sofia was in active labour.

'Is this part of your birth plan?' the midwife asked Sofia sincerely between contractions. She pointed at her exposed belly painted with a map of the world (Australia in the centre), which now sans body suit was even more of a statement piece.

'Absolutely. I wanted my son to arrive and really feel like a citizen of planet Earth. It's also a metaphor for how he's now my whole world.'

I stifled a giggle.

'Speaking of birth plans. I wrote a letter. It's in the suitcase.' Sofia turned to me, once the midwife had left, no doubt to share her tale of the painted lady in Birth Suite 4.

'I'm on it,' I said. I riffled through the bag we'd grabbed en route to the hospital, fished out a piece of paper and scanned Sofia's wishes.

When Sofia didn't need me by her side I hung up fairy lights, spritzed lavender room spray, Blu-tacked up photos of people Sofia loved on the wall (I was pleased to see I'd made the cut), warmed up a heat pack, applied a TENS machine and fired up the 'Birth' Spotify playlist.

For the next few hours, Sofia stoically breathed and clenched my hand through each contraction. Then she began to throw up. I held the tubular sick bags steady for her, and then fed her a small sip of juice through a straw, knowing she needed the sugar but probably wouldn't be able to keep it down.

I could tell things were ramping up a notch. The contractions were coming faster and harder.

'I can't do this anymore,' she whimpered so softly I could barely hear her.

I didn't know what to say. It said in black and white in her birth plan that she didn't want to be offered gas or drugs, that her preference was for a natural birth with as little intervention as possible. But her face was grey with pain. What was the right thing to do? I wanted her to have what she wanted – for her birth to be the way she'd imagined.

'What would your doula be saying right now?' I asked, knowing it was a cop-out of a question.

'She's not bloody here right now. But you are,' she said.

'I am. I'm here,' I said, holding her hand.

'Does an epidural make this all go away?' she whispered, even more softly.

'For me it did,' I replied honestly. 'Although, I hated actually having it put in. The part where you had to be still – I found that bit bloody terrifying, like the worst game of Dead Fish ever. But I wasn't as prepared as you. You know me. I just wanted to hide from the pain, I didn't want to feel anything. You're braver than I am.'

'Go get the anaesthetist. Please,' she said.

'Are you sure? Because your letter says you don't want any pain relief. That you'd like to use breathing techniques ...'

'Read the bloody last line of the letter again. And then get me the DRUGS!' she wailed.

I speed-read the last sentence of her letter aloud.

'*So, this is what I want. But things don't always turn out the way you think they're going to. And at the end of the day, the only thing that matters is that my baby and I are healthy. I know, that whatever happens, it's all going to be okay.*'

'I'm on it! I'll be back with all the drugs as soon as I can,' I said and raced towards the door.

There was a short wait for the anaesthetist. The grey-haired doctor with a can-do spirit bounced into the room, all jolly energy and bad jokes to deflect from the serious nature of her job and what she was about to do. Within minutes, Sofia was drugged to the hilt. Some colour returned to her face.

'Press the green button whenever you want a top-up,' she told Sofia, who clutched the button like she was Gollum holding the fabled ring.

Once the pain had dissolved, Sofia fell asleep. Every half-hour or so, her eyes would flutter open, she'd survey the room, press the button and then go back to sleep. Her active labour became very passive.

The midwife regularly checked her progress, and Sofia seemed completely disengaged from the whole process. So, I just sat on the armchair in the corner of her room, waiting for her now much-less-intense labour to progress.

I spent the first little bit updating everyone, calling Morgan again and again until he finally answered. I also made sure Kajal was still okay with Hazel ('All good – Hazel's asleep and perfect. Did you know the new purple Wiggle is really hot?' she replied). Then my phone died. The midwife, after some pleading, agreed to charge it at the nurses' station, but I was left without a phone or a fully conscious Sofia.

Here I was in a birth suite again, though this one was far nicer than the one where Hazel had been born. Sofia had private health insurance, which gave her access to the private wing of the hospital. I'd given birth a few floors below in the public hospital.

In my third trimester, I'd decided that if I was going to be a parent on my own, I needed to start with the birth. My due date came and went. At that point, time came to a standstill. I spent most of the day eating pineapple, bouncing on an exercise ball and tweaking my nipples – anything that might bring on labour.

Then in the middle of the night I'd felt a twinge, not so different from the Braxton Hicks that had been plaguing me for the past few weeks, but strong enough that I couldn't get back to sleep. I'd called the hospital. Once they'd realised I was on my own, they'd told me to come in straightaway.

At the start, I'd felt vindicated. I drove myself to the hospital, parked in the overpriced car park and carried my own suitcase up to the reception.

A few painful hours and then a couple of less painful hours (once the epidural was in) later, the monitor I'd been hooked up to began to beep. The face of the student midwife (who I was sure had been allocated to my room once they'd realised I was solo) registered panic. A more senior midwife jogged into the room and reviewed the spikes on the paper being spat out at regular intervals by the machine.

'I'm going to get the doctor,' she said, in a practised, steady voice. But I could tell that something was happening. For the first time, I felt properly afraid and properly alone. Was the baby okay?

Seconds later, the doctor was in the room studying the monitor.

'The baby's heart rate is dropping. If it doesn't pick up soon I recommend an emergency C-section,' he said.

'Fine. Whatever you think is best for the baby,' I said, now terrified. Suddenly, I desperately didn't want to be by myself. In that moment, I wanted more than anything else for Mum to be by my side. But even though she'd been excited about the pregnancy and had said nothing about the fact that I was going to be a single mother, she hadn't offered to be my support person for the birth. So, I hadn't asked.

At the bottom of my legs was a doctor, a midwife, my student (who had stuck dutifully by her post), and about ten other trainee doctors who apparently, at some point, I'd permitted to be there. And what was that? Yes, it was. A mirror.

I could see everything. And I wanted to see nothing.

'You can see the head. Focus on it while you push!' the doctor coached like I was his star ruckman.

I almost cricked my neck turning away from the proverbial ring of fire, wishing there was someone to firmly tell him to lose the mirror. And also, the army of students. On the monitor, I could see the contractions building.

'Okay, I need you to push hard through the contraction.'

I closed my eyes and with everything in me I pushed. It was so physical and exhausting. I needed to breathe. My eyeballs felt like they were about to pop out. But the doctor was still cheering me on, mirror and crowd in situ, telling me to keep going.

'I need you to keep pushing. The heart rate is dropping and we need her out!'

I desperately needed to take a deep breath. I had nothing left to give. In this room, surrounded by people in scrubs, I felt afraid, exhausted and lonelier than I ever had before in my life. I clenched my fists, feeling my nails dig into my sweaty palms, and pushed harder.

And Hazel was born. And I was still exhausted and afraid, but no longer alone.

She was handed to me. My daughter. And for the first time in my life, I fell in love.

'Sof! I'm sorry. I'm here!' Morgan rushed into the room, sweaty and out of breath.

'Gruuuuuh,' Sofia's eyes flickered open. She gave him a half-smile, acknowledging his presence, and then closed them again.

He turned to me wide-eyed. 'Is she okay?' he whispered.

I swallowed the jelly bean, one of Sofia's birth snacks, that I'd been nibbling on, and pulled myself up from the armchair where I'd been for the last few hours. I stretched out my back.

'She's fine. She's had an epidural, so she's not in any pain. She just wants to be on her own.'

'An epidural? Right. Okay. No birthing ball? Or water bath? Or chanting?' He seemed a bit confused.

I shook my head.

He spotted the carefully packed birth bag, now consigned to the corner of the room.

'We've pivoted from the birth plan a bit. Sofia was very philosophical about it all,' I said, in a low voice. Not that she showed any interest in our conversation anyway. 'I'll leave you guys alone. The doctor said it won't be long. You've got a big night ahead.'

By the time I pulled up in front of our house, there was a message from Morgan.

Meet Luka. Born at 9.42 pm. Sof doing well. Thanks again for today. We'll call tomorrow.

Sofia also had sent me a bunch of photos, including one of her deflated Earth stomach post-birth.

I squealed with excitement, zooming in on the photo of Sofia holding her new son. He was squished, had a tuft of dark hair and the face of an old man. He was perfect.

In the least patronising sense, I was so proud of her. What had she said in her letter? Lacking Will's photographic memory, I couldn't recite it word for word. But it was something like, *The only thing that matters is that my baby is healthy. And I know it's all going to be okay.*

She'd had a vision for her birth and then had ripped it all up and happily changed course. And it had been fine. She was healthy, and her son was perfection.

There was another photo of Morgan holding Luka. I zoomed in. It must have been taken straight after the birth – his hair was still wet and stuck to his head. They were staring at each other. Luka, face sticking out of a lemon, pink and blue blanket, was transfixed by his dad. Morgan, half-smiling, looked as if he'd happily spend the rest of his life just gazing at his son.

I searched through my phone until I found a photo of Hazel, taken by a midwife, a few minutes after she'd been born. Her scrunched face stared up at me, evidently a bit annoyed that her relaxing time floating around my tummy had come to an end. It seemed unbelievable that she'd once been as small as Luka, but there she was.

I hadn't thought about Hazel's birth since it had happened – I'd blocked out the day. But being in the hospital this evening had brought it all back, as well as the torrent of raw emotions that had consumed me as we'd become a family.

Opening a new message, I typed, It would be good to talk again, and pressed 'send'.

Will's house was lit up – he was home.

Standing on our street, I knew I should go home, do the sensible thing. I always tried to do the sensible thing; make people happy. But it was so rare that I felt like this, almost never – like I just wanted to feel, not think, that the real world could wait. A familiar stab of guilt assailed me as I remembered the last night I'd felt like this, desperate for a familiar pair of arms around me, then shook it off.

I walked up his path, across his verandah and knocked on his door.

CHAPTER 25

I had a million innocuous reasons to be knocking. Had he seen Hazel's green sleep suit? Did he mind staying late next Tuesday while I did an evening site inspection?

I heard footsteps pad down the hallway and the door opened.

'Hi,' I said, instantly forgetting all my excuses.

'Hey.'

'Sorry, I don't know why I came here.' I felt a strong need to go home and scream into my pillow. 'Although, Kajal's fallen asleep in my bed and I don't want to wake her.' She'd messaged me at the hospital to tell me she could stay all night and ask if it was okay if she slept in my bed. I'd said of course and sent through a stream of effusive thanks.

'Do you want to come in?'

I knew I should go home. But I was also very aware that I'd never been inside Will's house, and I was desperate to see it. And I didn't want to be alone tonight, didn't want to have to spend time with my thoughts.

I nodded and followed Will down his hallway, walking as slowly as I could so I could take it all in. The front room of the house was his study, which I could glimpse from the street. But I'd only been able to see his enormous desk and computer screen, which took pride of place by the window. What I hadn't been able to see was the shiny black piano with sheet music sitting in the stand. Behind it was a built-in bookcase jammed with books, that looked like they'd all been read. The armchair and coffee table fitted the room perfectly and I guessed were handcrafted as opposed to assembled from a flat pack.

I'd been right about his renovation – it had turned the house into a shrine to neutral colours. But what I hadn't guessed was that this served to showcase the art hanging on his walls – huge, mostly abstract canvases. Enormous Indigenous paintings lined his hallway. The door to what I assumed was his bedroom, was shut.

'I'm cooking a late dinner. Have you eaten?'

I shook my head. 'A home-cooked meal. We've gone from microwave, to reheating to cooking from scratch. We've reached peak us,' I babbled.

I checked my phone. There were no notifications on the monitor.

Will opened his fridge. It was a grown-up one – vegetables in the crisper, glass bottles of mineral water in the bottle section, dips and berries on the top shelf.

'Can I do anything?'

God, I'd gone from acting like a cretin, to a motor mouth, to a polite schoolgirl. What was wrong with me?

'Sit. Entertain me,' he said. He poured me a glass of white wine, topped up his own and used the same bottle to deglaze some onions that were already cooking in a frying pan.

The wine fumes drifted towards me and I felt heady.

'May I use your bathroom?' Again so formal. Will and I basically had spent the last two months together, and for a good week of that I'd been stuck on a toilet. So, why was I acting like I was at a job interview?

'It's in the same spot as yours.' He gestured behind the kitchen.

The floorplans of our houses might have been a mirror of one another, but whereas mine was 'a renovator's delight', Will's was 'impeccably finished' after his epic renovation. The white subway tiles in his shower gleamed. His Aesop handwash didn't even have a sticky drop down the front of the bottle. The only clue that a person ever used this bathroom was a faint hint of the woody aftershave he wore.

I splashed water on my face and stared at myself in the mirror. I'd expected to see a horror show, but instead I looked … alive. My eyes were sparkling, my cheeks were flushed pink and my hair was bouncy.

'You need to go home,' I told myself.

I opened Will's cabinet, very aware that I was violating his privacy. It was predictably ordered with all his bottles and skincare (he'd be embarrassed that I knew he owned a cleansing gel) lined up. I spritzed some of his aftershave on my wrist.

'I should go,' I said, when I returned to the kitchen.

Will had added bacon and tomato into the pan and turned down the heat to let it simmer gently. 'This will be ready soon.'

We stood facing each other.

'Are you wearing my cologne?' he asked.

Shit, I'd been caught. Would he be annoyed that I'd been going through his stuff? Would he think I was a total freak?

He smiled.

'I should go,' I repeated, but now much more weakly.

'You should go,' he said, taking a step towards me, the green flecks in his eyes dancing.

I took a step towards him. 'Kajal's been with Hazel today. I love Kajal. She's amazing. You should go on a date with her,' I said, in a voice so soft I was almost whispering.

'Kajal is great,' he agreed. 'But I don't want to go on a date with her.'

'Why?' I asked, but I already knew the answer.

'Because Kajal isn't you.'

He leaned forward and kissed me. He tasted minerally. His lips were soft and he smelled like I did, but a gentler version.

I kissed him back, tentatively at first.

'Are you sure about this?' he asked, when we finally pulled away from each other.

'Yes,' I replied breathlessly.

I stretched my arms up and he pulled my jumper off. Then I reached forward and unbuttoned his shirt.

When he ran his finger slowly along my collarbone, I involuntarily shivered, then held my palm flat against his chest.

'How many hours a day are you spending at the gym?'

'Whenever I wanted to be … doing this with you, I worked out,' he replied.

I glanced up from his chest to see if he was teasing me. He wasn't. He stared at me, with no hint of joke, or even of hesitation. Just raw desire. Which was exactly how I felt.

This time, I leaned in to kiss him. My whirring brain, which had been in overdrive now for days, weeks even, finally stopped. There were no thoughts anymore. Just his lips. And the faint grate of his stubble against my cheek. And the smell of his aftershave on both of us.

When he gently ran his hand down the side of my face, I felt like every hair on my body was on end.

Panic shot through me. It pulled me out of my blissful state of not thinking. What was the condition of my hair in various regions of my body? The hair on my head was fine – washed and blow-dried for the concert. Armpits and legs had been shaved for similar reasons. And my bikini line? For both logistical and financial reasons, no professionals had been involved for a long time in that region. But it hadn't been that long since our foray to the conference had required some grooming.

A million thoughts rushed to the surface, vying for attention and emotional energy. I hadn't had sex since I'd given birth. Would it be the same? Would it hurt?

But the kiss overrode my thoughts. And I didn't want to think. I just wanted to feel. More specifically, I just wanted to feel Will's hands all over me.

Were a million thoughts also racing through his head? I opened my eyes and pulled away from him. There was no hint of concern or worry on his face. He seemed the most … himself since I'd met him.

God, he was gorgeous.

'Can I?' I asked, as I put my hands on his belt. He nodded. I unbuckled it and then undid the button and the zip. His pants fell to the floor and he stepped out of them, standing in front of me wearing nothing but tight, navy boxer shorts.

Undoing my own pair of jeans, I wriggled out of them. I was thrilled I'd chosen a pair of undies from my old life this morning – fuchsia with a lacy band.

We pressed against each other again. He ran his fingers up and down my back, and then through my hair. I could feel desire building. Part of me wanted this moment to last forever. The other part wanted to pull him on top of me. I could feel, even with his boxers still on, that he might be up for the on-top-of-me option.

His hand moved to the edges of the lace. 'Can I?' he asked, his voice gravellier than usual.

I nodded, very aware that I was breathing heavily. I wanted him. And soon.

He pulled at the waistband and slowly removed my undies. They fell to the ground and I stepped out of them. And there I was naked in front of Will. Well, still in a bra.

He pulled off his boxers. 'Do you want to …' He jerked his head towards the bedroom. I nodded and followed him.

On the precipice of his bedroom, we kissed again. There was no awkwardness, no hesitancy. Just our two bodies, our lips. I nipped his lip and he groaned.

'Lie down,' he said.

I did as instructed on his slate-grey linen doona cover. He put his hands on either side of my ribcage and ran his hands down the side of my body, past my hips and then gently pulled my legs apart.

'I've been dreaming of doing this,' he said.

Had he? My mind threatened to go into a spin, but then my brain shut down again.

Time stopped. At some point, I started to quietly groan. And then waves began to build. And with a final flicker of his tongue I convulsed, suddenly miles away from reality. I tried to stifle louder moans and failed.

Taking a few moments to catch my breath, I pulled myself up into his arms and we kissed again.

'How was that?' he asked, looking pleased, not smug. Just genuinely content that he'd given me pleasure.

'Terrible,' I said, practically purring. 'I'm trying to work out if it was always that good, or whether you're particularly talented at it.'

He smiled broadly.

'I want you,' I said, touching him. 'And I think you want me.'

'I want you so badly.'

We fell together, Will on top of me.

'Wait … we need a … condom,' I said. There was a very slim chance I could actually get pregnant. But one I was very much not willing to take.

'Wait here!' He practically leaped out of bed and opened his wardrobe, revealing a series of identical navy-blue suits on hangers. Pulling open the top drawer, he grabbed a packet, which was reassuringly unopened, and walked back over to the bed.

'Have you … since?'

I raised an eyebrow. 'Yeah, I've been batting them away.'

Will laughed. 'Are you sure you want to?'

I nodded. 'Are you? I don't know if everything … still works down there.'

Maybe I should have got a mirror and done a site inspection before things got this far. But it wasn't as if I knew that tonight was going to happen. And he'd already been down there and hadn't run away screaming. And clearly, some things still worked.

'You're perfect.' He climbed back into bed and kissed my feet. 'These are perfect.'

Then he kissed my calf and then the outside of my thigh, and then the inside. 'And these are perfect.'

Then he kissed my tummy, my still-squishy belly with a slight paunch that I wasn't sure would ever disappear. 'This is perfect.'

'I want you,' I said again. And I did. I wanted to feel all of him.

I climbed on top of him, desperate for him. But I was also nervous. All the women in my council mother's group had got back in the metaphorical saddle once they'd been given the green light by their doctor at the six-week mark, with varying degrees of success. For some women, it had been fine. For others, painful or near impossible. Some had been prescribed vibrator-like devices to relax their vaginal muscles by evangelical physiotherapists. How would my much-traumatised, and then largely ignored, vagina react?

I exhaled. It turned out that six weeks, or maybe six years, of built-up sexual tension had primed things down there.

'Are you okay?' he asked, his eyes filled with concern and desire.

'I am so okay,' I replied with a smile. I held his gaze and we began to move together. I ran my fingers through his now ruffled hair and then brushed them gently over his nipples. He threw his head back.

Our bodies moved together faster, wordlessly in sync. He reached out and held my face and then pulled me towards him and kissed me deeply. Then he exhaled.

I rolled over and lay in the crook of his arms. We were both panting and sweaty and smiling, tangled up in his grey sheets.

My stomach rumbled.

'Do you want some dinner? The sauce should be ready now.'

For some reason, this seemed like the funniest thing on earth and we both burst out laughing. And our laughter somehow neutralised the lingering mood of sexual tension. Suddenly, it felt like we were us again. Just us naked. Which felt far more normal than I ever would have imagined it could be.

I didn't really want to get out of his comfortable bed, but my stomach betrayed me.

'Dinner would be amazing!'

Will filled two enormous bowls of pasta and we took them into his study to eat. I curled up on the armchair wrapped in Will's enormous navy towelling dressing gown, and Will sat on the piano stool eating his.

It should have felt weird. I should have been freaking out. But it all felt … completely normal. Over the last few weeks, I'd inhaled countless meals in front of Will. He'd seen me in every state of dress and undress. He'd seen me at my most deranged and my most polished. This felt like an almost natural extension.

'Play me something?'

'What do you want to hear?'

'Something you enjoy playing.'

He put his bowl next to the stool on the floor and turned his back to me. Then his hands were moving, gently but confidently, and music filled the room. I didn't know what he was playing, but I was sure I'd heard it before. The music swelled and I felt tears once more prick the edges of my eyes.

I'd been so wrong about Will. I'd thought he was an acerbic, unyielding workaholic. And he was all those things. But I hadn't known that he was so talented, so caring. And also so wry, so quick-witted.

The piece was short. After he'd played the final note, he paused for a moment and then spun around to face me. I dabbed at my eyes with his dressing-gown sleeve, and he pretended not to notice.

'You're so talented. And that song ... it's gorgeous.'

'It's called "*Le Cygne*" – "The Swan". It reminds me of you – trying to make it all seem effortless, attempting to hide all the work it takes to try to be everything to everyone.'

I stared at him. How did he see the thing that I tried so hard to hide and think it was ... swanlike?

'I feel like I've heard it before.'

'I play it quite a lot. Maybe you heard it through the window.'

Maybe I had, but just hadn't properly realised what was next door. Or hadn't wanted to.

'I wasn't sure you wanted ... this,' I said. 'After that time on the beach, you said you just wanted to be friends. And those messages you sent me after we kissed?'

'You asked me to sign a contractual provision promising that nothing would happen between us. I didn't want to take advantage,' he said.

'Can I take advantage of you now?' I asked. He nodded and smiled.

Pulling myself up from the armchair, I walked over to the stool. I sat next to Will and leaned in to kiss him. The next noise the piano made was far less melodious.

CHAPTER 26

I decided to sneak out of Will's house as the sun was rising. My monitor hadn't pinged – neither Kajal nor Hazel were awake. But I wanted to be home before they were.

As I got dressed, Will kissed my neck. I desperately wanted to kiss him back and pick up where we'd left off last night. But instead, I'd hauled myself out of bed.

As much as I did want to get home, I made a short detour (from the five-metre walk home) through my gentrified suburb, in the first light of the day. Our neighbourhood was always quiet in the mornings – a subdued mix of wide-eyed survivors falling out of the nightclubs on Commercial Road, retirees with shopping carts on their way to the market and parents with baby carriers hunting down caffeine.

I felt a deep sense of being at home, of belonging, in my village within a city. This was where we'd grown up, where we'd moved to with Mum after Dad had left, because it was cheap to rent then. This was where I'd built my own family.

And this morning reaffirmed why I never wanted to leave. I walked through a small reserve that was glistening with morning dew. A family of magpies chortled from bluey-grey peeling gum trees. It was swooping season, but today I felt like nothing could touch me.

I stopped for a moment, closed my eyes and inhaled the smell of sweet, damp grass and the minty eucalyptus. The early-morning sun warmed my face. This morning the world felt fresh, hopeful and filled with possibility.

My flashing phone interrupted my moment of gratitude. Had Hazel woken up early?

No, it was Will.

My pillow smells like your perfume, he wrote.

You'll never be able to wash it again, I messaged back, smiling. I still smell like your aftershave.

I was now smiling on the inside, too. For the first time since Hazel had been born, I didn't feel like I was being buffeted from all directions. I might have had even less sleep than usual last night, but rather than feeling drunk with exhaustion, I felt rejuvenated, content even.

Later that day, I was at my desk working through lunch when Will messaged me. I felt my cheeks begin to flush when I saw his name. Flashes of limbs tangled up in grey linen sprang to mind.

Robert has asked if we can meet this afternoon. Any chance you could work from home?

No worries. I'll sort it out! I tapped.

'I'm sorry, but no,' Monica said, not looking even slightly sorry when I asked her. 'It's an anchor day. Everyone else has to be here, so you do, too.'

I blinked at her in disbelief. She insisted her team come in every day, except for Fridays – a day I didn't work. I could do most of my job from home. And even if I didn't log on later tonight, I'd more than make up my hours this week. And well, every week. I often arrived early and I always worked through lunch. And since I'd returned to work, I'd barely asked for any flexibility.

'Right,' I said.

In the end, I asked Will to drop Hazel into the office. He was wearing one of his navy suits and was as frazzled as I'd ever seen him. Which made sense. Today he'd find out whether the thing he'd been working for, often night and day, for over a decade was about to come to fruition. Nerves were understandable.

'Inhale. Exhale,' I said, with what I hoped was a reassuring smile. I stepped forward and straightened his tie.

'I'm fine,' he said. The closed-off expression, the guarded mask he'd worn before I'd got to know him properly, was back. As was the phone in his hand.

Monica stomped through reception as Will passed me the nappy bag. She glared at Hazel in her pram. 'This is not what I had in mind,' she said, not pausing for a response.

Will glared at her, and for once I didn't care.

Kajal appeared at reception holding the green juice she must have popped out to get. Her face lit up when she saw Will. I saw him through her eyes – the picture of corporate gorgeousness – hair particularly floppy, his best pair of glasses on, shirt so white it almost gleamed against his tanned skin.

'Hey, Will,' she said. She wasn't using her professional receptionist voice. This one was far sultrier.

'Hi, Kajal.' He smiled warmly at her.

'Okay, you better go or you'll be late,' I said. 'Good luck! You've got this.'

'Weird question – is Will Hazel's bio dad?' Kajal asked, as soon as he'd gone.

I forced a laugh, as if her suggestion was the most ridiculous thing I'd ever heard. It came out sounding all wrong.

'No! He's my neighbour. He helped me out today when I had a childcare emergency. What made you think that?'

'He's just so great with Hazel.'

'Yeah, he's a natural,' I said, a memory of Will holding Hazel for the first time, like a wing attack trying to make a pass, leaping to mind.

I managed to finish my work by playing Hazel YouTube clips and constantly feeding her snacks. On the dot of five, I began to pack up. Once again, I was thankful for a job I could do in my sleep. Or in this case, with one hand and cartoons flashing next to my screen.

'Zoe. Quick chat in the meeting room?' Monica asked from her desk. She didn't acknowledge that now might not be the best time for a meeting. Nor invite Hazel to attend or offer an alternative plan.

I could tell she'd been watching the clock, too, waiting for me to finish the day, knowing I was desperate to leave.

'Yep, um. I'll just be a few minutes.'

I left Hazel with Kajal in reception, watching *Bluey* on the computer, then walked to the meeting room, my heart pounding. Monica was waiting, tapping her acrylic tips on the wooden conference table, like a shark eyeing her prey.

'I'll get straight to the point. I was very impressed when you returned from parental leave. It was a really strong start. But lately, things have been … slipping.

So unfortunately, I've been forced to put you on a performance plan.' Her voice dripped with feigned sympathy.

I could feel my cheeks beginning to burn from both embarrassment and anger. Performance plans were used to push idiots out of the business. I could do this job with half my brain. I might have been a bit … distracted. And then I'd got sick. But I had been doing my job. And I'd been doing it well.

I skimmed the sheet of paper in front of me that listed all my indiscretions.

Reduced output since returning from parental leave. Seriously! I'd gone part-time. And I was producing well over three-fifths of what I'd previously got through in a week. And for commensurate pay.

Regularly using phone for personal reasons during work hours. Was this a joke? Who didn't sneakily check their phone at work? Kajal spent most of her workday online shopping, only pausing to flirt with good-looking clients. Monica spent a huge chunk of hers on Facebook Marketplace, no doubt buying more hideous outfits or going straight from site inspections to beauty appointments.

I knew I could fight back, that her accusations were groundless. But what was the point? If she wanted me gone, she'd make it happen. I'd seen her do it before to women in my position. Why had I thought I'd be immune, that it would be different with me?

'Did I ever really have a chance at that promotion?' I asked, staring straight at her.

Before she could stop herself, she smirked. And I knew the answer to my question. God, she was a snake.

'Like I've said before, new parents often drop the ball. But we'll implement this plan and take it from there.'

She was a bully. I'd known this for a while, before I'd gone on maternity leave. But it wasn't until I'd seen how she treated me, through Will's eyes, that I'd been sure I wasn't just being sensitive, a weakling. I felt something inside me snap.

'I'll save you the paperwork. I quit.'

It was only once I'd collected my bag from my desk and Hazel from reception and was in the car that it hit me. How had I made such an enormous decision on almost zero sleep and probably still high on sex?

I had a baby daughter, was in charge of providing for both of us and was now unemployed. Would I be able to keep our place at the new childcare centre without a job? Probably not. Surely, I needed a job to be eligible for the childcare subsidy. Without the subsidy, I wouldn't be able to afford the fees. Or rent. Or anything.

Hazel fell asleep in her car seat, crashing after all the sugary snacks I'd bribed her with, and so I drove and drove, not even really noticing where I was going.

What had I done? Could I beg Monica for my job back? Had I properly quit? Didn't something need to be put in writing before it was legal? Maybe Will would know. Whenever I'd complained about Monica, he'd reel off all the workplace laws he was sure she was breaching – maybe he could help me legally dig my way out of the hole I'd created for myself in yet another moment of madness.

Will! He'd know by now whether he was a partner.

As soon as I parked outside our house, I dug up my phone from the bottom of my bag to call him. There was a notification of an email from the HR department at work, subject – 'Termination of Employment'. So, that answered that question. I really needed Will's help now – maybe it was time I took some sort of action against Monica. The business had to be liable for her toxic behaviour.

I also had a stack of unread messages. And a heap of missed calls. But before I'd had a chance to read any of them, there was a tap on my window.

I jumped in my seat from fright. The person tapped again.

'It's me. Adam. You messaged last night – said you wanted to talk.'

I wound down the window. 'I didn't mean come over to my house and wait for me to get home.'

'Well, I'm here.'

I carefully unbuckled a still-asleep Hazel from her seat and led him into our unlit hallway. When we were together, we hadn't stayed here much – he preferred that I went to his apartment, and I'd acquiesced.

'Are you okay?' he asked. He looked at me then at Hazel, who was nuzzled into my shoulder, his familiar face registering both concern and curiosity. I was glad it was so dark.

'I just quit my job.'

'What happened?'

'I realised that there are limits to how much you should put up with from a person.' I moved Hazel close to me, against my chest, feeling exposed as Adam watched us.

'Good for you.'

'Adam, I've got to put her down. And I've had a dumpster fire of a day. Can we talk another time?' I wanted, more than anything, for him to leave. Now.

'I'm happy to wait,' he said. 'Anyway, you shouldn't be alone when you feel like shit.'

I bit my tongue and said nothing.

By the time I'd got Hazel down, knowing that she'd fallen asleep way too early and would probably want to party during the night, all I wanted to do was roll into bed myself. I was half-tempted to hide in the bedroom until Adam got the hint and left. But instead, I snuck out of the dark room and crept up the hallway to face my ex-boyfriend.

'Adam, I'm beyond exhausted,' I tried again.

'Why did you message me last night?'

Why had I? Because I'd inhaled second-hand laughing gas? Because the hospital had unearthed a bunch of emotions I'd repressed for almost nine months.

'It was a mistake. It was meant to go to Sofia,' I bluffed.

'What did you want to talk about?' Adam pressed.

'Nothing,' I said, suddenly feeling very vulnerable. This afternoon already had sucked up all my fight, all my defences. 'I guess, just more of what we talked about the other day.'

'Zoe.' He stood up from the couch and pulled himself up to his full height. 'She could be mine. Couldn't she?'

CHAPTER 27

I hesitated for a moment and then nodded. And with that nod my world, my carefully constructed house of cards, crumbled around me.

Adam stared at me, his face contorted by disbelief and shock. 'But you told me … When you were pregnant and I asked, you said …'

'I didn't tell you the whole truth.'

'So, she might be my daughter?'

I noticed a water bill on the fridge. Had I paid it yet?

'Zoe?' Adam asked again.

I turned back to face him. 'I don't know for sure. But it's possible,' I said.

'But you told me that there was no chance she was mine. That you were one hundred per cent certain you'd got pregnant using the donor.'

'I was trying to protect Hazel. I promised her no one would ever leave her. And you told me you didn't want a baby.'

'I didn't think we should have a hypothetical baby together. But it's different now that she's here. And that I might be her father.'

'Biologically.'

'What does that mean?'

'She might have your DNA, but there's more to being a parent than biology, Adam. Being a parent means being there for your child. It means putting your kid's life ahead of yours. It means showing up.'

'How was I meant to do that if I didn't know I could be her dad? You didn't give me a choice.'

I felt a sting of guilt shoot through me. Adam ran his hand through his slicked-back hair.

Hazel wailed from the bedroom. We'd both been close to shouting and we must have woken her up.

'I need to go settle her,' I said.

'Can I meet her?' he asked.

My stomach contracted again. 'Not while she's upset and half-asleep. That wouldn't be a good idea, for anyone.'

He didn't push back.

In the bedroom, I held Hazel in my arms and stroked her head until she became heavy against me. Then I lay her down in the cot and watched until her eyes fluttered shut. She looked so peaceful. She had no idea that I'd just cracked open her life in the next room.

When I was sure Hazel was asleep, I reluctantly returned to the kitchen. The bottom drawer, where Adam knew I kept all my important documents, was now open. A messy pile of papers was in front of him.

'What's this?' He no longer appeared shocked. His cheeks had now gone blotchy. He held up the printout of the draft newspaper article Sofia had sent me.

'It's nothing,' I said, grabbing it from him. But it was too late – he'd read it.

'You let another man fill the role of Hazel's father, before you'd even given me the chance to find out if she was mine?' he asked. 'You were never going to tell me the truth, were you?' His nostrils flared.

'None of that article is true. It's a draft that never ran, I promise.'

'You promise? How am I meant to believe anything you say?' He stood up and slammed his chair back under the table.

'Shhh, you'll wake Hazel.'

'Did Will know about the donor?' Adam asked.

'Yes,' I said, after a pause.

'And did you tell him that I could be Hazel's father?'

'No! I haven't told anyone that. I didn't even let myself think about it. I just pretended what happened between us that night didn't happen.'

Adam was now clutching the side of the table so tightly his knuckles were white.

'I promise that article's fake news. Will and I aren't a couple. We just lied to his work so that he could take paternity leave and help me with childcare. And he agreed to do it because it was going to help him make partner. It's all a total lie.'

Adam stared at me.

'I know it sounds crazy. But I thought it was the best thing for Hazel. Every decision I've made was for her.'

'How was hiding a possible parent the best thing for Hazel? It was the best thing for *you*.'

Each word felt like a knife in my heart.

'Hazel is my everything. I was just trying to protect her.'

'From me?'

There was no good way to reply to his question. And I knew that once he'd lost his temper, and I'd never seen him this angry before, that reasoning was useless anyway.

Adam paused for a moment. 'We need a DNA test, obviously. And I'm going to find out exactly what my rights are here. You'll be hearing from my lawyers.'

Adam loved to use expressions he'd heard in a movie. But he delivered this one with total sincerity. Then he stormed out.

I heard the door shut. I stood there for a few minutes just staring down the dark hallway in shock. I'd told Adam the truth and he'd demanded a DNA test. And if she was his, what would happen next?

Shaking, I picked up my phone. Usually, she was one of my two most recent calls. But we hadn't spoken since Sofia's baby shower. I scrolled and pressed 'dial'.

'Hi …' It was all I managed to get out before I burst into tears.

'Are you okay? What's wrong?'

'Is there … Could you please … Come over?' I managed to get out between sobs.

'I'll be there as soon as I can,' she said.

I'd stopped crying by the time she arrived. Camille, still in a black work dress and heels, found me sitting on the couch staring at the wall, numb.

'Sorry. You were working,' I said dumbly.

'It's fine. What's going on?' Normally, she'd wrap her arms around me and hug me, but tonight she remained standing.

'Adam's furious at me. What if he can take Hazel from me?' I replied.

'Adam? What's he got to do with anything?' she asked, confused.

'You know how I told you I got pregnant after a one-night thing. Never even knew the guy's surname?' I said. 'That's not the truth. I haven't told anyone the truth. I've barely been able to admit the truth to myself.'

'Okay. Well, maybe it's time you did,' she said. And so I told her the story.

CHAPTER 28

It had all begun on the day I was meant to get married. I was wearing a white gown and a doctor in scrubs was about to insert a speculum between my legs.

'Now this might feel a bit uncomfortable, but it will be over quickly,' Dr Saliba said.

I winced silently. 'When the clinic called this morning and said that today was the best day in my cycle, my first reaction was – no way, not today. But then I thought, I don't want to waste another month. And maybe it's ... actually perfect.'

I always babbled and overshared when I was nervous or uneasy. And right now, I was both.

'Why's today perfect?' Amelia, the ultra-perky ultrasound technician assisting Dr Saliba, asked.

'I'm going to insert the cannula now,' Dr Saliba said. I felt a pinch.

'Today was meant to be my wedding day,' I said, before I could stop myself.

'You abandoned your wedding for this?' Amelia asked, as she swivelled around from her machine to stare at me. Dr Saliba shot her a look from between my legs, which she missed.

'Oh no, sorry – it was cancelled ages ago,' I explained. Six months ago, to be precise.

She pursed her lips, sympathetically. Still in her twenties, I bet she believed that the fairytale ended with a glinting ring and an expensive white dress. That first came marriage, then the baby in the baby carriage. That happily ever after meant that you'd been chosen. I knew better now – over the past few months, I'd learned that we lived in a world where women could choose their own adventure. And I'd chosen mine – to be a mum. On my own.

'Now I need you to confirm that the details on this vial are correct,' Dr Saliba said and handed me a tube. I read the printed label. *Zoe Julianne Harper.* Then I read the label another five times.

'That's correct,' I said finally, and carefully handed it back. It had taken me three slow months to reach the top of the sperm-donation waiting list, and the contents of this vial had cost me a chunk of my savings.

There were a few minutes of concentrated silence. Amelia manoeuvred the ultrasound machine, Dr Saliba deftly connected the vial to the tubes and I stared at the ceiling.

'And we're done,' Dr Saliba said.

'That's it?' I asked. This moment had loomed large in my mind for months, but the whole process had taken less than five minutes from start to finish. It almost felt a bit … anticlimactic. 'So, I could be pregnant right now? If all goes … swimmingly?'

The doctor chuckled behind his surgical mask, and I felt a rush of pride. I wanted to be Dr Saliba's favourite patient.

'Well, not right at this moment,' he said. 'You need to ovulate first. And with your PCOS … as you know, it's likely to take a few goes.' He whipped off his rubber gloves with a thwack.

'Is someone picking you up?' he asked.

'I can drive myself, can't I? I called reception yesterday and they said I'd be okay to drive because you didn't use any anaesthetic.'

I had to get used to doing things on my own.

'Yes, that's fine,' Dr Saliba said gently. 'Now you lie here for ten minutes until …' he checked the clock affixed to the wall, '… three. Then you can get dressed and head to reception.'

'Perfect,' I croaked, swallowing the frog in my throat. Today, at three o'clock, in another version of my life, I'd be following Sofia and Camille in matching shades of silk down the aisle.

Was there a word for trying to reconcile the gap between how you'd thought your life would turn out, and how it had? There probably was in German.

'Thanks, Dr Saliba,' I said, with the biggest smile I could muster. 'Thanks, Amelia.'

'Would you like me to wait with you?' Amelia asked gently.

'I'm okay. But thank you,' I said.

'Some people find the next two weeks while they wait can be difficult. So, make sure you ask for the support you need,' Dr Saliba said, as he washed his hands.

'I will,' I said.

Amelia turned off the ultrasound machine, Dr Saliba

dried his hands and I was left, lying on a thinly padded bed covered in medical tissue paper, alone.

A jolt of nerves shot through me. Could I actually do this solo? I'd never changed a nappy. I didn't understand how breastfeeding worked. Birth sounded like a horror movie.

I felt a sudden visceral longing for my mum. But she was in Bendigo. And I'd already decided not to tell her what I was doing.

I checked the clock. In a few minutes' time, in an alternative life, Adam and I would have been making our vows. We would have been promising to be together till death do us part.

My phone was within reaching distance. I could pick it up now and call Sofia. She'd be on her way within minutes.

I shut my eyes and put both my hands on my belly, over the hospital gown.

'Baby. I know you don't exactly exist yet. But you might soon. So, I want to make you a promise,' I whispered aloud. These vows weren't carefully prepared, or being made in front of all my friends and family. This small grey room in an East Melbourne fertility clinic that smelled of disinfectant was almost the aesthetic counterpart of the Yarra Valley winery I'd been so excited to book and so devastated to cancel. But somehow, this moment still felt sacred. And I felt a deep sense of calm – that I'd made the right decision and that everything was going to be okay.

'Baby. I promise I'll do everything I can to give you the best life possible. I promise to give you all my love.' I took a deep breath. 'It'll just be the two of us.'

*

After the procedure, I drove myself home and got catastrophically drunk. I hadn't meant to. But one small glass of wine had led to many.

I knew that there was no certainty that I'd even get pregnant after one try. I had sticky ovaries, after all – Dr Saliba had told me it could be a long journey. But the enormity of what I'd done, with no one to share it with, hit me that evening. Hard.

And I'd felt so alone. I tried to tell myself that this day was special – it was the beginning of a journey to have a child. But the day also involved an enormous cash payment and spread legs in a doctor's office.

A bottle of wine in, having had no dinner, I called Adam.

He came straight from the office because he'd been worried. In the six months since we'd broken up, I hadn't done anything like this. I'd been determined to avoid the cliché, and in my darkest hours when I'd been desperate to speak to him, to hear answers, I'd always called Sofia or Camille instead.

We opened another bottle, then one more. He ordered pizzas, which remained largely untouched. And for a while, we pretended that things were like they'd been. Before everyone else got engaged. Before they got married. Before I wanted a baby.

And the evening ended how most of our drunken evenings did – in bed. We'd had sex. It had been perfectly ordinary sex. But it had felt so familiar that as we lay in bed next to each other, I'd burst into tears.

Naturally, Adam assumed I was crying because of the breakup.

'I'm sorry, Zo,' he said. 'I honestly didn't mean to hurt you.'

'It's not that,' I croaked. 'Today I might have become pregnant. With a nice stranger's baby.'

Adam sat up in bed looking, understandably, confused.

And it all poured out of me. How after months of dates with men who were in no hurry to have children, another specialist declaring my fertility prospects dwindling, a few appointments, a large chunk of cash and finally making the almost impossible decision of which donor I should pick, I'd done it – I'd chosen to have a baby on my own. My daughter or son would be able to contact the donor, if they wanted to, when they were eighteen. The procedure had been uncomfortable, but not totally awful. And in a few short weeks, I'd find out if it had been successful.

Adam listened without comment. I didn't know if it was genuine shock or a sense of guilt that had rendered him virtually speechless. But I was glad when he just gave me a short but tight hug and then spent the night with me.

Obviously, I'd had a monster hangover the next day. My brain had felt woolly and it wasn't until late in the day that I'd realised what I'd done. I'd had sex, unprotected sex, with my ex-boyfriend on the same day I'd had a procedure to be impregnated. On the day I knew I was most fertile.

Some frantic research online confirmed my fears – it was possible that either encounter could get me pregnant. And short of a paternity test after the baby was born, I wouldn't know who the father was.

But, I reasoned, becoming pregnant wasn't a sure-fire thing. In fact, statistically, there was more chance that it wouldn't work than it would. I'd try again next month at the clinic, and do it properly this time.

But then, a few weeks later my period was a day late, I felt exhausted and my boobs were sore. Even as I peed on the stick, I already knew. It was happening.

Maybe Adam and I had used protection? I was a bit blurry on the details of the night. And if he hadn't, wasn't conception a race to the egg? The donor had had a good few hours' head start.

But I knew as the second line turned blue that there was a chance that Adam could be the father.

I hadn't announced my pregnancy, but our worlds were still close enough that he found out. He turned up on my doorstep on a Sunday morning when I was in my second trimester.

'Could it be mine?' he'd asked, stressed.

'No,' I'd said. 'I didn't get pregnant that month.'

He didn't know how many weeks I was, or my due date. He'd believed me and left.

It wasn't a calculated lie. I'd vaguely known that one day I'd have to face up to the truth, that I'd want my child to know their own story. But I'd ignored the issue, tried not to think about it and locked all memories of that night away. Until now.

CHAPTER 29

Camille finished listening to the story and stared at me.

'I wanted to do it on my own. But I … made a mistake, a huge mistake,' I said, my lips wobbling. 'I didn't want it to be like this.'

Camille handed me a roll of paper towel and I tore off a sheet and dabbed at my eyes.

I took a deep breath. I needed her to answer the questions that were bubbling up and smashing around my mind. 'If it turns out he is her dad, what can he do?'

'He can request that he's recognised as Hazel's legal father. And there's a range of things he can ask for – visitation rights, certain custody arrangements.'

'Would he get those?'

'He'd probably get something.' She paused for a moment. 'A court's primary consideration is what's best for the child, not the parents. And the court will often form the view that where there are two parents wanting involvement in a child's life, it's in a child's best interests to allow that.'

'But I didn't mean for there to be two parents. It was just meant to be me. I knew, I thought, Adam didn't ever want kids. So, I just … considered him to be an alternative sperm donor. Part of me thought I was doing him a favour, setting him free.'

'The man who donated to the clinic knowingly and legally forfeited all parental rights. Adam very much didn't. There's a big difference – you know that,' she said firmly.

She paused again to let me absorb everything she'd told me.

'If Adam is the father he could assist you with child support,' Camille said, as if this was a silver lining.

'I don't want Adam's money! I can support Hazel.'

Although could I? I'd resigned a few hours earlier, I had no income and limited savings.

'I quit my job this afternoon.' I buried my hands in my face.

'Why?'

'Another emotional and self-destructive decision,' I said. 'That wouldn't look great to a judge, would it? If Hazel's mum can't pay the rent, or afford groceries. What was I thinking?'

'How did Adam find out?' she asked.

'After Hazel was born, I tried to lock away everything that had come before that moment. And then you had a go at me about how I can avoid reality ...'

'And I was right!' she said.

'And Will gave me this pep talk about how if you face up to things they normally turn out okay. So, I went to see Adam. I think I wanted concrete proof that he didn't want Hazel – that I'd made the right decision in keeping him out of her life. Except he didn't say that. He sort of said ... the opposite.

'And then I was with Sofia during her birth. And I saw Morgs with Luka. And ... just, felt things. So, I messaged

Adam last night. And he was waiting here when I got home tonight. And he knew I was hiding something. He asked me if Hazel could be his. And I told him the truth. And then he saw the newspaper article about Will being Hazel's dad.'

'Article?'

'There was almost an article. But we made it go away.'

'Okay,' Camille said weakly.

'He totally flipped out. I've never seen him so angry. Not even when someone ran into his new ten-thousand-dollar titanium racing bike. And he said he's going to get lawyers involved. What if the court finds out that I'm an unemployed fraudster?' The room felt like it was spinning.

'I need you to calm down.'

'I can't lose her, Camille! What do I do?'

Camille reached across the table and held my arm. 'You get a good night's sleep and try to stay as calm as possible. Then tomorrow you go and speak to Adam, once he's had a chance to process everything. You tell him you'll agree to a DNA test and that you can both go from there.'

'Okay,' I said. Sleep. Speak to Adam.

'Why didn't you tell me the truth? About the sperm donor. And Adam,' Camille asked. She was trying to keep her expression neutral, but I could tell she was hurt.

'It was my business. I didn't owe it to you to tell you how I conceived my daughter.'

'But you have no problem calling me the minute you need family-law advice to untangle your web of lies,' she shot back.

'Sorry,' I said. 'Thanks for coming over.'

'It's fine.'

I scraped at my raw eyes and cheeks with the rough paper towel. 'I didn't tell Adam the truth because I didn't want Hazel to be left, to be hurt, the way we were by Dad. I thought I could protect her from feeling unloved, from … the way I've felt my whole life. I was going to face up to it … one day. Just … not yet. I didn't expect it to all come out like this.'

'Okay. But you didn't tell me you were even thinking about using a sperm donor. You used to tell me everything. But you didn't tell me you were going to do this huge thing. Did you tell Sofia?'

'Yes. And I wanted to tell you. But you …' I paused. 'I didn't want Mum to know.'

'Why not? She wouldn't have cared that you were using a donor. *Don't rely on anyone.* You were literally living out her mantra!'

'I thought that if she thought I'd been left by a guy, like she was, she might … I don't know. Want to help me out, or whatever.' I sighed. 'I was wrong. She left me to bloody sink. I was an idiot.'

Camille took a deep breath. 'You're blaming our parents for this mess?' she asked, incredulous. 'You're a grown-up. With a child. You need to just … let go of all these negative feelings.'

'Seriously!' I felt my last shred of self-restraint snap. 'At least I acknowledge I have some feelings rather than just burying them in work, being busy and getting mad at me instead of your husband.'

Camille stared at me for a moment, her lips so tightly pursed they'd almost disappeared. 'I'm not listening to this. I raced here from the office because you asked me to.

I'm here instead of spending time with my kids. I know you're scared, but don't take it out on me,' she said with such forced calmness her voice almost quivered.

'Camille. I've had a big day. I didn't mean all that.'

'Get some sleep,' she said, in a dangerously steady voice. 'Speak to Adam.'

Then she slowly picked up her bag and left.

By the time I finally crawled into bed, it felt like days had passed, weeks even, since I'd put Hazel down. Years since I'd been in Will's arms.

I checked my phone for the first time since I'd been in the car. There were messages from Kajal making sure I was okay. And a few missed calls from Will.

A sting of guilt broke through my angst. He'd had his big meeting. He'd know if he'd made partner. I should have checked in with him by now. I should have bought champagne and baked him a cake to celebrate, or soften any blow.

He hadn't come around tonight. Maybe he thought I was freaking out about what we'd done and didn't want to see him. Or maybe he'd been out with Charlie and his other uni friends celebrating or commiserating. Either way, I was glad I hadn't had to see him and pretend that everything was okay.

I tapped out a message.

How did it go?

CHAPTER 30

I woke up the next morning to a knock on the door. It was almost seven-thirty. I'd been up most of the night tossing and turning and soothing Hazel, who'd woken up on the hour, every hour. I'd only fallen asleep as the sun had risen. I turned over – Hazel was awake, calmly playing with one of her dummies.

Picking her up, I groggily walked to the front door and paused. My heart began to pound. Could it be Adam? I needed to speak to him today. But first, I had to work out exactly what I wanted to say.

'Hello?' I asked through the door.

'It's me.' It was Will.

'Why didn't you use your key?' I asked as I opened the door.

'I'm a bit early today. I didn't want to catch you off guard.'

'You didn't write back. What happened?'

A smile lit up his whole face. 'I wanted to tell you in person. They invited me to join the partnership.' He was trying to be coy, but even with his expert ability to mask his emotions, elation broke through.

I threw my free arm around him, feeling a frisson of electricity.

'Congratulations!' I said, pulling away from him. 'That's amazing news. You deserve it. Wow. How do you feel?'

'I feel …' He searched for the right words. 'Relieved. I feel like everything that happened at school, all the late nights, The Arrangement, even. It all means something now.'

'Great,' I said weakly. 'Let's have a toast. It might be a bit early for champagne, but a celebratory orange juice?'

'Sorry I'm here so early. I knew you'd be exhausted last night. And you guys are normally up, and I just wanted to tell you. To thank you for the part you played in the whole campaign. Robert said the partnership were really impressed by us at the conference, and that was all you.'

He leaned forward and kissed me. His lips were soft, and as they grazed mine, I felt my knees weaken.

'Thank you,' he said, his voice slightly gravelly again.

I led him through to the kitchen, very aware I was only wearing the oversized T-shirt I'd slept in.

'Are you okay?' I saw him take in the bottle of whisky and single glass on the table sitting next to a pile of scrunched-up tissues covered in mascara.

Flashes from the previous night carouselled through my mind, and I had to blink to make them go away.

'I'm fine,' I said, feeling a stab of guilt at the lie. But this was Will's moment – his victory. 'Overtired. Hazel's routine was a bit out after yesterday.'

'You're a bit pale. Maybe you've got a bug?'

'Hey, this morning isn't about me. It's about you!' I poured orange juice into two cloudy champagne flutes.

'To Will.' I raised my glass and he smiled. 'I've been lucky to be your fake partner. They're beyond lucky to get you as a real one. And I'm just so happy that you got everything you wanted.'

I clinked my glass against his, and he then tapped his glass against Hazel's plastic sippy cup.

'It's my second-last day with Hazel. I thought I might do something special with her today … maybe take her to the children's museum?'

This was the moment to tell Will I'd quit my job, that I needed his legal brain to try to get it back. But I needed to see Adam today, and it was better if I did it without Hazel.

'And let's have dinner together after Hazel's gone to bed. We can talk. Or we can not talk …' There was a smile in his voice and his eyes were bright.

'Sounds great!' I said, instead. 'Well, I better hustle and get ready. I'm late.'

I spent the morning in a cafe trying not to think about Will and trying to work out what to say to Adam. Writing had always been the thing I could do without a second thought. But for the first time in my life, I felt completely stuck. I stared at the list in my notebook.

- *I should have told you that Hazel might be your biological daughter. Obviously.*
- *But you told me you didn't want kids. And ghosted me when I told you I did.*
- *I was so hurt by how our relationship ended, so I was wary about letting you in my life, and Hazel's life, again.*

- *I am a great mother. Don't get the legal system involved.*
- *I shouldn't have pretended to be in a relationship with Will. But I was desperate – childcare is a nightmare.*

I shut my notebook. This wasn't helping. I just needed to speak with him. Surely, in the light of day, he knew all of this.

I called him, my heart beating faster with every ring. When he didn't pick up, I sent him a message and waited. And when he didn't reply I went to his apartment building, but no one answered the buzzer. At his office, a skyscraper at the bottom of the city, a battle-axe of a receptionist firmly told me, after I'd given my name, that he was out and wasn't expected to come in. I was almost certain she was lying.

I spent the rest of the day on a bench outside Adam's office building, waiting. At four o'clock, my phone pinged. I'd received an email with the subject heading, 'Request for DNA test – Hazel Julianne Harper'. It had been sent by a law firm. I opened the attachment and skimmed over the officious letter filled with terrifying words; 'custody', 'fraudulent', 'Department of Human Services' danced off the page.

A few minutes later, my phone pinged again with a text from Adam. I think it's better if we communicate through our lawyers.

My stomach tightened. If I'd learned anything via osmosis from Camille's work, it was that involving lawyers rarely made things better. She always told potential clients that she should be a last resort – that things would get expensive and messy if lawyers ran the show.

I knew Camille would be able to make sense of the letter. Part of me wanted to dash to the other end of the city where she worked and ask her what to do right this second. But we'd both said things to each other last night, and it was getting late. Will and Hazel were both waiting for me.

'How was your day?' Will asked, when I got home.

'Same old. You know, work,' I replied, glad I wasn't facing him as I gave Hazel a big squeeze hello.

'Kajal dropped off your stuff,' he said. 'She wanted to make sure you were okay.'

I swung around. His face was as expressionless as I'd ever seen it.

'I should have told you,' I sighed. 'I quit yesterday. Monica was going to fire me anyway. I actually was going to ask you if there are any legal actions I could take.'

'What did you do today?'

'I just … wandered around the city. Tried to process it all.'

'I got a call from Adam Hall.'

CHAPTER 31

My heart sank. Adam had lashed out at me, through Will.

'What did he say?'

'He asked me why I was pretending to be his possible child's father. And whether my firm knew the whole picture,' Will said. 'He, in not so many words, threatened to tell work what we'd done.'

'He won't do it,' I said. 'He's got a shitty temper and can be stupid sometimes. But his bark is way worse than his bite.'

'You're defending him?'

'No. I'm just …' Hoping that it's true. 'He wants to hurt me, not you.'

'I called Robert and told him the whole story, all about The Arrangement, this afternoon,' Will said. 'I wasn't going to wait around for a guy like Adam to drop the blade on my neck.'

Clearly, Adam's threat had been enough to send Will over the edge. He'd lived by his own advice – he'd faced the situation head-on and risked the thing that mattered most to him.

'So, you're not going to be a partner?'

'I'm not going to be a lawyer,' he said. 'I resigned from the firm this afternoon. First thing I've ever quit.

Robert made it very clear that if I didn't they'd be forced to fire me for cause. And then I self-reported to the Law Institute. I'll probably lose my practising certificate – they don't typically let lawyers who commit fraud keep them.'

'Will. Jesus. I don't know what to say.'

'How did Adam know what we did?' His voice was devoid of anger, or any emotion. His restraint was unnerving.

'I told him. Last night.'

Will stared at me for a moment, then he picked up the TV remote and switched it on – *The Wiggles*, a sole mum's best friend, was already loaded. He pressed 'play'.

I popped Hazel into her playpen. She barely moved, already transfixed by the colours and music.

Will opened the courtyard door, and stepped outside into the space between our houses. I followed him.

'Why did you tell him?' he asked.

'You know how I used a sperm donor to conceive Hazel?'

'Yes.'

'I slept with Adam around the same time. Which means, I don't exactly know who Hazel's father is. Until yesterday, I hadn't told anyone, not even Adam,' I said.

'Why did you tell him what we'd done?'

'He saw the article – the draft Sofia sent me. He thought that you were adopting Hazel and was pretty furious about that. So, I told him the truth to try to calm him down, to try to make things better,' I said. 'I spent the whole of today trying to talk to him, to try to sort it out. But all I got was a letter from his lawyer. He said he wants part custody of Hazel.'

There was a moment's silence while he processed what I'd told him. His poker face had never been more impenetrable. I had no idea what he was thinking. Was he feeling anything? Or had he totally shut down and reverted to survival mode?

He sucked in a slow, deep breath. 'I take full responsibility for what's happened in my life. It was entirely my own fault. I was the one who committed fraud, not you. I never should have agreed to do what we did.' He paused. 'But you need to take responsibility for your own life. And Hazel's life.'

'That's what I was trying to do. All I wanted was some bloody childcare!'

'No, you didn't. You're addicted to things that aren't real. You put up with that arsehole Adam for years because there was no chance you could ever actually feel something real for him.'

'Stop. Will. Stop.' I didn't need to hear all this. Not today.

'No, I'm not going to stop. I love Hazel, so I'm going to say my piece and then get the hell out of your life. The reason you felt so comfortable with our whole lie from the beginning was because it suited you to hide behind a lie. It suited you to have a fake dad for Hazel. To be my fake girlfriend. Because then, nothing had to be real. Because you're terrified of feeling anything real. Because then you'd have to admit to yourself that you shouldn't spend your whole life settling, that you're actually someone worth loving.'

Now I wanted to scoff, '*No, I wasn't.*' And in front of me was proof – the person who'd got to know me better than anyone, better than Camille, and Sofia, even. And I'd infiltrated his world and ruined his life. Just like I'd ruined my parents' lives.

'I'm really sorry about … everything.' It was the only thing I could think to say.

'I honestly thought that this whole … whatever we did, was the right thing to do. The moral thing to do,' he said.

'What?'

'I did the research before I agreed to our arrangement. Did you know single mums are more likely to suffer from mental illness and poverty than nearly any other group? I thought … I could give back. I thought I was doing the right thing. We do pro bono cases all the time, and I thought, how is this really any different?'

I stared at him in disbelief. 'I wasn't some charity case you took on! You did this to get ahead, because you wanted to make partner more than anything else. God, Will, you think that I'm addicted to things that aren't real. So are you! The chip on your shoulder is enormous. You think I don't believe that I deserve love. Well, maybe that's true. But at least I believe that I deserve to be happy. I might end up alone, but you'll end up miserable – stuck on this unforgiving and soul-destroying treadmill that's all wrong for you. And for what? To prove to your moronic relations that you're as good as they are. To show your bullies that you're a big man now? I don't get it. You're the smartest person I know. But when it comes to your own happiness, you're a total idiot.'

'I'm sick of being the punching bag when you're angry at other people but too scared to tell them what you think.'

'No, trust me, Will, right now I'm angry at you.'

'Right. Well … you've already made it crystal clear that you don't agree with my career choices, Zoe. And, guess what, you win – I no longer have a career.'

I stopped in my tracks, taking a deep breath. 'Surely, there's something you can do? Can you say there's been a misunderstanding? We were together, sort of, in the end – that's not a lie.'

'I didn't get parental leave because we were together, Zoe. I got it because I told Robert that I was Hazel's co-parent with plans to adopt her. And we don't have a single piece of paper to show any of that. We have nothing to back up our story. In fact, all we have is the opposite – a contract binding us to a lie.'

'Hazel loves you. And you've been a better father figure to her than half of those male lawyers at that stupid conference. I saw them all that weekend – they left their wives to do all the parenting. Surely, I can write a letter saying that you've done the work of a parent, or something?'

'It wouldn't be enough,' Will said.

'Adam might not be her biological father. We can get a test. And if it's not him we can begin the process of adoption. Fill out enough paperwork to convince your firm that we didn't lie. You can tell Robert that you weren't thinking straight when you spoke to him today – that we'd had a fight and you weren't in your right mind. Tell him that Adam's my jealous ex-boyfriend.'

He gave me a piercing look. He searched my face, as if trying to work out if I was hiding something. 'You think it's Adam,' he said. For the first time since I'd got home, there was a hint of emotion in his voice – resignation.

'How do you know?' I asked.

'Because I know you,' he said. 'And I can see on your face that you guess she's his. You've thought it for weeks. You avoided giving the doctor the donor's medical history when Hazel was in the hospital. I thought it was weird, but I didn't know why. But you already thought that Hazel was his daughter then, didn't you?'

I paused for a moment then nodded. 'She looks like him. I mean, not like a doppelganger or anything. But … in the last few months, I've started to see it, hints of him,' I said softly. 'I've seen Adam's baby photos – she's becoming more and more like him. It could be my mind playing tricks, but I don't think so.'

'That's why you got so upset when you thought a photo of Hazel was going to be in a newspaper?'

'I knew if he saw a photo of her, and saw what I saw, he probably would have worked it out. He's not as smart as you, but he's sharp.'

'You know he would have seen a photo of her one day. Or bumped into you guys?'

'I know. He saw her last night. And he was staring at her, trying to work it out,' I said, taking another deep breath to try to steady myself. 'I think I was just … in total denial.'

It was the truth, that I'd tried to ignore reality and what that meant for my life and Hazel's.

'And you let me do this whole … thing with you,' he said. 'When you knew that it could end like this.'

'I didn't think there was any chance it would. I'd convinced myself she was the donor's baby. I was going to keep the possibility that she wasn't all safely locked away. I'm … sorry,' I said. There was nothing else to say.

'Just to be clear, I don't give a shit that Adam is Hazel's dad. Who Hazel's dad is, is actually none of my business,' Will said. 'But you lied to me – again and again. And you let me tangle up my life, my dreams, with your lie because you were too afraid to confront reality. That's what's unforgivable.'

He walked back into the house, where Hazel was still absorbed in her show. I stood at the door, clinging to its frame, watching.

'Bye, Hazelnut. I love you and I'll miss you a lot.'

Hazel smiled at Will, oblivious to his sentiments. I swallowed an involuntary sob.

CHAPTER 32

For the next few days the world felt like it had come to a standstill. Somehow, I kept the wheels turning on our routine. I shampooed Hazel's hair and pulled it into a mohawk. I stroked her head while I fed her. I read *Spot* with silly voices. I changed and tucked her into bed for her naps.

In some ways, I was glad I had to keep moving, and I tried to engross myself in whatever task I was doing, tried to give my full attention to Hazel. But just when I thought I was succeeding, my imagination would take hold. I'd picture Will alone and trying to process what had happened, trying to get his head around the fact that the life he'd wanted, the one he'd fought so hard for, had been so tantalisingly close to getting, was all gone. Because of what we'd done.

And I had no idea where he'd gone – no lights had been on in his house since our fight. I liked to think he was on a well-deserved holiday, but I doubted it. Although I drafted a million messages to make sure he was okay, I hadn't actually sent any. No combination of words sounded right.

Finally, I sent a message to Charlie, who'd given me his number, and asked him to please check in on his friend. I needed to know that someone was looking out for him.

Thanks for letting me know. He's taking some time out. Hope you and Hazel are feeling better. Charlie, he replied.

I tried to reach out to Adam, but he still wouldn't return my calls or messages. I emailed his lawyer, agreeing to the DNA test, and booked an appointment.

I had no one to talk to. Every time I messaged Camille, she replied that she was snowed under at work and would call me later. But she never did. I knew that Sofia and Luka were home from the hospital, but she didn't need my misery puncturing her blissful baby bubble. And I couldn't bring myself to call Mum.

And so, it was just me and Hazel – exactly what I'd thought I'd wanted, the two of us back in our cocoon.

On Monday, I still felt numb, but I knew I had to get out of the house for Hazel's sake. I decided to take her to the music class Will had enrolled her in.

When Will had told me about the class, I'd imagined it would be at our local library, where parents would sit in an awkward circle and sing some nursery rhymes led by a slightly embarrassed librarian, while the babies lolled around obliviously on the carpet. That's what I would have signed up for.

But Will's commitment to excellence had extended to Hazel's extracurriculars. He'd found a class at the Melbourne University Conservatorium. Tramming into the city seemed like a faff, but I knew that Hazel needed more stimulation than another day at home could provide.

The music school, in the arts precinct on the edge of the city, was a squat red brick building. Students, almost invariably in head-to-toe black, streamed in and out, some holding instruments in cases.

Hazel, much more alert now that we'd finally left the house, stared at the procession of pierced, tattooed and dyed-hair students with interest. A few smiled at her, but we were invisible to most of them. I didn't blame them. It was only when I hit my thirties that I noticed babies were absolutely everywhere. The whole world was full of them.

I spotted two women with prams ahead. I guessed they were here for the same class and followed them into the foyer of a large auditorium, where a circle of cushions had been arranged on the scarlet carpet. Most of them were already occupied by women holding their babies and chatting.

'Is this one free?' I asked the pair I'd followed in, pointing to a spare cushion next to them.

'Yes,' one of them replied. She was effortlessly cool in black denim overalls, a white puff-sleeved shirt and sneakers. She was together. She'd got dressed and done her hair and makeup before she'd left the house. Her baby's socks matched. When she wasn't mothering, she was probably a neurosurgeon or similar. And she'd found the best class in the city for her child. No free local class at the library for her progeny.

'Hi, Hazel!' She seemed a bit confused. 'Where's Will today?'

'He's … I had the day off today. I'm Zoe. Her mum.'

The woman's eyes flicked from me and then to Hazel and then back again. 'She's a real mix of both of you,' she said.

I wanted to scream. Was everyone an expert on genetics? I couldn't escape it. Luckily, before I could think of a reply, a woman wearing a bright linen shift clapped her hands and began to sing.

I'd wanted to hate the class, but by the halfway mark, I had to admit that it was pretty fantastic. Its theme was 'Happy and Sad'. We'd danced along to Pharrell's 'Happy' and I'd almost exploded with pride when Hazel had clapped as we'd all warbled, 'When you're happy and you know it clap your hands.' She'd been the only one to do it. Had Will taught her that?

At the end of the class, the teacher pulled a violin out of its case. 'Now I'm going to play some music that might make you feel sad,' she said.

Did she have to? The happy music had made me feel, for the first time in the last few days, like the world wasn't going to end in spite of all evidence to the contrary.

She pulled the violin up to her chin and moved the bow along its strings. I gulped. It was 'The Swan' song. The one Will had played to me that night, which now seemed like a million years ago.

As the elegant, mournful tune filled the auditorium, I felt my eyes prickle with tears. Will had told me I reminded him of a swan because I was frantically trying to be everything to everyone. He'd been wrong – I'd failed to be anything to anyone. I'd let everyone down. Tears began to flow, pour really, down my face.

The cool mother in the black overalls gave me a concerned, sideways glance. I ran my sleeve across my face to dry my tears.

'Hormones,' I mouthed at her, and she nodded then turned back towards the music.

Happy and sad. Apparently, these concepts were so simple we could teach them to babies who hadn't even hit their first birthday. So, why was it such a struggle for me to work through these feelings?

Happiness. Snippets from the last few months flashed through my mind. No big moments, just lots of quotidian ones. Will and I both hysterically laughing when I dropped the pie he'd bought and it splattered all over the kitchen floor. We'd eaten the floor pie anyway, still giggling. Acerbic texts arriving in a steady stream throughout the day making me laugh out loud, as Will opined on the world and everyone he found annoying in it. Coming home from work to find Will giving Hazel her bath, not realising he was still wearing my shower cap to make her laugh. Hazel laughing – Will could always make her laugh. He'd pull a funny face or lift her onto his shoulders or tickle her left foot (not her right one) and she'd dissolve into peals of laughter. The most beautiful sound on earth. Far more glorious than anything that the teacher, no doubt an expert musician, could ever extract from her instrument.

Now I felt sad. And other things, too. All those emotions I'd kept under the surface for so long continued to bubble up. And for the first time in my life, I didn't push them back down under the surface and try to keep gliding along. I let myself feel them and it was awful. I felt angry – at Adam's self-righteousness, at Camille's repression. And guilty – at the damage my lies had caused. But mostly, I felt exposed. I'd spent so long hiding the truth from everyone – about what I wanted, the mistakes I'd made and the things I was afraid of. And now it was all out in the open.

We continued in this state of inertia for the next few days – long ones only punctuated by walks around our neighbourhood. I knew I needed to do adult things – contact recruiters, scour LinkedIn ads, email service providers and ask if I could defer payments. But I felt paralysed, with only the energy to cater to Hazel's minute-to-minute needs, nothing more.

On a rainy morning, I was sitting on my couch, while Hazel napped, staring at a blank Word document and willing it to magically become my CV, when my phone pinged.

Are you free this afternoon? I'm doing an event today and I'm worried about Sofia. It was from Morgan.

Sofia answered the door, holding a screaming Luka. Her hair was greasy and her face was washed out by exhaustion.

I'd assumed that she hadn't replied to my messages offering backup or answered my calls because she was inundated with help and company from Mary.

'Come in,' said Sofia, in a weary voice.

I'd guessed wrong.

CHAPTER 33

Sofia's apartment was a total mess. Laundry was piled high onto an armchair, coffee cups and plates with crumbs were scattered over the table and the floor, and the kitchen counter was filled with painkiller packets and empty water bottles.

'I know you might not want me here, but I can't not help. I brought you some things. I'll give them to you, then I'll leave if you want me to,' I said. Sofia seemed too drained to muster the energy to reply. 'Bad night?'

'Terrible,' she said, biting her lip, as Luka grizzled in her arms.

'Want me to have a hold?' I offered. I popped Hazel in front of Emma Memma on my phone, then Sofia handed him over.

'He hasn't stopped crying all morning. I don't know what to do. Maybe he's allergic to dairy. Do you think I should stop eating dairy? Or maybe it's coffee. I'm drinking one a day, which the nurse said was okay. But maybe it affects him more than other babies.' She was talking at a million miles an hour, careening from one thought to the next. I'd never seen her so wound up.

'Sit down, Sof,' I said gently. Luka's whimpers were getting quieter and quieter.

'He hasn't shut up all morning, and the minute you hold him he's happy,' Sofia said, her lips now quivering. 'I thought I'd be a natural at this, but I'm so crap.'

She burst into tears. I wanted to hug her, but Luka was now quiet and snuggled against me. And I didn't think that his cries would help the situation.

I didn't know what to say, or what would help. That she was doing amazingly. Or would that sound patronising? That she should speak to a doctor or nurse before she started to eliminate foods. That cutting out coffee might make things harder for her.

'It gets easier, I promise,' I said, after a pause. I knew she wouldn't believe me. I hadn't when Camille had told me the same thing. But she'd planted a little seed of hope, which had helped during the darkest, toughest moments.

'Did you tell me how hard this was?' Sofia asked. 'Or did I just not hear it.'

Had I? I'm sure I had told her a version of the truth, but maybe not the whole truth. First, because she'd been struggling with fertility issues when Hazel was born. But I'd also probably downplayed the tough bits because I wanted to seem like I was doing okay.

'I mean, I had such a great pregnancy. I thought that breastfeeding would be a breeze, too. But it's so bloody painful,' she said. 'My nipples are a battlefield. They're cracked and bleeding and lumpy. I dread feeding my own baby.' She sniffed and rubbed her nose on her sleeve.

'And Morgs was so helpful when he was on leave. But he's had to go back to work now, and it's so hard on my own all day – just feeling exhausted and broken.'

'Has your mum been around?' I asked. Mary had been so excited about being a grandmother. I thought Sofia would be complaining about too much help, not languishing on her own.

Sofia let out a frustrated sigh. 'She won't listen to me. She put Luka to sleep on his stomach wearing a million layers. And a beanie. And she got angry when I told her it was dangerous – that safety standards have changed in the last thirty years. We started fighting. It wasn't worth the help.'

I upturned my handbag onto the floor. 'Your nips are a mess?' I asked.

'Beyond a mess,' Sofia answered.

'I've brought a few packs of these absolutely magical nipple compresses. Whack one on each boob after every feed and they work like a dream. Electronic heat pack because I'm sure your shoulders and neck are aching like hell. I've brought some nipple shields – some nurses aren't a fan, but they're not the ones in excruciating pain. Lanolin cream. Ohhh … my breast pump and some bottles in case you wanted to express a feed.

'And I've brought some lollies – because sugar. I brought some of my breastfeeding pyjamas. And singlets …'

Sofia burst into another round of tears.

'I'm sorry. I didn't mean to upset you. I just wanted to help, so I put everything I could think of in here,' I said.

'I've wanted you here so much. But I was so blasé about having a baby – about how I'd be able to handle it, about how nothing would change. And look at me, I'm basically still at the mum starting line and I'm already a a total shit show.'

I cleared a path through the pile of stuff I'd brought then crawled over to Sofia and gave her an enormous hug.

'Shit. Your tits are rock hard! When's Luka due for a feed?'

'In an hour,' Sofia said, fear on her face.

'Okay. Here's what we're going to do. You're going to go and get in a scorching-hot shower. Take as long as you need until you feel human again. Then when you come back we're going to use the breast pump to express his next feed, to give your nipples a chance to heal. Then you're going to go have a nice long nap and Hazel and I will take charge of Luka.'

I helped Sofia up from the couch and led her to the bathroom.

A few hours later, Sofia stumbled into the living room.

'Is Luka okay?' she asked blearily.

'Totally fine. An absolute dream,' I said. He was sleeping in his pram bassinet and Hazel was napping in his cot.

While the babies slept, I'd cleaned up the place. And so when Sofia emerged, it looked like her apartment again. I'd also prepared a plate filled with the cookies and cakes I'd stress-baked throughout the week. My time with Will had weaned me off microwave meals – I now craved real food, albeit lately with as much sugar and chocolate in them as possible.

Sofia grabbed a cookie with each hand. 'I feel like a new person,' she said. 'Like my brain is less foggy.'

'No one feels human when they haven't slept for more than two hours in a row for days,' I said. 'Don't hate me, but I've booked an appointment for you with a lactation consultant. You can cancel it if you want. But, just in case.'

'I should have asked for your help earlier,' she said, tucking her still-damp hair behind her ears. 'I just couldn't admit that …'

'Hey, I get it.' I gave her another bear hug. 'And to cheer you up, I'm going to tell you a story that might help you feel like you have your shit together,' I said.

While Sofia ate, I filled her in on what had happened since she'd had Luka.

'Wow – you win. Your life is way more screwed up than mine. What a gift!' Sofia said with a grin when I'd finished. I threw a pillow at her.

'Are you okay? Have you heard anything else from Adam?'

I shook my head. 'We did the DNA test yesterday and now have to wait for the results. I've messaged and called him a million times. He hasn't replied. I check my emails a thousand times a day expecting another letter from his lawyers. And every time there's a knock on the door, I'm convinced it's going to be the Department of Human Services to accuse me of being a crap mother. So … I've had better weeks.'

'What's Will going to do now?' Sofia asked.

I shrugged. I didn't know, and perhaps I never would.

'You don't think you should see him? Or call him?' she asked.

I thought of all the times over the last week my finger had hovered over the dial button and shook my head. 'He'll never forgive me. What happened between us was just too … tangled and complicated. I think we both need to move on with our lives.'

I felt my throat constrict. I believed what I'd just told Sofia. But the idea that I'd never see him again seemed incomprehensible and made me feel winded, in desperate need of oxygen.

The four of us spent the rest of the afternoon curled up in Sofia's freshly made-up bed. We entertained Hazel, while Luka slept in his nest in the middle of us.

'Hey … I have an idea. You wanna dance?' I asked.

Sofia slowly nodded. I put on 'Rocket Man' and the two of us danced around her bedroom, with as much enthusiasm and laughter as our respective pelvic floors could handle, to our audience of two.

Morgan arrived home in the late afternoon. He peered around the bedroom door, sweaty and red-faced, with the fear-filled eyes of a man who didn't know what he'd find. Sofia smiled at him, and Morgan's shoulders dropped with relief.

'Thanks,' he mouthed at me, and I smiled back at him.

Luka began to make mewling sounds. Sofia gingerly picked him up from his nest and passed him to Morgan.

Before I realised what I was doing, I'd picked up Hazel off the bed and held her tightly against my now pounding heart. Suddenly, it felt like it was just the two of us in this bedroom, as if Sofia, Morgan and Luka had disappeared.

I gazed down at my daughter and took in her cheeky smile, enormous, inquisitive, bright-blue eyes, round, chubby cheeks, arms that were never still, mouth half-filled with teeth – she was my baby who wouldn't be a baby for much longer.

I'd made so many promises to her. I'd promised her it would just be the two of us. I'd promised her I would never let anyone leave her, that I would never let her be hurt. But seeing Sofia and Morgan with Luka, my almost-toddler against me, I realised that I'd got it wrong.

And it wasn't Morgan's face, full of fierce love, that had made my stomach tighten and my arms reach out towards my baby girl. No, I knew that I could love Hazel enough for two people. I'd never doubted that. She didn't need a father. She was surrounded by good men. That wasn't it.

It was the way Sofia handed Luka to Morgan that had rendered me breathless and turned the room sepia. She trusted him, completely, without hesitation, with this helpless thing she loved more than anything else in the world. I'd never been able to do that. I'd thought that I'd had to be enough for her.

I'd thought, I'd truly believed, that if I never properly let anyone into our little family of two, I could save her from our family legacy of being abandoned. The one that had ripped its way through Mum's life. The one that had dismantled mine.

But I wanted better than that for Hazel. I wanted her to have a life filled to the brim with love. I wanted her to be loved, by someone other than me, by as many people as possible.

So I realised, with a gulp and an even tighter squeeze of my daughter, that I needed to show her how to let people in, even if that meant accepting the risk that they could leave.

CHAPTER 34

Over the next couple of days I worked like a fury, Hazel by my side. I typed up a CV and arranged meetings with any recruiter who would talk to me. I rang Hazel's new childcare centre and asked Anh, the manager, if we could please keep our spot. I told her that I was a single mum and unexpectedly unemployed, though job hunting, but I'd pay whatever fees they charged. After weeks of free childcare from Will, I'd been able to save up a little – I could use it for this.

Anh, herself a single mum she told me, made a counteroffer – she agreed to hold the spot for a few weeks and told me that if I was job hunting then I was still eligible for a subsidy.

Then we ambushed Adam. We turned up at his apartment building on Friday afternoon, the day I guessed he'd be working from home. I knew it was a risky move, but Sofia agreed we needed to talk. And given he wasn't taking my calls or replying to my texts or emails, this was the only way I had a chance of catching him.

He answered the buzzer then let me in, I thought mainly because he couldn't bring himself to close the door on Hazel.

'We've done the DNA test. And there's a chance she's not yours. But I wanted to talk to you before the results come back.'

I let him process the news for a moment. He couldn't take his eyes off Hazel. It was the first time he'd properly seen her, in the light of day.

'I should have told you that you could be her biological father when you asked me. But I was scared. I didn't feel safe telling you the truth. Because that day, when you turned up at my house, I could see that you weren't really sure if you wanted her to be yours. And I wasn't sure that I should tell you the answer to the question you asked until you were sure what you wanted the answer to be.

'Because Hazel is the most incredible baby in the whole world – honestly, she's completely amazing. I love her more than anything and I will do everything to protect her. But I'll also do anything for her.'

I paused for a moment and gave Hazel a kiss on her head. She put her pudgy hand against her mouth and thrust it out again towards me and said, 'Mwaaah!'

I blew her a kiss back and turned to Adam.

'I came here the other week because what I wanted to hear was that you were glad that you hadn't had a baby with me. I wanted closure. But instead, you finally actually told me what you really felt about our relationship. And how you felt about a baby, or the possibility of a baby. And honestly, it really wasn't what I expected you to say.'

I took a deep breath. 'Look, I know we can do this through lawyers and go to court if we have to. And I know it's likely they'll think that you have a right to be part of Hazel's life. But it's not about your rights, and it's not about my rights. It's about Hazel and what she deserves. And I think she deserves a parent or parents who are all in. And being a parent is way more than biology. So, if you're her biological father, then Hazel needs you to be her real father and be all in.'

I finished my speech, the one that had been percolating in my mind for weeks. And not because I wanted it to sound impressive, or even convincing. But because I wanted to say what I absolutely believed – not what I thought anyone wanted to hear. I wanted to tell the truth – not a version of it.

Adam's focus was all on Hazel. He'd been staring at her the whole time I'd been speaking, and she'd also been watching him, interested by this new person. There was a silence between us. Then Adam cleared his throat.

'I did something stupid after you told me about you and Will Flemming pretending to be together,' he said.

'I know,' I said. 'After your call, Will spoke to his boss and told him the whole story. He lost his partnership and his job. His whole career, really.'

'Shit,' Adam said, pressing his fingers into his forehead. 'I didn't mean to actually screw things up for him. I was just … really pissed off that day.'

'I get it,' I said. 'But in spite of the whole pretending-to-be-in-a-relationship thing, Will has pretty strong views on what's right and wrong.'

'Is there anything I can do to fix it?'

'I don't think so.'

'Is he okay?'

'I don't know,' I said. 'Probably not.'

I felt my throat constricting as I tried to hold back the tears welling. I saw understanding cross Adam's face.

'Oh. You and him. That part was real.'

I nodded and blinked the tears away. 'It's over now. Obviously.'

'I'm really sorry for calling him, Zoe. This was between you and me, not him. It was a bloody childish thing to do.'

'It was,' I said.

He finally looked at me, dead on. 'You weren't totally wrong,' he said. 'That day when you were pregnant and I turned up and asked you if she was mine?'

'Yes.'

'I wasn't sure I wanted her to be mine that day. You were right about that,' he said. 'And I understand why you didn't want to trust me with her. After I basically dumped you without an explanation, after all those years together. I was so angry the other night. Partly because you didn't tell me the truth after I'd told you how I really felt. But mostly, I was … angry at myself. That because I was such an arsehole I missed the chance to be part of her life for almost a year.'

'It's not too late to be part of her life, Adam. But if you're her dad she needs you to be all in,' I repeated.

I could see that he was about to speak, but I interrupted him.

'Don't say anything now. Just think about it. Please.'

He nodded. 'Can I … hold her?'

'Hey, muffin. Do you want to have a cuddle with Adam?' I asked, then handed her to him. I knew that soon separation anxiety would kick in and she'd begin to fear strangers. But for now, she happily settled into his arms.

Adam held her like she was made of porcelain, an expression of total wonder on his face.

'What if I'm not good enough for her?' he asked, in a voice so soft it was almost a whisper.

'I ask myself that a lot, too.'

CHAPTER 35

The next morning, I bundled Hazel into the car before her nap. After two hours of driving, and one hour of blaring hideously upbeat music in a desperate bid to entertain her, we arrived in Bendigo.

I drove through the centre of the town, past the bank branch where Mum worked and down the promenade of grand Victorian buildings into the suburbs. Her car was parked outside the house. She was home.

I knew I had to have this conversation, but as I knocked on the front door with Hazel on my hip, my confidence wavered. Maybe we could just say hi and be on our way …

No. There were questions I needed to ask. Things I needed to say. And the time to do this was now.

Mum opened the door in an old pair of flared tracksuit pants and a fleece covered in flowers – one of her classic weekend outfits.

'Well, this is a surprise,' she said. I was pretty sure she didn't mean it was a good one. I willed her to reach out and grab Hazel from me, like Will's mum had.

'Hello, Hazel. Aren't you a big girl,' she said. It was the kind of innocuous comment you made when you encountered a baby in the street, not your own flesh and blood. She waved a hand, held close to her body, at her granddaughter.

Mum made us both a cup of tea and then led us through to her gloomy, south-facing living room. I perched on one of the floral tapestry couches and surveyed Mum's domain. She had been renting this house for almost five years, but I'd only visited a handful of times. The room was filled with furniture that seemed barely used. A remote sat on top of a neatly folded newspaper on the side table. I guessed Mum only used it in the evenings after work.

'I wanted to talk to you about … Dad,' I said.

She raised an eyebrow and pressed her lips together. We'd barely ever talked about him, growing up, and it was clear she didn't particularly want to start now. My heart was pounding so hard I wondered if Hazel, against me, could feel it?

'Did he leave because of me?'

'What?' She appeared genuinely surprised. 'Of course not!'

I carefully sat Hazel down on the faded carpet and scattered toys around her, giving myself a moment to work out what to say next. I couldn't shy away from these questions. I needed to know the truth, whether the story I'd told myself my whole life was real. Pulling myself back up to the couch, I faced Mum again.

'I need to know, Mum. Was it my fault?'

'What are you talking about? You were a young child when he left. How could anything have been your fault?'

'I just always felt that it was. I mean, he left on my first day of school.'

She froze. I thought she was going to stand up and leave the room. Then she shuffled up the couch towards me and pulled my hands into hers. I noticed that they were now the hands of an older woman – the skin over her bones was thinner and marked with sun spots.

'He left because of me, because of our relationship.' Her voice cracked slightly. 'He stayed for so long because he loved you so much.'

I let what she said sink in. Had Mum known this, thought this, my whole life?

'But he barely saw us after he left.'

'I … was very angry after he went. I didn't make it easy for him to see you two.'

She held my stare, but I could see a flicker of apprehension in her eyes. Her clasp on my hands loosened.

'What?'

'He chose to move to another state with another woman. And he was terrible at paying child support,' she said, now slightly more defiant. 'But … I still made things more difficult than they needed to be.'

'So, Dad did want to see more of us?'

She paused for a moment and then nodded.

I pulled my hands away from her, feeling a flicker of anger spark, in the same spot where I'd always felt shame.

'And then you left, moved here as soon as I finished school. Like you couldn't wait to get away from us,' I said. 'It made me feel like … I'm the kind of person people want to leave.' My lip wobbled and I bit it. I needed to hold it together.

'I got a new job. I thought … you were grown up …

you didn't need me anymore. I'd raised you both to be independent.'

I stared at her, searching her face for any trace that she didn't believe her own words. Did she really think that just because I'd turned eighteen I'd stopped needing my mum? Obviously, I could make my own way in the world then – look after myself, earn my own money. But I'd still needed her.

I could see her pointed chin, Camille's chin, begin to drop. Her bright-blue eyes – the same colour as mine and Hazel's – began to fill with tears. But now I couldn't stop, even if I'd wanted to.

'And since I had Hazel, I've needed you more than ever. There have been so many times when I just wanted my mum. But you've avoided me, you've avoided us.

'I know how hard it is doing it on your own. And I know that it's impossible to be a perfect parent. I've already screwed up a million times. But I would never abandon Hazel. I would never let her feel like she's not wanted.

'Jesus. You kept Dad away from us to punish him. I've spent decades thinking it was my fault that our family fell apart. *Never rely on anyone* – you taught us that like it was gospel. I tried to do that with a newborn and almost fell to pieces. I needed you, Mum. When I barely got any sleep and thought I was going to go crazy. When I needed a few hours to have a shower and buy food. When I was so dehydrated that I had to go to the hospital and was put on an IV drip.

'Camille's done her best to fill the gap, but she's driving herself into the ground trying to do everything. She needs you, too. We both do. You're our mum.'

I kneeled down on the floor and began to stuff Hazel's toys back into the nappy bag.

'I thought I could protect Hazel from ever feeling the way you made me feel. But it didn't work. It just made things worse,' I said.

Mum didn't say anything, she just stared at me. Then she sucked in a gulp of air, lifted her chin and straightened her spine. I stiffened. She was going to deny it. She was going to tell me that I was a big girl who'd made a grown-up decision and where did I get off insulting her, expecting too much.

Then she exhaled and her head fell into her hands.

'I'm sorry,' she said softly, into her palms. And I knew then that I hadn't been imagining it – she had been avoiding me.

I didn't reply. I'd said everything I'd come here to say – everything that had been swirling around, making me put up barriers between my heart and the world, for decades.

She slowly lifted her face and looked at me straight on. I held my breath.

'It's just – you, being a single mum. It … when I saw the two of you together, it was like I was reliving … those years.'

Hazel, who'd been happily playing with a ball, wailed as it rolled under the table. Before I could move, Mum leaped up, crouched under the table, then sat down next to Hazel and handed her the toy.

'Those years, after your dad left, were so tough. I didn't want to … remember,' Mum said. 'I always felt like I was a terrible mum when you were both little. Too busy, too cold, too selfish. I thought the best thing I could do was stay out of your lives.'

I began to breathe again.

'Your name is her middle name. I've always wanted you in my life, in Hazel's life, Mum,' I said. And before she could say anything else, I picked up Hazel and left.

CHAPTER 36

That evening, I knocked on Camille's door. She answered dressed up in one of the floaty dresses she loved but rarely got a chance to wear. She'd done her hair and her makeup and seemed uncharacteristically excited rather than flat-out stressed.

She looked confused when she saw me and Hazel on her doorstep.

'Um … did I forget you were coming? Ed and I are going out for a date night.'

Ed appeared behind his wife, his expression sheepish. 'Actually, that's not exactly the plan. Um … Zoe wants to take you out. I'm staying home with all the kids,' he said.

'What? But you told me …'

'We'll go out another time. Zoe wants to talk to you. Please, Camille, I'd really like you to go,' Ed said.

I'd called Ed on the drive back into the city and it turned out he'd been just as worried about Camille as I was.

'Okay, fine.' Camille relented.

I'd booked a table at a bar. As soon as we were seated, I ordered a bottle of wine.

'Will told Robert everything and lost his job. He's also

reported himself to the Law Institute,' I said. 'I'm sorry I put you in a compromised position.'

'His career will be over,' Camille said, and I nodded.

'I suppose envy isn't a normal reaction to that?'

'Probably not,' I said carefully. 'You … wouldn't mind if your career just disappeared?'

A waiter deposited the wine bottle on our table, and I poured us both two large glasses.

'No, I would. I really love my job, I love being a lawyer,' she said. 'But I feel like I'm wound up so tight that I can't enjoy anything anymore. Everything feels hollow. I can't enjoy the work. I can't enjoy time with Ed and the kids. Holding everything together the whole time is just so … excruciatingly exhausting. I have nothing left in the tank.'

'I know,' I said.

'The stuff you said to me the other week, about not letting myself feel anything, and hiding behind perfection …'

'It wasn't a helpful time to say it,' I said.

'But it's true.'

'I know,' I said.

'I'm sorry about all that stuff I said at the baby shower. I was resentful, but it was about Ed and our lives, not about you. Well, it was a bit about you. But mainly my marriage. I saw Morgan more than pulling his weight, and Sofia just so content, and I was green with jealousy. And I guess that day was the straw that broke the camel's back.'

'Honestly, I'm surprised you lasted this long before you cracked. Will, who's now separately done both the jobs you do at once, was impressed too. It's a real testament to your threshold for being miserable.'

Camille smiled as she took a small sip of her wine.

'I bought you something,' I said. 'But don't bite my head off, okay?' I handed her a small present.

She slowly pulled off the wrapping paper. 'A game?' she asked, confused.

'Sort of,' I said. 'I read about this online. It's this system called Fair Play. Every task that a family needs to function is on a separate card in this pack. And then you work out which tasks are relevant and fairly divide them up between a couple. The person holding that card is responsible for that job from start to finish.

'For example, if Ed's holding the "Extracurricular activities", card then he's responsible for finding a swimming class for the twins, enrolling them, buying bathers and towels and taking them there each week. The whole lot. You won't have to think about it at all. You can have that mental space freed.'

I braced, not quite sure how Camille would react. She picked up the bottle of wine and refilled our glasses.

'That's really … thoughtful,' she said. 'As subtle as a sledgehammer, but thoughtful.'

'Speaking of sledgehammers,' I barrelled on. 'I went to see Mum this morning. And three decades' worth of anger poured out of me. I told her I'd needed more from her.'

'What did she say?'

'I left before she could really say anything.'

'How do you feel?'

'Lighter. Naked,' I said. 'I spent so many years believing I wasn't angry at her, I really thought that. But it was all bubbling away, metastasising under the surface. And occasionally, it would surface, but I didn't know what it was. So, I mainly just dealt with it by having a ridiculous feud with my neighbour.'

'I'm sorry. I tried to … fill her shoes for you. But I didn't do a good enough job.'

'You've been amazing. Having a newborn isn't a one-person job. And all those times you stayed over with me so I could get some sleep. I would have lived on cereal if you hadn't filled my fridge. I would have fallen to pieces over the last year without you. I may have always wanted Mum to be there, but I was so lucky to have you. You've got to stop being so hard on yourself. You've got to stop trying to do all the parts of your life perfectly.'

Camille's thin lips began to wobble. 'I thought if I was … good enough, she'd … come back to us,' Camille said. 'I worked my guts out at school and university. I got the law degree and the fancy grad job. I climbed up the ranks and made partner. I have an entire pro bono practice helping women like her who were left without enough money and resources. I always thought that if I got the next shiny thing she might … notice, care. And then I married the guy and had the kids – one of each – and took out the enormous mortgage on the fancy house.'

She twisted a pearl earring with her fingers. 'Trying harder, putting in more effort, isn't going to make anyone love me more, is it?'

I shook my head.

'And I get it. I see women in her shoes all the time. Left by their husbands for another woman. Not enough money and without the skills to earn a decent wage. It's …' she searched for the perfect word, 'fucked.'

I laughed.

'I was older than you. I saw her fall to bits and retreat into herself. I think for years, she shut down because she had to. But then she chose not to reboot,' she said. 'And I'm sympathetic, but I can't just shut away all the other feelings, too. Because I'm also … a bit broken by it.

'And I'm sorry I minimised your pain. I realise I was basically gaslighting you. But I just … if I acknowledged your feelings I knew that I'd actually have to deal with my own. And it was way easier to hide behind the pursuit of perfection.'

She picked up the bottle again, and poured the remainder of the wine across our two glasses. Mine was filled almost to the brim.

'So, I give up. I give in,' she said. 'I choose mediocrity. And happiness.'

'The twins love you for being you. That's all they want. And Mum would be lucky to be part of your life on your worst, most unproductive, least perfect day.'

A waitress stopped by our table and collected the empty wine bottle. 'Would you like another one?' she asked.

'We're okay,' I said.

'I want shots. Could we please get a round of shots? Tequila!'

I raised an eyebrow, but Camille wasn't joking.

'I want to get drunk. I can't remember the last time I had more than a single glass. Or did anything fun,' she said. 'Will you get drunk with me?'

'I mean, yes. You know I love a good session,' I said. 'But are you sure that's what you want to do?'

She reached across the table and held my hands. 'I know I have a lot of repressed emotions. And I know a few shots won't undo years of my metamorphosis into an uptight control freak. I will get a mental health plan on Monday and see a therapist, even though that's my idea of hell. But tonight I just want to get drunk. With you. Are you in?'

'I've left Ed with lots of formula. I'm in!'

The first round of shots that Camille ordered was not the last. By the time we left the bar, our table was covered with salt and bitten-into lemon wedges, and the only food we'd eaten were the olives in our martinis.

'I'm sorry I didn't tell you about the donor. I was really proud that I was choosing to make a family following my own rules. I wanted to be a proud solo mum by choice. But then on one stupid night, I stuffed it up. And I was just … so ashamed of myself and felt so guilty.'

'I'm always here for you no matter what mistakes you make. Always will be,' she said. 'Hey. And I didn't mean to be flippant about Will before. About his job. I am sorry that's how it ended.'

'I feel so terrible.'

'It's not your fault. He was the one who lied to his work, not you.'

'I'm the one who talked him into it. And I'm the reason he felt the need to tell his work. I just … want to know he's okay.'

'You should talk to him.'

'He won't want to talk to me. He made that very clear.'

'I'm not sure that's true. Sofia said he was pretty into you.'

'You spoke to Sofia?'

'I was worried about you,' Camille said. 'I wasn't ready to talk, but I wanted Sofia to know that I was here for you. And to make sure that you went to see Adam.'

'I did.'

'How'd it go?'

'If I end up in court I'll have the best family lawyer on my side.'

She raised her glass and I clinked mine against it. Liquid sloshed out of both.

Camille suddenly burst out laughing. 'I forgot it's Father's Day tomorrow. I have to be up early to get lunch ready.'

'That's tomorrow? No, Camille, I can't see Mum tomorrow.'

'She's not coming. She cancelled this morning.'

'After I saw her?'

'It must have been.'

'You should cancel lunch.'

'There are four kilos of lamb sitting in my freezer. I've already set my alarm so I'm awake in time to slow-roast it.'

'Leave it there. Cancel the alarm. We'll order pizza! *I'll* order pizza.'

'But I want Ed to have a special day.'

'He won't care whether there's lamb or not. It doesn't need to be perfect to be special. Lower the bar. Let us help.'

She stared at me for a moment and then grinned.

*

As I was getting ready to leave for Camille's lunch, there was a knock on the door. For a moment, I felt a jolt of hope in case it was Will. But I knew it wouldn't be.

I opened the door.

'I'm all in,' Adam said without preamble. 'No lawyers. Just us trying to figure out what's best for Hazel. What do you think?'

'Okay,' I said. 'Come in.'

Hazel, who was happily finger-painting with the remnants of her yoghurt on the highchair tray, smiled at him when he entered the kitchen.

'We're running late for something. I have to finish getting ready. Do you think you could watch her for a sec?'

Adam nodded. From the hallway, I saw him bending over to talk to her. He grabbed a piece of paper towel and began to gently dab at her mouth, which was ringed with food.

I sat on my bed, feeling winded, like someone had punched me in the stomach. I didn't move for as long as I could bear, then returned to the kitchen. Hazel was now playing on the floor with Adam.

'Happy first Father's Day,' I said. 'In spite of our track record of terrible timing, at least the results came before today.'

'The results?' He looked confused.

'You haven't got them yet?' He shook his head.

Reaching down into my bottom drawer, I pulled out the folded piece of paper sitting on top of the pile, then handed it to him.

CHAPTER 37

Adam took the piece of paper with slightly shaking hands.

I'd received the results of the DNA test late Friday afternoon by email. I thought he'd have received them, too – Adam's law firm had also been copied in. But the email must have arrived after end-of-week drinks had begun.

He carefully opened the piece of paper and read the results.

'It's real. She's mine. She's ours,' he said, his voice full of joy with an undercurrent of shock.

'Hazel has something for you, too. A Father's Day present.' I pulled a thick envelope out of the same drawer and handed it to Hazel. She clasped it in her pudgy hands, then handed it back to me.

'Muffin, can you give it to Adam?' I pointed at him. She now understood the game and thrust it at him.

'Thank you, Hazel,' he said, gently taking it from her and gingerly opening it.

I'd filled it with photos of Hazel – from the first nine months of her life, or longer really because I'd included copies of all her scans. I'd planned to give Will a photo in a nice frame as a thank you at the end of The Arrangement, and had gone a bit mad with the printing.

'Thank you,' he said, without taking his eyes off the

photo he was staring at – the first one taken of the two of us, the one a nurse had snapped only moments after she was born. He slowly flicked through the pile of photos and then carefully slipped them into the envelope.

'I love her already, I promise you I do. And I want her. I want to be her dad, a really great one. And I'll always be there for her, always.' He looked up at me, from where he was kneeling on the floor next to Hazel. 'Zoe, will you let me be part of her life?'

I stared at him for a moment. 'Yes. I will.'

Camille answered the door in active wear.

'Sorry! We all slept in, even the twins. I feel like absolute death!'

Her hair was scraped into a bun and her only makeup was last night's mascara under her eyes. The twins were both in their pyjamas flopped in front of the TV watching *Bluey*. Instead of preparing a picture-perfect lunch, she'd enjoyed a slow morning with her family. That alone made my hangover worthwhile.

She led me to the kitchen where the Fair Play cards I'd given her were spread out on the table. 'Rubbish', 'Weeknight dinners', 'Extracurricular activities', 'Medical appointments', 'Thank you cards' – one giant paper patchwork of Camille's current mental load.

'Zoe, you're here!' Ed said.

'You've already started. And on Father's Day,' I said, catching Ed's eye and suppressing a smile.

'No time like the present!' Camille was the happiest I'd seen her around Ed in … well, since they'd had the twins. 'I read up on it this morning. It's actually really smart – just applying simple organisational management principles to the proper functioning of a household.'

'So, who's got what jobs?' I asked.

'We were just about to do that part,' Camille said with a small frown.

No wonder Ed had been so pleased that I'd turned up when I had.

'We'll do it after lunch,' Ed said, placing two mugs of coffee in front of us. 'Now, I might just pop into my study and leave you guys to chat.'

I'd barely had my first sip before a sports match began to blare from Ed's study.

'I really think this is the answer,' Camille said, with the zeal of a convert.

'Sounds amazing,' I said, trying to match her enthusiasm.

'And pizza was a great idea. Ed loves pizza. Much better than lamb. And I know you said you'd order them, but it's super easy just to whip up a base using Greek yoghurt and flour. And I just chopped up some things we had in the fridge.'

A tray of homemade pizza bases rested on the spotless bench, a vat of fresh tomato-and-basil sauce simmered on the stove and a row of matching Marimekko bowls filled with chopped-up capsicum, ham and cheese were in a straight line.

'I thought the kids could make their own. They might make a bit of a mess, but it'll be fun!' Camille said. 'Because things don't always have to be perfect.'

'Grandma Julie's here.' Arti appeared at the kitchen door with Mum a few steps behind him.

'Mum!' Camille bounced up. 'I thought you weren't coming.'

'I wasn't,' Mum said. 'Then … I was hoping I could talk to you girls.'

'Lead the way back to the TV, Arti. We're going to absolutely obliterate your screen-time limits today!' Ed appeared and ushered her out of the kitchen. Camille and I were left alone with Mum.

'Can I get you anything? A drink? A homemade pizza?' Camille asked.

'No. I'm fine, thanks,' Mum replied. 'I just wanted to talk to you girls.'

'Okay,' I said. I wasn't overwhelmed by the same bubbling anger that had consumed me yesterday. Maybe it was the hangover, or maybe it was because I'd finally said what had been buried for so long, but today I just felt wrung out. Lighter, but also emotionally exhausted.

'I just came to say I'm sorry. To both of you,' Mum said. She was looking older than the picture of her I held in my mind. Her lipstick ran into the creases around her mouth and her blonde hair was awash with greys. 'It was hard to hear what you said yesterday, Zoe, because it was all true. I put up a drawbridge after your dad left and I never let it down again.

'I told myself that it was okay – that I was teaching you independence, to be self-reliant. Except … of course you were meant to rely on me.

'I am unbelievably proud of both of you. You went and got everything I only dreamed of – good degrees and jobs. And you're both wonderful mothers.'

Camille suddenly burst into a high-pitched wail. It was a visceral cry from somewhere deep.

'Sorry,' she blubbered. 'It's just … I'm really hungover.'

Mum sat down next to Camille and gently stroked her arm while she sobbed. As Camille's breathing returned to normal, I sat silently at the other end of the couch.

'If you'll let me I'd like another chance to do better. I'd like to help you girls. And be a better grandmother.'

'That would be good. The kids would love that. I'd love that,' Camille said, between sniffs.

'Zoe?' Mum turned around to face me.

'Would you give us a hand with the pizzas? We're both a little … wobbly today,' I said. 'And Happy Second Mother's Day, Mum.'

She had done the work of two parents during most of our childhood, so why not double the recognition? The day had been invented by a greeting-card company – of course we could make it whatever we wanted it to be.

'Oh, that was just something I made up for you kids so you wouldn't get upset that your dad wasn't around. I don't need a stupid, made-up day! Now let's go make some pizzas.'

I raised an eyebrow at Camille behind Mum's back and she shrugged. We both giggled.

While Mum manoeuvred around the kitchen helping the kids make up their own lunch, Ed poured each of us a glass of champagne, while Camille and I sat at the table.

And I knew it would all be okay. I could forgive Mum, and myself. And I might not have a manny, but I was no longer doing this on my own.

CHAPTER 38

'Shit!' I yanked at the strap on the car seat and it finally loosened. Slipping Hazel out, I scooped up her overflowing nappy bag with my spare arm.

Cars converged upon the car park, toddlers and parents spilling out of them.

'Ready for an adventure, Hazel!' I said. Six weeks after The Arrangement had abruptly ended, it was Hazel's second first day of childcare and I definitely wasn't emotionally ready, still. But I never would be. And this place was amazing. Last week, we'd completed the orientation and I knew that she'd be happy here. The place felt like childhood – all bright colours, controlled mess and a duck and a chicken in the enormous outdoor play area.

She'd cried when I'd left her for her orientation. And I'd bawled in the car on the way home. But today, as I handed her over to the educators in charge of the baby room, there were no tears.

Anh stood at the reception entrance greeting all the families.

'Our newest family!' she said, when she saw me.

'Thanks for having us.'

'Your application was very compelling! It showed a real commitment to community spirit,' Anh said.

All I'd done was fill out a basic form online, sent Will on a tour and called them every few weeks for an update. My vibe had definitely been more desperation than community spirit.

'What do you mean?' I couldn't help asking.

'You volunteered to help out with the centre's marketing. We'd love to get you involved in our newsletter. You work as a copywriter, right?' she said, seeing my confused expression.

I nodded. 'That's my background.'

She pulled out a sheet of paper from the file she was holding and handed it to me. It was a printout of an email.

Dear Anh,

Thank you for your time on the phone and for the update on Hazel's application.

We are so impressed by the work you are doing for our community that we would like to make a donation to be used for something fun for the kids – a sandpit or some play equipment?

Hazel's mother, Zoe, is very experienced in marketing. As a member of your community, she would love to put her many skills to good use if that would be of assistance.

We look forward to hearing in the future if a space becomes available.

Yours sincerely,

Will Flemming

I suppressed a giggle. What Will had done was just short of bribery. Actually, it pretty much was bribery. But it had worked.

I wondered how much Will had donated. Enough to secure a coveted spot here, evidently.

I reread the email. Perhaps it wasn't the donation. Will had also offered up my skills. And Anh seemed keen to get me involved. Had that tipped the scales? Or maybe it was the cold, hard cash. Whatever it was, I was grateful.

I felt a familiar pang of sadness. The one that swallowed me up whenever I thought of Will.

When the dust had settled, I'd finally told Camille and Sofia how I really felt about him. How I'd fallen head over heels for a geeky, competitive, generous, kind man who'd made my now broken heart turn to mush. About how I'd been sleeping with my enemy, had made a total mess of everything and had destroyed any chance we ever had together.

'I told myself so many things that weren't true. That he ruined my birthday party. That he was an arrogant arsehole. That he could never be interested in someone like me. That I couldn't risk falling in love. And none of them were true.'

'Are you sure there's no hope?' Camille asked.

'He's the most stubborn man alive,' I said.

'Maybe you're wrong about this, too?' Sofia suggested. 'He called me.'

I stared at her, my heart beginning to pound.

'No, not since everything combusted,' she said. 'He called me about that newspaper story. His boss was being an arsehole and refusing to call the journalist to have the bits about you and Hazel removed because it made the firm seem so progressive. He'd promised you he'd fix it, so he wanted to know if they'd pull the story about you if he offered the journalist another one, instead.'

'What story?' I asked.

'I can't tell you the details – he told me in confidence. But it would have been a disaster for his firm – it was about the unsafe working conditions of their junior overworked lawyers, and would have ended his career for sure. And in the end, his boss agreed to make the call so it all went away.'

Will had been prepared to destroy his own career, to throw himself on his sword, to protect me and Hazel? He'd always felt that we were more important. And I hadn't trusted him.

I felt guilty using a childcare spot when I didn't have a job. But Sofia had told me to pull my head out of my arse. And Camille had backed her up.

'Finding a great job is a full-time job!' Sofia had said. When I'd confessed that I secretly wondered if I could do something more with my career, they'd been thrilled. Camille spent far too much of her limited free time doing practice job interviews with me. And Sofia tapped into her vast network of creative people and arranged a stack of coffee catch-ups so I could network.

Before I'd even told them I was worried about money, I got a message from Camille. I've transferred you cash. It's a loan and I know you'll be good for it, but no hurry. Don't have an existential crisis about it.

Obviously I had an existential crisis, but in the end I accepted it. My hand was forced when Hazel and I were evicted from our cottage.

I finally had worked up the courage to ask our landlord to make some repairs to the house. The next day, we were given a Notice to Vacate. Camille told us that this was totally illegal and she was happy to help me fight it, but I didn't want to. It was time for us to move on.

We moved into Sofia's building. She'd called me one day to say that a small ground-floor apartment was up for lease. I'd been reticent. I didn't want to impinge on her life. But she'd insisted and put in a good word for us with the owner.

And so far, it was going well. The apartment was tiny, but I was used to tiny. We had a small courtyard where Hazel could crawl around, and the apartment was filled with wonders like air-conditioning and a reliable oven. We were far enough away from our old house for a new start, but still close enough to our old world.

And Sofia and I were able to help each other out. Whenever she had an appointment or was exhausted, I could pop up and watch Luka. We'd go for long walks together on slow afternoons and often have a glass of wine before the chaos of dinner, bath and bedtime shift began.

I hadn't seen Will again before we'd moved. As we were packing, an auction board had gone up on his front fence. He was selling.

I missed him. I thought that moving away from his house would provide closure. But he'd become so entwined in our lives that the smallest things, like Hazel's farmyard books or her music class, reminded me of him.

When she did something ridiculous, I'd make a mental note to tell him, before remembering what had happened. When Hazel began to stand, I felt an urge to send him a video. But I couldn't.

I readjusted my beautiful new silk dress shirt. It fitted perfectly – not an elastic band in sight. Camille had insisted on taking me shopping and had spoiled me. It felt good to be wearing something that wasn't straining to fit a body I didn't have anymore, and maybe wouldn't have again.

Checking the clock on the dashboard, I took a deep breath and reversed out of the car park. I had plenty of time to get across town for the job interview. I really wanted this one – head of content at a real estate listings website. Camille and I had worked through the job description and she'd convinced me I was absolutely qualified for it. And Sofia had rustled up Alison, the sister of one of her dance-class friends who worked at the company, so I could get the inside track.

'Sofia said you have a baby?' Alison asked me when we'd met up for a coffee. She was slightly older than me and nailing a tech casual outfit in light denim jeans, a crisp white T-shirt and layered fine gold jewellery.

I'd nodded, though not too enthusiastically – I'd planned to very much hide this fact during the job-hunting process.

'The company is properly flexible – working from home, job sharing, part-time – they take it really seriously.'

I raised a cynical eyebrow before I remembered I was trying to impress her.

'You've been burned before? At one of those "family-friendly" businesses – unless you actually have a family?'

'I was, yeah,' I admitted.

'Been there, got the T-shirt when I had my first. I promise you, this place walks the walk,' she said with a friendly smile. 'How old is she?'

Our coffee went far longer than the half-hour it was scheduled for as we went back and forth chatting about our kids. Then Alison's phone lit up and she noticed the time.

'Shit – I have to race to pick up the kids. Don't get me started on the madness of childcare pick-up!'

Will sprang, as he often did uninvited, into my mind.

'I'll put in a good word for you,' she said as we left the cafe together. 'I think you'd be perfect for that role.'

I thanked her and really hoped that what she said was true. Although, I suspected that she was eager to go into bat for me not just because she thought I'd be a good fit, but because she wanted to help another mum get ahead in the world.

After the interview, with time before I had to collect Hazel, I sat in a cafe then opened up my laptop and began to type.

The Love Contract

[Note to Will: It's actually, according to Camille, a deed poll, not a contract, because it's a set of one-way promises from me to you. But 'Love Deed Poll' just didn't sound right, so we're going to roll with it being a contract, okay?]

Recitals: The purpose of this agreement is for Zoe to tell Will how she really feels.

My fingers flew over the keyboard as I wrote sections one ('Apology') and two ('Thank you'). The words poured out of me. Then I reached the next one – the headline section – and paused.

Section 3 – Love

(1) Zoe promises that she now knows:

(a) she is worthy of love and that's what she deserves ('Real Love');

(b) she won't settle for anything less than Real Love;

(c) if she can't have Real Love, she'd rather be on her own;

(d) but not because she's hiding from anything.

[Note to Will: I know you won't like this legal drafting, but the greatest artists take a form and experiment and make it their own, okay?]

I took a deep breath and kept typing.

(2) Zoe loves Will because:

(a) he's got the zippiest, most curious brain possible (and nerds are v. hot);

(b) he's funny (in like a sharp, good-mean way);

(c) the piccolo is actually the sexiest instrument;

(d) anything he does he does well (cf. he went from being terrified of babies to making one – the best one – feel cared for, safe and loved);

(e) beneath the muscles and the tan and the twinkly eyes and the floppy hair, is a truly kind guy (don't roll your eyes, it's true); and

(f) you make me feel like the most me version of myself and I want to help you to be the you-est version of you, while wanting to be together with you.

I reread what I'd written and then pressed 'save' before I could overthink it, or delete it. Then I changed the font to Comic Sans and inserted a clip-art cartoon of a judge banging a gavel. I hoped, at the very least, it would make Will laugh.

I attached the document to an email and kept typing.

Subject: Final draft – The Love Contract
From: Zoe.Harper@gmail.com
To: William.Flemming@flemming.com

Hi Will,
I'm not sure where you are, but wherever it is I hope you're well.

Please find attached the final version of The Love Contract, for your records. Because I love you. And if you can't say it with a contract, how can you say it?

I've also attached the invitation to Hazel's first birthday party/our new building's Christmas party in a few weeks. I'm going old school – think fairy bread, Cheezels and mini-Frankfurts. If you want to come I'll even let you have a lolly bag.

We miss you.

X Zoe

It was time to collect Hazel. I pressed 'send'.

CHAPTER 39

I'd meant for Hazel's first birthday party to be low key, I really had. But it had sort of… escalated. Particularly when Sofia and I had combined it with our small apartment building's inaugural Christmas party.

Because it felt like something worth celebrating. We'd done it. We'd made it. It hadn't exactly been how I'd envisaged, but here we were, and Hazel was happy and healthy.

I'd been manically watching the weather forecast all week. It had threatened rain, which was problematic as the backup venue for our local park was my apartment. And I'd lost count of how many people I'd invited. But the weather gods had looked benevolently on us – it was a crisp, sunny summer's day with no clouds in sight.

I surveyed our handiwork. A rainbow of helium balloons were tied to every inanimate object in the area. One table heaved with the party food that Camille and I had stayed up far too late making – sausage rolls and Christmas-tree-shaped ginger biscuits. Another was filled with drinks in tubs of ice and an enormous unicorn cake that Sofia had helped me decorate. Morgan had created a Christmas tree-esque creation out of wire, native foliage and red banksia, and

Mariah Carey crooned from a speaker sitting next to a vat of mulled wine.

People would begin to arrive at any moment. I pulled a bottle of champagne, a nice expensive one I'd sprung for, out of my handbag.

'Guys, before everyone arrives – a toast!' I passed a filled plastic flute to Camille and Sofia, who'd helped me set up.

'I just wanted to say – thank you. Hazel and I couldn't have done this past year without you two.' I raised my glass. 'To our village.'

'The village!' We clinked our glasses.

Camille took a big gulp. She was lighter than usual. Over the last three months, we'd spent many evenings together talking about our childhood over a bottle of wine. There had been a lot of tears.

And she seemed to have given herself a permission slip to enjoy her own life again. She'd pulled back at work a bit, which meant she could spend more – silly – time with the twins. And it had helped that Ed had surprised us all, and even himself probably, by taking a new job – one that kept him in Melbourne most of the time.

'Oh, Ed's here!' Camille said.

She seemed genuinely pleased to see him. Marital relations had improved. Ed had started to help Camille with pick-ups and drop-offs and the car pool to dance class and soccer, and preparing the occasional dinner. Enough had been taken off Camille's load that she could breathe again.

Sofia took a swig. Today, she was wearing tangerine overalls and a unicorn-horn headband sat precariously on top of her curls. Concealer almost hid the shadows under her eyes, but she was wearing a defiant shade of orange lipstick.

Luka wasn't a great sleeper, but she had more help now. Mary was staying over one night a week to give Sofia a proper break, and Mary was getting more comfortable with letting Sofia be the boss of her baby.

'Guess who's here!' Sofia said, with a glint in her eyes. My heart skipped a beat. I tucked my hair in place behind my ears. I'd made an effort to look nice today. Of course I had, it was a party. Everyone I knew would be here. Maybe even …

It was Adam, walking towards us with a monstrously large present.

Since Adam had been back in my life, we'd had a few wobbles – I didn't always find it easy to let go of Hazel, and he was still learning the parenting ropes. But we'd begun to find our groove.

Adam visited our place a few evenings a week and often stayed for a glass of wine and dinner. Hazel now called him 'Dada' and we were building up to our first sleepover.

I was never gladder that we'd moved than during those nights with Adam; they were far too similar to all those dinners Will and I had shared together. Except with Adam, I never had to repress any feelings. We were co-parents, nothing more. I hoped that we could, one day, become proper friends – for Hazel's sake.

He kissed me on the cheek. 'Something small for Hazel,' he said, as he put down the gargantuan gift. 'It's a ride-on tractor.'

In no universe was this a sensible present for a family who lived in a shoebox-sized apartment. But she'd love it.

'Where is she?' he asked, looking around.

'Mum's bringing her as soon as she wakes up from her nap,' I said.

Mum, a woman of extremes, had decided to spend her long accrued long-service leave in the city. And suddenly, we went from having next to no Mum in our lives to arguably far too much Mum. And while she drove Camille and me slightly mad, our kids adored her. Once she'd decided that her grandchildren weren't merely reminders of a difficult past but rather a chance for a do-over, she'd thrown herself into the new role.

And she'd been invaluable as Hazel cycled through all the illnesses she picked up from childcare. When she'd passed on (another) bout of gastro to Mum, it had taken all the self-restraint I possessed not to suggest that lemonade might do the trick.

'I got something for you, too,' Adam said, pulling a small box out of his backpack.

I opened it up and stared. It was a sparkling diamond hanging on a silver chain. 'Is that …?'

'Yeah, it is,' he said. It was the largest stone from the engagement ring I'd spotted in his drawer so many years ago, the one he'd never given me. But now, instead of being set in a ring, the stone was hanging off a delicate chain.

'I bought it for you. Lots of women get jewellery when they have a baby. It just seemed right,' he said, trying to act coy, but evidently thrilled with his present. 'My therapist thought it could be a symbol of a new stage in our lives.'

'Thank you,' I said, gently lifting it out of the box and holding up my hair so that Adam could secure the clasp.

Other people had begun to arrive – Ed and the twins, Kajal, Alison and her kids, Mary and our neighbours.

'Look who's here!' Sofia squealed. My heart began to race again.

'Mama!' Mum put down Hazel, wearing a truly hideous glittery dress she'd bought her, and she toddled a few wobbly steps towards me.

'My muffin!'

I felt like I might explode with love. One year with her. So many firsts – smiles, teeth, steps. Months of sleepless nights. A full photo roll. Two bouts of gastro and a handful of other viruses. Three bottles of baby Panadol. Four sizes of clothes outgrown. Two childcare centres. One manny. And endless love.

'Oh, and we have one more special visitor,' Camille said and winked at me.

I spun around. Walking towards us was … a unicorn.

Well, obviously it wasn't a unicorn – it was a pony that had had a glow-up. I burst out laughing.

'Was this you?' I asked Camille.

'Nope.'

I turned to Adam and raised an eyebrow.

'Well – her favourite book is *Thelma the Unicorn*!'

Hazel's eyes lit up. As the birthday girl, she got the first ride and her eyes were wide open as she gently trotted around the park, Adam holding her up, as I took a million and one photos.

The next hour was chaos, with kids running

everywhere and adults chasing after them. I noticed Adam attentively making sure that Kajal's glass was always full.

I checked my watch – party time was almost over. No more were the days where my events would spill over into the early hours of the morning, necessitating a sneaky run next door to empty the overflow of bottles into Will's bin. Soon everyone would do battle with their car seats and head home for dinner, bath and bedtime. And those without kids would be off home to get ready for their Saturday-night plans. Or in Adam and Kajal's case, I suspected that they might be headed to Adam's penthouse for a festive nightcap.

It was cake time. And time to accept that, of course, he wasn't coming.

'Ready for your first taste of cake, Hazel?'

I scooped her up and spun her around. She giggled with glee.

And then out of the corner of my eye I saw him, and all of a sudden I felt dizzy.

It was Will. He strode towards us and my heart did a cartwheel. He was even more handsome than I'd remembered. As he got closer, I searched his face for signs of stress or strain, for the dark shadows of tiredness that had marred his face when he was working to make partner. But they weren't there.

'You came,' I said, when he was close enough.

'You invited me.'

'I did.'

'And so did Camille, Sofia and Kajal. And Adam. So many people forwarded me the invitation, I thought I was being spammed.'

'Adam did?' I asked. 'You know he's here?'

I didn't know how Will would feel being around the guy who'd been a catalyst for his career imploding.

'He sent it to me with an obnoxiously expensive bottle of whisky,' Will said. That sounded like Adam. 'He also sent me a heartfelt note to apologise for his call. And to thank me for looking after his daughter.'

Hazel lunged and pulled his glasses from his face with a cackle of laughter.

'I think she remembers you.'

Will smiled and ruffled her hair. 'Happy first birthday, Hazelnut.'

Sofia appeared out of nowhere and whisked Hazel out of my arms. 'People want to say hello to the birthday girl!' she said.

We were left alone.

When I'd emailed him an invitation and The Love Contract, I was almost certain he wouldn't come, that he'd probably see my name and delete the email without opening it.

But here he was. The same Will, with his dark flop of hair, flashing chestnut-coloured eyes and wry smile.

'I'm really sorry about … everything,' I said.

'I know. I got your email.'

I nodded, glad.

'And I came here to say that … I'm sorry, too. I wanted to reply sooner, but … I've been working through some stuff over the last few months.'

I felt the final knot, the one that had sat curled up at the bottom of my stomach for the last few months, untangle.

'Are you … okay?' I asked.

He smiled, and I knew that he was. None of the heaviness had returned – his phone was still in his pocket, there were no dark rings under his eyes and he wasn't twitchy.

'I took a break and went to stay with my parents. They're teaching at a school in the Northern Territory. I spent a lot of time on my own, and with them, just thinking and working out what I wanted to do next. And … I've been accepted to do a doctorate.' I could hear the pride in his voice.

'Congratulations!'

'I got the idea from Hazel's music class. Being back on a university campus, I'd take her on long walks after class and soak it all in. And it made me realise that I still really love the law, just not the way I was practising it.'

'What's it going to be on?'

'How law reform could help to remove systemic gender inequality embedded in our care paradigms.'

'Really?' I replied, surprised.

'No,' he said with a laugh. 'I'm going to do a survey of international capital markets.'

I smiled. Will was still Will. And I couldn't think of anything more perfect for him. The university would be lucky to have his ridiculous brain.

'Congratulations to you, too. I saw you have a new job.'

I did. I was now a head of content. I had a team, a small one, but still. The job terrified me on a day-to-day basis, and I felt like a total fraud most of the time. But I knew the growing pains were good. And that I was far closer to becoming the role model I wanted to be for Hazel.

'I also came here today to talk about this,' he said, pulling a piece of paper out of his back pocket and unfolding it.

It was The Love Contract.

'You called it the final version, but it's not.' He handed it to me.

My hands began to shake as I skimmed the printout. Will's amendments in blue ink were all over it, most of them on the 'Love' clause. I could feel his gaze on me as I read them.

(3) Will loves Zoe because:

(a) she's the warmest, funnest, most thoughtful person he's ever met;

(b) her brain doesn't work like other people's (in a creative, fizzing way);

(c) her capacity for joy and love is inspiring; and

(d) you make me feel like the most me version of myself and I want to help you to be the you-est version of you, while wanting to be together with you. [Note to Z: This is plagiarism, but you're a v. good writer (I know you know this!) W]

(4) Will's promises:

Will promises Zoe Real Love.

'I've added a promise from me to you in there. Now that it's got mutual promises, it actually is a contract,' he said.

I gazed up at him. Who'd have thought a legal document could move me so deeply, could make me feel so wobbly.

When our eyes met, I felt every part of my body tingle. And then he leaned forward and kissed me and the world disappeared. It was just him and me. I'd only had a single sip of champagne but felt woozy. The smell of his cologne, the brush of his cheek against mine, his hand resting on my hip – they were the most intoxicating sensations I'd ever experienced.

'Wait.' He took a small step backwards. 'You know, I'm never going to be a rich partner at a law firm,' he said. He was doing his best to keep his tone light, but I knew that there was still some genuine insecurity there, that he was still getting used to this new version of himself.

'Because that was my favourite part of you,' I said, and he smiled, relief in his eyes. 'Anyway, I got a pay rise and plan on being very successful.'

'And I know I'm never going to be Hazel's dad. And I'll never pretend that I am. I'd just be happy to be involved in whatever way you and Adam want.'

We both smiled, understanding the irony of what he'd just said.

'I know. I trust you with her.' My smile widened into a big grin. He was happy. He loved me. And I was going to let him.

'Hey, you two. Stop acting like teenagers. Everyone's ready to eat the cake. I'm lighting the candle now,' Sofia yelled at us. But I could see she was thrilled by this development.

We seemed to have inspired our guests. Camille and Ed were giving each other puppy-dog looks across the party as they each wrangled a child. Morgan gave Sofia a cheeky pat on her bottom as she held a match to the candle. And Kajal winked at Adam, who blushed.

Will held up a paper bag he'd been carrying. 'I bought a Santa costume,' he said. 'I thought we might want to do a group photo. I assumed you'd want to reprise the elf look?'

'I always knew you had a thing for me in those gold leggings,' I said.

He laughed and then he offered me his hand and I took it. Hazel toddled towards us and I scooped her up with my other arm. And as we walked towards the crowd that had gathered around the cake, I wondered if anyone else in the whole wide world had ever felt less alone.

ACKNOWLEDGEMENTS

I adore Grace Kelly so much that I named my dog after her. When she won her Oscar (not that I'm comparing) her acceptance speech was brief – two lines thanking all those who made her award possible. I always thought this was a very elegant and aspirational approach to thank yous. But I'm not Grace Kelly. And this story, about how parents (and people, really) need a village, took an incredible village. So enormous thank yous are in order …

My gratitude to the team at HarperCollins Australia. Anna Valdinger, the warmest and most incisive dream publisher. Rachel Cramp, for being such a fabulously smart, creative and supportive editor. Alexandra Nahlous – for an amazing copy edit. Pamela Dunne – for such a thoughtful proofread. The Banjo Prize team who made my dreams come true. Louisa Maggio for a cover that is so perfect that it made me smile for days. And, of course, everyone in the team who helped turn this into a real-life book.

To Kate O'Donnell for her brilliant feedback and insights which, at risk of hyperbole, were life changing.

To the team at Curtis Brown Creative who taught me so much – in particular Anna Davis, Nikita Lalwani, Jenny Colgan and Christina Pishiris. And all my classmates who are so talented.

To the generous readers who gave me early feedback: Josh Fisher, Georgia Hill, Jack Peters, Michelle Nicholas-Wright, Rachel Yeoh and Stephanie Carty.

To the people who gave me sage advice and cheered me along: Claire Desmond, Mark Klemens, Andrew Knight, Greg Basser, Sophie McNaught, Rebecca Cahill, Veronica Lando and Michelle Upton.

To the 2023 Debut Crew and all the Australian writers I've met in real life and online who are the most supportive gang you could imagine.

To my friends, the great loves of my life.

To the Vizard and Griffiths families – including Tom, Mad, Jim and Liv – whose obsessive creativity is an inspiration.

To Mum for the passion. To Dad for the belief. And for everything else.

To Poppy and baby boy – my world.

And my endless thanks to Hugh. I love romance stories and can't believe I am lucky enough to live out my own with someone as smart, funny and supportive as you. Thank you for backing me every step of the way.

And to you the reader, who picked up this book. My aim when I set out on this journey was to write something entertaining, something that showed the lives of women as I know them and something romantic (and a bit funny). My hope is that I've delivered on that. Thank you for your time.